The Croatian Outlier

A NOVEL

FRANK BUCHAR

The Croatian Outlier

Copyright © 2025 by Frank Buchar

The Croatian Outlier is a work of fiction. All incidents and dialogue, and all characters, are products of the author's imagination and invention and are not to be taken as real. Where historical personages appear, the context, incidents, and dialogues concerning these persons are entirely fictional and are not intended to depict actual events or to change the entirely fictional nature of the work. In all respects, any resemblance to actual persons, living or dead, is entirely coincidental.

Cover design by Marco Buchar

ISBN 978-1-7782251-1-6 (print)

For all members, past, present,
and future, of the Croatian Hall
in Schumacher, Canada (1932)

Pronunciation Guide for Croatian Names and Places

Č is pronounced like the 'ch' in church

Ć ć is a somewhat softer 'ch' sound

J, j is pronounced like the 'y' in yet

Š, š is pronounced like the 'sh' in 'share'

Ž, ž is pronounced like the 's' in 'measure'

IF WE THINK ABOUT IT, we find that our life consists in this achieving of a pure relationship between ourselves and the living universe about us. This is how I "save my soul" by accomplishing a pure relationship between me and another person, me and other people, me and a nation, me and a race of men, me and the animals, me and the trees or flowers, me and the earth, me and the skies and sun and stars, me and the moon; an infinity of pure relations, big and little, like the stars of the sky: that makes our eternity, for each one of us, me and the timber I am sawing, the lines of force I follow; me and the dough I knead for bread, me and the very motion with which I write, me and the bit of gold I have got. This, if we knew it, is our life and eternity: the subtle, perfected relation between me and my whole circumambient universe.

- D. H. LAWRENCE

VARAŽDIN
SAMOBOR
RETRO ZAGREB
KARLOVAC
CROATIA
SENJ
PULA
GOSPIĆ
NIN
ZADAR
ADRIATIC SEA
KLIS
SOLIN
SPLIT
OMIŠ
MAKARSKA
TUČEPI
DUBROVNIK

Definition of Outlier

1. An outlying part or member
2. Geol. A younger rock formation isolated in older rocks
3. Statistics. A result differing greatly from others in the same sample

Oxford Canadian Dictionary

CONTENTS

Hamilton
Canada

PART ONE

23 February 10:16 2023

1.1

ANOTHER DAY FALLS. I HOPE today is a better day. Yesterday wasn't so good. As I was going up the stairs from the basement I saw a man who wasn't there. He was sitting on the landing between the outside door and the stairs that lead to my landlord's place. He was just sitting there, his back against the wall with his forearms resting on his bended knees. He looked straight at me, just watching me. He had a baby face with blonde hair that was balding at the front and pink peach fuzz on his chin that looked as if he was trying to grow a beard. He wore a dark blue military uniform with brass buttons buttoned to the neck. His trouser legs were tucked into fine looking black boots that were polished and shiny. I pretended not to see him. I knew he wasn't there because I passed right through him as I opened the outside door to leave the house. He didn't move at all.

Now, today, I'm about to leave my apartment 221B again. I know I need to get out for a walk in the fresh air. I hope I'm not losing it. I pause for a moment not knowing what I'll encounter around the corner. I close the door behind me and turn to walk up the basement stairs that are painted a light blue colour that could use another paint job. Sure enough, the same man I thought I saw yesterday is there again today. He is sitting in the same place on the landing and watching me. I walk through him again, effortlessly, open the heavy door with its large brass doorknob, and close it firmly behind me. It makes a satisfying sound as it shuts. I take a deep breath wishing he'd stay away. The mid-February air is cold and I adjust my scarf. I pull it close around my neck. I hope he's not there when I return.

I turn left from my apartment entrance and walk several paces to Queen Street South. There is no traffic and I cross the road to the sidewalk. Then, I turn right and continue walking past two houses and the Laundromat on the corner where I turn left towards the middle school a short distance away. It is a squat one-story brick structure that fronts a large playing field and park. I touch the rough brick wall for reassurance and walk past the empty school-rooms towards the park. No one is about. There is a light dusting of snow on the frozen grass, but only in spots. I walk across the track that serves as a perimeter to the football field and continue westward towards Locke Street South. To my left I see the commemorative brass plaque to fallen Hamilton soldiers from World War One, young men who played on this very football field. I trudge on, aiming for Starbuck's until I see the Antiques Shop and decide to go in. The front display window shows a sumptuous red-and-gold tasselled tablecloth tastefully draped over a fine old oak dresser. The shopkeeper is at the back of the store and looks to be heavily involved in paperwork. I nod to her in greeting and proceed to take a closer look at the objects within. The curious flotsam of the past has always beguiled me.

A low pine cupboard catches my eye. The top of it is made of two planks that have shrunk over time, creating a gap between them. It looks rustic with signs of wear and tear and the marks of the maker's tools upon it. A note upon it reads *Quebec, late nineteenth century*. I absentmindedly run my index finger along the length of the gap and feel the smooth wood on either side.

Suddenly, out of nowhere, a human figure is in front of me. An old woman with round wire spectacles. Her white hair is tied in a bun. She places her hand on the top of the cupboard and gently weeps. She is thin and slightly hunched over. I am oblivious to her, simply not there. She is crying quietly and her tears are falling onto the cupboard top. Oddly, I am seeing her in black and white. I cannot tell the true colour of her long dress or her broach. My eyes are seeing only in black and white though I suspect the pine cupboard is a soft blonde colour. The old woman is leaning against the cupboard for support as if she had just been told something terrible.

It would appear that she is in the first wave of grief and her sobs are heart wrenching to me. The antique dealer approaches me, smiling, and just about to speak when I turn away and hasten out of the shop. This can't be happening, as I make my way south and then east towards the park again on Charlton Avenue West. Twice on the same day, spirits, visible spirits. I hope the man in the blue uniform isn't there when I get home. I've got to get free of this. If I don't I know I'm lost.

Just as I'm walking by the Hamilton Amateur Athletic Association building that anchors the park on Kent Street, I hear the songs of dozens and dozens of birds in the bare winter bushes, singing away happily and loudly. It's a joyful sound. As I get closer, I see several of the sparrows clearly, and can almost touch them. And then the chirping stops abruptly, as if I had suddenly fallen from grace. I look away and quicken my steps, half in dread of what I will find when I open the side entrance door to my apartment. It is my apartment, it's all I have, and I will not be forced out by fear. Not now. Not ever.

My courage abates somewhat as I cross Queen Street South and insert my key into the lock. I hesitate just for a second and then pull the door open. The man who wasn't there isn't there, and I feel a great wave of relief course through me. I descend the stairs, turn right, and enter my apartment. I am alone.

I felt much better the next day and decided that I needed to get out more, breathe in fresh cold air, and put the past behind me. Perhaps then I wouldn't be having hallucinations of people who weren't really there, like the old woman at the antique store and the soldier on my basement stair landing. It was bitter cold outside so I put on my scarf and down parka and headed for the Jackson Square Mall, downtown. It seemed to me that if I focussed more on everyday details around me that I'd be able to rid myself of seeing things.

I locked the side door securely behind me and walked north on Queen Street to Robinson where I turned right. I walked at a brisk pace and within a few short minutes I was at Bay Street where I turned left and continued walking several more minutes, past City Hall, until I was at the west end of the Mall. A homeless man was sitting on the ground against a concrete pillar with a baseball cap in front of him. He asked if I had spare change for a coffee, and I dropped a toonie in the pocket of his cap. I entered the Mall and walked past the small fountain beneath the escalator, past the liquor store and the small shops that lined the broad corridor, until I reached Tim Horton's where I bought a large coffee and a double chocolate doughnut. I sat at a table and watched the passers-by through the floor to ceiling plate glass. The coffee was fresh and piping hot, and the doughnut melted in my mouth. From there I walked past the bookshop towards the drug store where I turned left and continued past the theaters towards the food court. It was busy with many people sporting Bulldog hockey jerseys for the afternoon game. They sat in happy animated groups eating burgers and fried KFC chicken and subs. I was going to go into the library next to the food court, but when I checked my wallet I discovered I didn't have my library card with me.

1.2

I returned home along the same route and within fifteen minutes I was descending the stairs to my apartment. It was then that I heard the voices. More than one. I stopped for a moment and listened. The voices were saying something about the quaintness of the furnishings not quite being of museum quality, and then raucous laughter. They were speaking Croatian, the language of my grandparents. It felt familiar and good to hear it spoken once again. I opened the inner door hesitantly, and there they were.

There were three of them. A tall striking woman with abundant white hair stood next to the faux fireplace, smiling. She had turned it on and had placed her hand on the small built-in shelf above the fireplace. A portly man sat leaning forward in the pine rocking chair with a quizzical look on his heavily wrinkled face while a huge man in his early fifties occupied half the pull-out couch that I used as my bed. They were all dressed strangely in a style and manner I hadn't seen before. Their clothes were tight and accentuated their figures.

"What are you doing here?" I shouted.

"Easy, easy," the big man said. "We are here to talk with you. That is all. We mean no harm." He spoke very loudly, close to shouting. I don't think he was aware of it. It was his natural manner I guess. He was easily six and a half feet tall and two hundred and sixty pounds.

"Don't be afraid," the fat man in the rocker said quietly, in almost a whisper. His voice was gentle and reassuring, almost jolly. He was bald and pink with a round face and a red and white chequered scarf neatly tied around his throat. He looked to be in his late sixties.

The tall woman lifted her chin slightly and squinted her eyes as if examining some rather strange and unpleasant object as she looked at me. She was elegant and fit, a woman in her fifties, with thick white hair that framed a handsome, almost masculine face.

"Who let you in here? What's going on?" I edged my way backwards towards the door hoping to make a run for it if I could. I could hear the panic in my own voice.

Sensing my intent, the big man rose from the couch slowly, the top of his head brushing against the dropped panel ceiling. "Listen to us," he bellowed, "just hear us out. No one will harm you." He motioned for me to sit on the couch. I felt very small beside him. He was a very large, imposing man, unlike the soldier on the stairwell that I had encountered the day before.

The woman, in a dark purple outfit made of cloth and rubber-like material that I had never seen before, looked intently at me and began to speak in a slow, deliberate manner as if she were addressing an idiot.

"What we are about to speak of, will no doubt sound strange to you, the stuff of dreams or nightmares perhaps, but believe me, it is as real as our encounter here in this moment. Unfortunately so. The soldier, Goran, that you met on your stairway, is from the future, like us. We sent him. Both we and Goran are projections only, three dimensional, non-physical projections. We wanted to give you a premonition of our visit though we should have done it differently as we can see that it has unsettled you. We are experiencing a crisis and so we are seeking out whatever resources we believe may be of assistance. We are deputy ministers in the Croatian government, a coalition government of the Blues and the Browns, but we need no formality here. I am Inez, and this is Boris, and last but not least is Darko. Our world, where we're from, is a future Croatia, one under dire threat, and you are a part of the diaspora from an earlier version of our state. Our scientists have corroborated the results of an ancestry search that you took. A small, seemingly trivial analysis of you and your forebears has taken on a new significance. But besides that, we have observed you over time and we have learned that you see things that others cannot. You are quite remarkable and gifted though you are unaware of your talents. I'm sure you can remember times when you felt you were being watched. And indeed, you were." At that point she glanced at the stout man in the rocking chair and nodded sharply.

He stood up and rubbed the palms of his hands together vigorously. "I am Boris Hodnik. The crisis that our fellow deputy minister Inez Jakovac, speaks of, is nothing new, only we had hoped the endless eras of invasion and war were finally over. However, that is not to be. We have been given an ultimatum. A simple one. An invader has promised us a place if we give up our own. If we do not, we will be pacified. That was the word used: pacified. They want us out. Very simply, we are to remove ourselves from our land and then act as frontier guardians for them. These aliens, who resemble us, are from a distant planet in the Milky Way Galaxy. They will also give us a great fortune in gold, for each and every one of our citizens. Croatia is to be theirs and theirs alone. That is the bottom line." He clapped his hands together and pointed to the man sitting next to me. It was as if they were passing a baton, transitioning from one speaker to the other.

The big man stood up suddenly. He glanced down at me. "I am Darko Yamich. Even in this projected three-dimensional reality, I need to stand. Poor circulation otherwise. I will continue. Can you imagine our predicament? This is the first time an alien force has decided to make a move on our planet, and the entry point is Croatia. Why? Because of stone, karst stone, which we in Croatia possess in abundance. As it turns out their own planet is no longer habitable, and in their search of the universe it appears that our little portion of the galaxy most resembles their own. They look like us, human featured, but are very pale. They are very polite. At least the ones we've met with during negotiations. But they are deadly intent on having Croatia and appear to have the resources to take it. Initially, when we challenged them during our first negotiations, they offered an object lesson while we were still at the negotiating table.

They asked us to keep a watch on the city of Varaždin. Not knowing their purpose we sent a company of our military to defend the city. They gave us a date and time to leave the city and its environs. They pinpointed the target zone and circumference precisely. The epicenter was the City Hall located in Tomislav Square, the very heart of the city. We had advised the general population to leave. Many did, but not all. At the appointed time, at noon, on Saturday, January 06, in 2323, just after the changing of the guard, the celebrated Purgari, there was a blinding flash of orange light above the city center and afterwards, everyone within the circle was gone. Everyone. Buildings and infrastructure were left intact. But there were no people about nor animals. It was bizarre. All property was left untouched.

We were told that this necessity was unfortunate, but since we needed proof, they had regrettably obliged. Most regrettably they said. They were exceedingly polite and their emissaries even looked distraught but the deed was done." At that the big man sat down once more, and cradled his head in his large hands. And then through his fingers he muttered, "Politeness be damned."

The other two looked at me to say something. An awkwardness filled the air, and there was silence, except for the electric fireplace that made a slight humming sound. I was puzzled, but said, "I'm sorry but what you're saying is totally nuts. You said the year was 2323? That's three hundred years from now. You need a reality check. Is this a weird joke of some kind? Who are you people? Am I going crazy? Are you for real?" I asked them. "Tell me I'm dreaming after eating tainted food."

"Time is an elusive concept," the elegant woman said softly, "and you will find that out when you join us. I can see your fear. We expected that. All of this is truly strange to you, but we will come through with your help and the help of many others from the diaspora."

"I can't help you. I think I need to see a doctor or psychiatrist or something. Maybe with medication you people will go away."

I watched them as they glanced at each other and smiled. The woman Inez spoke again. "We'll be in touch through Goran. Take some time to process all of this. You won't see us here again, but we'll send Goran back to give you instructions when it's time. We need you and we can offer generous incentives."

"I need some water," I said. I rose from the couch and hastened to my kitchen. I filled a glass with cold water from the tap and gulped it down at one go. When I returned to my living room they were gone. There was no trace of them, nothing. I shuddered uncontrollably for a moment and then stopped abruptly when I heard footsteps on the stairwell. Someone was coming down. There were three sharp knocks on my door.

1.3

It was Peter, my landlord and friend. He was carrying a tray of what looked like shortbread cookies and a small pot of golden marmalade. He was smiling broadly and placed the tray on the small glass coffee table in front of the couch. His smile faded instantly as he looked about.

"Where are they? Where are your guests? I heard voices coming from your apartment. A group of people. I'm sure I did. Evie and I just made a batch of cookies, and they're warm and fresh, and I wanted to share it with you. I know how you love pastries and sweets." Peter was tall and thin with freckles and a thatch of red hair that made him look younger than his thirty years. We had met at Mohawk College where I was studying media arts part-time, and he was taking a course on Classic French Cuisine.

"Oh I just turned off the television. Maybe that's what you heard." I looked away, not meeting his eyes. I hated lying to Peter because he was the kindest, gentlest person I had ever met and he was my closest friend.

"But I could swear I heard real voices. I couldn't make it out, what was said I mean, but this old house carries sound, and I knew you had guests."

"Must have been the TV," I said again. Looking down on the tray, I swallowed involuntarily at the sight of the delicious-looking shortbread cookies. Peter smiled, and we both sat side by side on the couch. He had even brought china dessert plates and a silver spoon for the marmalade. I asked him if he wanted some coffee, but he shook his head.

"No, let's just enjoy the shortbread," he said. We talked for a bit about how his French cuisine course was going and the great sauces he was learning to prepare. But he seemed to be preoccupied with something he was thinking about, and suddenly he turned to me and spoke earnestly.

"I'm worried about you Marin. Several times now I've heard voices down here from upstairs, but it turns out there was no one here but you. A couple of days ago I heard you talking with someone when we had that late afternoon snowfall. When the voices stopped, I know whoever it was you were talking to must have left. But when I looked the next morning there were no tracks in the snow, none at all. Are you OK? We haven't talked about it, but I know it must be hard for you since the breakup with Keira. Losing your part-time job and your girl within the same week, and then having to move to a small apartment like this must have been hard. I'm thinking you need to see someone if you need help. There's nothing wrong with getting help when you need it. And I don't mind helping out. I can connect you with someone who can help. What do you think?"

'So do you think I'm going nuts, or do you think I'm already there?"

"I'm not saying that. I'm just saying that I've heard voices coming from down here when I know you've been alone."

"Maybe you're the one who needs help Peter."

"Look, I'm sorry. You're my friend. I just want to help if I can. That's all."

"You're already helping me out a lot. You're giving me a break on the rent. I don't know what I'd do if you hadn't. Homeless in Hamilton and camping out in parks wouldn't be fun. I know that for sure."

"That's what friends are for," Peter said, his voice soft and gentle and tinged with compassion.

"I promise I'll pay you back. And look, I'll think about what you said. I give you my word on that."

Suddenly a voice was heard coming from the stairwell. It was Evie calling for Peter. He smiled tenderly at me and then placed the few remaining cookies on a paper napkin. He gathered up the plates and piled them on the tray, leaving the pot of fine cut marmalade for me as well. That was Peter.

Just as I was about to go for a walk I felt my iPhone vibrate in my pocket. A text message from Peter. He wants me to check out a dating app he's heard good things about. He says I'm spending too much time alone. He says I've got nothing to lose. I guess maybe I haven't. The only things I'd like to lose are the hallucinations I've been having. I open the website and the first thing I'm asked, after the hype, is to describe myself in thirty-five words or less. Short and sweet.

Twenty-four years old. Just under six feet. Athletic build. Hazel eyes. Sandy brown hair. A mature part-time student. Studying Media Arts. Love video games, hiking, and dining out. Love desserts of all kinds.

I answer a few more questions, attach a digital photograph, and send it away. Who knows what'll happen. Nothing ventured. Nothing gained. I can still back out. Money is tight and dating can be expensive. I know I've got to be careful.

I needed some fresh air. After I did some stretching exercises, I left my apartment and headed north on Queen Street until Hunter where I turned west. The day was brilliant and blue and very cold. There was a bounce in my step as I quickened my pace. The fresh snow crunched under my feet, the sound of it reassuring and inviting. I turned right on Pearl Street and crossed the pedestrian bridge over the railway tracks. In the middle of the iron, rust-coloured bridge there was a slight arch where I stopped to admire the clean lines of the engineering. It was a fine bridge and solid and meant to last. I think it must have been satisfying to build it. I removed a woollen glove and knocked on the metal for good luck and then continued on my way. I walked west as far as Dundurn Street and then south past the Beer Store and the liquor store until I hit Charlton Avenue West where I turned left. It was a familiar route and a favoured one. Not many people were about. One person walking his dog, and an old woman with a shopping cart carrying empties to the Beer Store for recycling and a small remuneration for her efforts. She was hunched over with age and trouble and wore a weathered tartan scarf that framed her thin face. She didn't look at me as I passed her.

And then it happened. Just as I'm walking past the solid brick building of the Hamilton Amateur Athletic Association grounds, I look to my left and see a group of men at the far end of the field. Perhaps a half dozen of them. I can't make them out clearly but they are running and moving swiftly across the snow-covered field and headed in my direction. As they advanced I noticed they were dressed in old-fashioned football kit. They were tossing a football amongst themselves. They were cheerful and having fun. But curiously, the human figures, as I saw them, were in various shades of black and white. I was not seeing them in colour. They appeared in black and white only like an old classic film. They stopped about thirty feet from me, they on the field, and I on the sidewalk, and they simply looked at me, smiling, but it was as if there was an immense chasm between them and me. We were on either side of a great divide. They smiled and played and waved at me. Though I was a little shaken, I sensed their warm friendliness and smiled back at them and waved. They were young men playing on a field that I knew was once theirs. I felt it in every inch of my being. They turned away and ran the length of the field in a broken circle, until they disappeared in the far distance. They left me with a sense of wistfulness and yearning for their fate. As I continued walking home I noticed there was something that wasn't there. An absence, a vacancy. There were no sparrows singing in the bushes as they often did. I missed that. Another moment or two, and I crossed Queen Street, and then turned right for my basement apartment.

I got the sense that I was being watched. Just like the three future visitors had said I was. Not all the time, but occasionally. It was a feeling. My basement apartment is very small, so sometimes, when I came from the kitchen to the living room, a space that also serves as my bedroom, I'd think I saw something on the periphery of my vision. A dark shadow or shape, but when I turned around quickly to look, there was nothing there, nothing at all. I determined that it was not an hallucination. The shadow was just a large overstuffed pillow on the couch. But still, the feeling persisted. I didn't like it. I didn't like to think that I was losing it. Maybe I was spending too much time alone like Peter had said.

1.4

But then I saw him, and the skin on the back of my neck tightened. The ancient, reptilian parts of my brain were roused and alerted. I saw the soldier the three visitors had told me would be returning. The soldier, Goran. He stepped out of my bathroom and sat on my rocking chair and rocked.

He was smiling with small perfect teeth. He was rocking gently. He was dressed in his blue uniform, and with his baby face he looked too young to be a soldier. Peach fuzz on his chin.

"So, here I am once again. You were honoured with the recent projected visit of our leaders, the three ministers. Greatly honoured. It happens rarely. They usually send only a projection of someone like me."

"What do you want with me?"

"Your help. You have gifts, that if aligned with our technology, allow us a chance, a slim chance, for survival. Those gifts, of course, need to be honed, but first we need your agreement and promise of secrecy."

"What? Who would I tell about this? I'd be put away if I spoke to anyone about this, about hallucinations, and alien invasions."

"Quite, but still, we require absolute secrecy. A few months of your time is all that is needed. I can promise you that you will find it interesting, intriguing, and far more engaging than what you are experiencing right now, in this time and place." At that, he waved his hand summarily to signify my apartment and the world around it.

"OK, I'm a little down on my luck just now but it's better than going off to somewhere and to some place that I know nothing about. I mean give me a break. Sure, my background is Croatian, and I'm proud of it. I'm part of the great diaspora, but that doesn't mean I have to follow blindly. After all I'm Croatian-Canadian, an outlier."

"More to the point. I'm authorized to compensate you richly for your time and trouble."

"With what? A cheque or money transfer from the future, cashable a few hundred years from now?" I shrugged at the folly of it.

"I can see I've piqued your interest." He reached into the inside pocket of his tunic and pulled out a folded sheet of paper. He stood up from the rocking chair and passed it over to me. It was a lottery ticket with next Saturday's date. "You will find that ten million in lottery winnings provides a suitable upswing in your luck." He smiled warmly at me and waited for me to take it all in.

"Those are winning numbers on your ticket. That is the advantage we have in coming from the future. Of course, you must sign the ticket."

"I don't know what to make of all this," I said, as I studied the numbers on the ticket.

"Are you in or out?" He reached over to take the ticket back, but I held on to it as our eyes met. He laughed cheerfully and rocked in the chair. "Ah, the Croatian in you definitely wants in. Or is it the Canadian? The prize is compelling, isn't it? Ten million to take you away from all this," he said, with just the slightest trace of sarcasm in his voice. "After your service with us is over, you will be returned precisely here, to 221B, Queen South, Hamilton, Canada, though there is some risk involved, of course. In all great ventures there is some degree of risk."

"What kind of risk?"

"That remains to be seen. That part of the future is yet to unfold. Perhaps, with your intuition you may experience glimmers of it. That is my guess only. After all, your profile indicates that you're some sort of magus or have the potential to be one, or perhaps you are a warrior poet. Who knows? I am to be one of your principal handlers, or coordinators. My job is to make sure you receive the best training, and that entails linking you up with the right people. The rest is up to you."

"What do I do?"

'You facilitate. Yes, that is the right word. Facilitation. You move things along and empower us to meet and defeat an enemy. An alien enemy."

"That sounds bizarre. I need to know more. My role isn't clear. I need to know what I'm getting into."

"You will, soon, if you decide to join us. You have until Saturday to decide. Three days. If you claim the lottery winnings, we'll know you're in. If not, you are not to take the money. Understood?"

"Yes."

"Good." At that, he rose from the rocker, winked at me, stepped into the bathroom, closed the door, and was gone from my sight. The rocker was still moving back and forth in smaller and smaller motions from the time he had stood and left it.

I sat dumbfounded on my couch. A few more seconds passed and the oak rocker stopped moving, and came to a still point. Abruptly. The Lotto 649 ticket was cradled in my right hand. I looked at the numbers: 03 15 18

21 28 37. There was nothing special about them. They were just numbers. I signed the ticket. I thought about it. Ten million.

1.5

I needed to think, and the best way for me to do that was to walk. I bundled up and headed out. There was a light snowfall in the air, but it wasn't that cold. The snowflakes were large and fell slowly to the ground. They were the kind of snowflakes that made me think about Christmas and happy times when my grandparents were alive. It felt good to be out. I walked the short distance to Aberdeen and then turned left. I continued walking east past the stately old homes and laid-back properties, and up the gradual incline towards James Street, the finest street in the city.

The snow was falling thickly now and with it, old memories from the past. An image of my grandfather reading to me in Croatian about Croatian princes, peasants, and pirates. He made history come alive with a great booming voice and grandiloquent gestures. With every sweep of his powerful arm the four-year old child in me grew quiet and wide-eyed at past glories and stunning sights on turquoise seas. Ancient tales of Illyrians and Romans and Byzantines paraded before my eyes, while my eyelashes, wet with the newly fallen snow, made me feel I was in a waking dream and both here and there simultaneously. Here, turning north on James Street on a snowy afternoon, and there, in Grimsby, decades earlier, in a modest kitchen with my grandfather's tales transforming the place into a pirate's castle beside a storied sea. The snow on my tongue was like a gift from some capricious god.

My pace quickened with the downward slope of the street. I stopped once and turned on the corner at Herkimer and James to look at the Escarpment behind me. Everyone called it the Mountain. As I continued on my walk, I remembered the time I had spent with my grandfather after my grandmother had died. He was heartbroken and would burst into tears often throughout the day. When I hugged him he would begin laughing uproariously through his grief and tell me how lucky he was to have a grandson like me.

Shortly after my grandmother died we went to live in his house in Lika, Croatia, near Gospić. I think it was called Ribnik. We spent two happy years there. One of my earliest memories was of seeing the Velebit mountains there. It was the height of summer and everything was green and gold and magical to a small boy. My grandfather said that there were great caves beneath the mountains and treasures hidden there by people from the past. Wide-eyed with wonder, I begged to be taken to the caves to see for myself.

So long ago from this time and place. As I walked I could see the hospital, St. Joseph's, across James to my right. Within a minute I was passing Robinson Street. I looked over at the small stone inuksuk in front of the art gallery. Snow was already covering parts of the sculpture. The Inuit figure was pointing east. I continued walking several blocks down James Street North until, just near the bay and harbour, I saw it. The stone face. I walked closer to the old customs building to admire the carving suspended in the concrete artistry of the public entrance.

Looking at the concrete face of the chieftain wearing his headdress in the prow of a stone ship, I remembered a sad tale. A native friend that I met at Mohawk College, Silas Wesley, had told me a tale I didn't want to remember, but one I could not forget. We carry our family with us wherever we go. Our brothers and sisters and parents and grandparents, all of them, are with us in the gestures and memories and the stories they leave behind. My friend said that his grandfather, a man named Edmund Cheechoo had told him of his experience at a Catholic residential school. He had been beaten countless times, brutalized, and treated with contempt and hatred. He suffered at the hands of Christian overseers, ministers and priests and nuns, for simply speaking in his native tongue. The Canadian political system supported their cruelty, indeed actively encouraged it for decade after decade. His grandfather said that the nuns were shapeshifters and could transform from angelic creatures singing hymns in the morning to violent furies in the evening, as adept in administering punishments with beaver tails and pussywillow switches, as singing praises to the Lord.

Right before his eyes they would change into creatures of mad hatred. And there was more. Children were not allowed toys or dolls of any kind.

So, they made a toy of a stone found on the road. The priests and nuns took these away too, and soon there were mounds of stones in the front yard, forbidden to the children. The love for a stone was not permitted, nor love of any kind. Who'd have thought there could be the magic of a child's love in a stone? Some of the little ones chose to die in despair because they could not fathom the cruelty of the black-clad demons in a world without love. I turned and walked back home heartbroken and grieving for lost children. It was just then that I remembered the incident as my pace quickened.

1.6

My grandfather and I had gotten up very early one morning and had driven to the mountains nearby. At the entrance to a great cave we were met by a small wizened man with more wrinkles than I had ever seen on a human being before. He embraced my grandfather warmly and spent a few moments just looking at him with unabashed delight. My grandfather called him Brujo. I liked him instantly and wasn't afraid at all. He was smiling as he spoke, and he never stopped smiling throughout all the time that we were with him. Indeed, he seemed to chuckle with delight at times, for no apparent reason, out of the blue. He was dressed quite simply in a kind of white smock and white baggy trousers. A dark purple sash was tied tightly around his waist.

He led the way and guided us deep into the caves. Electric lights were fixed high on the walls and illuminated the passageway. I pulled at my grandfather's sleeve and whispered that I wanted to see the hidden treasures he had talked to me about. He put his finger to his lips and then held my hand as we followed the strange, cheerful man. There were great stone icicles coming from the ceiling and the floor of the cave, some ivory coloured, some sand coloured, others dark. The little man stopped by a naturally formed pool filled with still black water where he told us to stop. He said he had some objects for us to see.

The memory of it was quite clear and sharp like the blade of a knife. He bid us follow him closely, and he led us into an adjoining cavern that was well lit. There, on the floor before us, were several objects. I tried to recall them in my mind's eye as my eyelashes squinted through the snow that continued to fall as I walked towards Jackson Square. Within a few minutes I was at James and King, the very heart of the city, with Gore Park and the gray imposing statue of Queen Victoria to the left of me. I trudged on and then the long forgotten incident floated up into my consciousness.

Set atop a blue tarp there were tools of various kinds and silver goblets and gold coins, and neatly folded peasant garments. I squeezed my grandfather's hand with excitement and joy. Here was the treasure he had told me about. My eyes scanned the objects.

As soon as I saw it I knew it was meant for me, and I cried out for it. I let go of my grandfather's hand and walked over the tarp and grabbed it with both hands, laughing with delight. It was a field axe and the wooden shaft of it was almost as tall as me, and had intricate designs carved into it, designs that resembled snowflakes. The strange man nodded towards my grandfather who followed me onto the tarp and gently removed it from my grasp. He was afraid I might hurt myself but the blade was covered with a dark brown leather sheath.

The little man smiled and asked me if I saw anything else that was mine. With a sweep of his arm he pointed to the other things resting on the tarp, the precious looking goblets and some items carved from wood. Only one other object caught my eye, and I howled with delight at seeing it. It was a wooden flute with a simple pattern incised into it. I blew into it, making several sharp sounds as my fingers danced over the six holes on its surface. While I played with it, I saw the strange little man talking intently with my grandfather who nodded meaningfully at his words, and every now and then he looked across to me with a quiet sadness in his eyes that was tinctured with pride.

And then the memory images faded as I found myself walking steadily past the old Eaton Centre and on past the small shops along James Street North. The snowfall was abating somewhat, and the walking was easy until I neared home. There were a few flurries that fell, but no other old memories with it. I kept on thinking about the ten million and how I would spend it. I would have taken the lottery ticket out to look at it again but I was worried the wet snow flurries might damage it.

1.7

The next few days were a blur as I confirmed the ten million deposited in my savings account. I didn't want to have my photo taken, but the lottery officials insisted so I complied. Peter was very happy for me, and even happier when I gave him one hundred thousand in cash for his kindness. He shrieked in delight and danced about my living room beside himself with joy. I told him there would be more coming, much more, but I needed to put my life in order first. I told him I would be going away for a few months, and that when I returned we would party. He hugged me and said he'd look after the apartment for me. He pulled out a joint, but I told him that would have to wait for a bit. I needed my mind to be crystal clear.

Despite the money, I started thinking hard about what I had gotten myself into. I knew what I had seen was real enough, the soldier Goran, and the other officials I had seen and heard in my apartment. They weren't hallucinations after all. They were projections from the future, and that made a difference to me. In taking the money I had committed myself to them. I didn't have to wait long for what came next. One afternoon as I entered my apartment, Goran was there, sitting in my rocking chair, smiling and rocking slowly. His uniform was the same, dark blue with shiny brass buttons. It looked as if he were trying to grow a moustache without very much success. There was an uneven line of golden fuzz above his lip. I couldn't help but look at it. I sat on the couch beside him.

"So, you have your money, yes?"

"Yes," I said.

"You are ready then, for several months work with us?"

"Several months?"

"About that. Probably under a year. We want you to join us tomorrow. Can you be ready?"

"That soon?"

"Yes. Tomorrow evening, around ten, a small airship will pick you up at the park across the street. Beside the tennis courts at the northern end of the field."

"You're serious?"

"Here's what will happen. The electric light standards, about eight of them, on either side of the field, will fail just before ten. Within seconds, all electric power to the surrounding homes will be momentarily lost. That will be the signal. You will run down the field from the athletic building at the southern end, and as you do so a small gray airship will descend and a door will open. You will enter and the door will close. No one will be inside. A fine blue mist, as if from a vaporizer, will issue from the vents on the ceiling. You will sleep very soundly and when you awake you will be in a future state. Literally. Nothing to worry about. You will be in good hands."

"I had hoped I'd have more time here."

"To do what?"

"Well, to get ready, that's all."

"Everything is taken care of. We will supply everything you need. Just come with the clothes on your back, nothing more. I must leave now." Suddenly he stood up, smiled, and walked into the bathroom leaving the door behind him partially open. In an instant he was gone.

There wasn't much for me to do the next day. I checked my bank account several times, and the money was still there. Peter and I enjoyed some wonderful homemade biscotti with freshly ground Colombian coffee in his apartment upstairs, and I told him then that I would be away, beginning that evening. I said that I wasn't quite sure where I was going, that I wanted to make it an adventure. He nodded enthusiastically, wished me well, said again that he'd look after my apartment, and then gave me a packet of vanilla biscotti to take with me. I felt as rich as a king.

1.8

Shortly before ten I made my way to the park and stood in front of the brick athletic building, somewhat apprehensive. No one was about. It was a dark, unpleasant evening with moisture in the air that held the threat of imminent rain. I felt strange but unafraid. I was ready. The lights went out on the tall electric standards surrounding the football field and then the lights within the surrounding private homes were out as well. I started to run down the field. It was sodden and patchy with tufts of grass here and there. I saw something descending at the far end of the field just in front of the tennis courts. It was the small airship that Goran had said would arrive there for me. I started to sprint towards it when I slipped and fell suddenly and found myself face-down on the cold ground. I turned my head upwards to see the door of the airship open and a small light shining within. Suddenly, a fine blue mist covered everything within as Goran had said it would, but I could see through it. I raised my head, but couldn't stand. I tried to get to my knees but slipped again. I felt lost for a moment when suddenly my body was lifted by my armpits, and I was pulled up and forward. Somehow, I regained my footing but I was barely touching the ground. I felt the light mist against my face. Then I was carried forward without any effort on my part. With a light push from behind by someone, I entered the airship and the door closed. I turned and looked through the small porthole on one side of the door. There, on the field just beyond the goalpost, were several figures that I had seen before. I still wasn't seeing them in natural colour. They were black and white figures. They were the football players, the young men whom I had seen running on this same field. The ghostly apparitions of a bygone war. They were waving at me. I waved back just as the airship began to ascend. As I buckled in, the fine blue mist hung in the air for several moments and then disappeared. The only physical sensation I felt, apart from feeling completely relaxed, was a light, fluttering movement within my stomach that lasted several seconds and then departed. It was like an anaesthetic. That was the last I remembered of my journey before drifting away into sleep.

Retro Zagreb

PART TWO

2.1

I CAN'T REMEMBER ANY DETAILS FROM the flight or voyage or whatever you want to call it. But I can remember being helped to my bed and someone covering me with a large white duvet. The bed felt so comfortable and warm and soft. I sank into it completely. My body felt leaden from the journey and I craved sleep. I have felt fatigue from long distance flights before but those experiences were nothing compared to this. I felt like a stone at the bottom of a deep dark well.

When I regained a full alert consciousness, I looked about not knowing where I was. I was still so tired, so very tired. It took me several minutes to rise from the bed and feel the plush oriental carpet beneath my feet. The guest room was very opulent and spacious with high ceilings, heavy drapes, antique furniture, and the huge canopied bed that I had slept in. Everything around me felt somewhat strange, even though the furnishings were similar to hotel accommodations at home, high end accommodations. I didn't understand how this could be the future, but then I didn't know what to expect. The large window overlooked a broad expansive park. When I opened the window, I could see to my left a magnificent gazebo and park benches. People were strolling about. It was a magnificent sunny day with skies as clear as a child's dreams. I looked about. I was situated on the third floor of what appeared to be a European palace from the nineteenth century. Around the perimeter of the grand park below I could make out several pieces of sculpture, the head and shoulder busts of important people

I assumed. Massive plane trees stood like sentinels along the pedestrian paths below me. Everything was bright and in full colour.

There was a deft, polite knock on my door and suddenly a young fresh-faced waiter pushed a white, linen-covered cart into the room. He had sandy brown hair, an infectious smile, and barely contained enthusiasm as he set the dining table. Within minutes I was enjoying a sumptuous breakfast of scrambled eggs and bacon, fresh brioche buns with strawberry jam, and wonderful piping hot coffee served from a steaming silver pot. Fresh fruit, cheeses, and a cold meat platter on a silver tray were set before me. The waiter smiled broadly and asked if there was anything else I desired before he took his leave. I shook my head and told him everything was perfect. He seemed sincerely disappointed that he couldn't serve me any longer. Unfortunately, I had nothing to give to him as a tip so I simply smiled as he left. I was hungry. Soon I was picking away leisurely at the fine cuts of meat and relaxing in the luxury of the place.

Some time later a short, balding middle-aged man in a white lab coat came into my room unannounced and bid me follow him with a curt wave of his arm. He didn't speak to me at all and walked very briskly. I had to exert myself just to keep a few paces behind him. He turned to me once with a look of annoyance on his face.

We walked through an elegant corridor and then down three flights of stairs and past the hotel lobby area where I noticed there were several black and white glossy photographs of Hollywood film stars and celebrities. Everything had a retro feel to it. I heard some raucous coughing as we walked down still another corridor. Then, we proceeded to a spacious common room with large upholstered chairs where a tall, thin man was waiting. He smiled perfunctorily, nodded, and the impatient man in the lab coat left. I sat in the wingback chair opposite the gaunt-looking man and waited for him to speak. He welcomed me formally, said that I could call him Matija, and then told me that he would provide some preliminary instruction that he hoped I would find useful in making sense of what I would experience.

The room was predominantly green and gold in colour with tasteful urban prints of the city on the walls. It seemed an incredibly large room for just the two of us. I leaned forward slightly. I was curious about what he meant by preliminary instruction.

"It begins here," he said, "and it is fitting that it should." Upon saying that he coughed violently for a moment, and then cleared his throat.

I noticed he had a very slight lisp, and that his warm brown eyes shone brightly as he spoke, as if he had something of great importance to relate. Indeed, I was to realize just how important it was soon enough.

For the first forty minutes he gave an introduction to the life and accomplishments of the inventor Nikola Tesla, citing in particular two of his creations, the induction motor and the Tesla coil, as being especially important in underpinning the technology of the old world as he phrased it, my world. He said these inventions were significant but small when set against something else. As he spoke, he grew excited with his subject, and his lisp became even more pronounced. It was an intermittent hissing sound. I tried to ignore it. Listening is difficult enough, I thought, without distractions.

"One of his greatest legacies to the modern world is something he briefly mentions in his curious autobiography. He writes about being able to visualize his inventions, to do so in his mind without having to painstakingly develop his experiments. He could picture them in his mind, clearly, without having to build a model. For the moment you construct a model, you're beset by details that drag you down from the great concept, the underlying principle that contains your vision. That was his genius, and his gift to us. He was encouraging us to work with the concept in our mind, to allow it to play within the sphere of our imagination. He was able to develop and perfect an idea, a concept, without having to construct anything in a technical shop setting. Within his imagination he could fine-tune his invention and make it work through continuous improvements and countless reconstructions using his force of concentration to always keep the invention uppermost in his mind. He could do this and obtain results without sacrificing quality."

Just then the same waiter that had served breakfast to me earlier brought in a tray of coffee and cakes and set it down on a mahogany table beside us. Matija flashed a warm smile and urged me to partake with a generous wave of his hand. The waiter poured the coffee into fine porcelain cups, and placed them before us. The walnut bread looked wonderful, and I smiled in great appreciation of it. The waiter was pleased and chuckled when he saw me swallow involuntarily at the sight of it. With his gracious manner and beguiling smile, he obviously enjoyed his work, and waited a moment before he left.

"It took us a long time to realize the implications of Tesla's approach. It is perhaps as artistic as it is scientific. The vision, the concept in the imagination, guides product development. The process behind it, behind the invention, whatever it happens to be, is more expeditious, more efficient, and incredibly cheaper. The savings are stupendous." Matija took a long slurping sip of his coffee and grew silent in the contemplation of Tesla's practical genius. I began to wonder where this was leading.

"Your room is comfortable, yes?"

"Yes Matija, very. But I had expected the future to be different, to look different. Actually, it's as if I went back in time, rather than forward. This place and the park outside my window could easily be nineteenth or twentieth century Europe." I refilled my coffee cup and reached for a crescent shaped almond cookie that melted in my mouth. It was so delicious I ate several more leaving just one on the platter. Matija took notice of my enjoyment and smiled.

"Yes, yes, that was our intent. We will be back in the future soon enough, Marin. The park below your window is the famous Zagreb Park known as Zrinjevac. It was totally destroyed, along with most of the city, in the great earthquake of June fifth, 2205. This palace too, where we sit, and indeed the entire city was reconstructed from drawings, photographs, and memories. All of it was remade meticulously to imitate the way it appeared originally. I will show you the city later. Have you been to Zagreb before? I mean, in your own time, back then, in the twenty-first century?

"Just as a small boy with my grandfather. We spent a couple of days here in Zagreb, on a sightseeing tour, but I don't remember anything much other than the statue of a man on a horse with his sword extended. My grandfather bought me a small plastic replica of it, and so I remembered. But only that."

"Ah yes, our hero, Ban Jelačić, in the central square named after him. We will create new memories for you Marin. Rest assured of that. You speak very good Croatian, charming, with a slight accent of course, but we will correct that."

"I was raised by my grandparents after my parents died in an automobile accident. They taught me to speak Croatian in Canada. They were from Lika. After both of my grandparents died I was raised in foster homes."

"Yes, I know. I was given your complete profile. I'm sorry."

"It was many years ago. I hardly remember my parents anymore. I was so young." It bothered me that Matija seemed to know everything about me. I don't know why. There was a long, uncomfortable silence.

"So sorry," he said, his lisp producing the gentle hissing sound that I was growing accustomed to.

Matija suggested then that we go on a walking tour of the city and continue what he termed my instruction. First, we walked the perimeter of the park, Zrinjevac, and walked south from there on the western side of the street, past an adjoining park area, Strossmayer Square, he called it, that contained a Gallery of Old Masters, and we continued on, south from there to another square that contained the impressive statue of one of the first Croatian kings, Tomislav. We didn't cross the street to the train station, but rather made a circuit and walked north on the eastern side of the park towards the center of the city. I was trying to get my bearings as we walked, so I would remember it.

Matija made a point of pointing out attractions and pairing it with his instruction. For instance, he would stop at one of the head and shoulder busts of famous Croatians that lined the park and discuss a particular topic.

"Now, this man was not only a political leader. He was also a poet. With him you have the prose of utilitarian politics complemented by the poetry of the human soul. An appreciation of finance and iambic pentameter within the same rib cage. And why should it be any different than this. The two fields are not mutually exclusive, are they? The question you must ask yourself is how this relates to you and your work with us. But more of that later."

Several people were walking by us in the opposite direction, in small groups, and all of them I noticed were wearing clothing similar to what people were wearing back home. If this was the future I thought, clothing styles hadn't progressed or changed much. That struck me as odd. When I asked Matija about this, he motioned to a park bench where we sat quietly for a moment and watched the passers-by. An elegant, elderly woman was walking her dog, a small black terrier, on a silver leash. A teenager was tossing a small blue ball high into the air and catching it repeatedly. He wore a t-shirt that read **Big Fish**. He dropped the ball once and the terrier immediately leapt for it, pulling the leash from the woman's grasp. The terrier held the ball in his mouth triumphantly and wanted to play.

A group of musicians carrying stringed instruments made their way up the stairs of the gazebo, and I watched as a diminutive bass player gamely struggled with his burden. There was a happy, contented hum in the air of people enjoying themselves on a splendid summer's day. It was far different from the cold weather back home in Hamilton.

Matija turned to me. "All of this," he said, "all of this that you see before you is a re-creation from the past. Several places across Croatia have been rebuilt in this way. What we call Retro Zagreb is in Zone One of the national Heritage Project. Tourist officials have designated this particular month as representative of the year 2023. Everyone is expected to wear clothing from that era. You will see this everywhere in Retro Zagreb. Outside of Zone One, beyond the old city, it is June 01, 2324, of course."

"What?" I shouted. "This year is 2324! You've got to be kidding!"

"Not at all," he said. "You will see when we leave the Zone, how things change. Tesla's concepts were just the beginning. We've progressed in some ways, to be sure, but not unfortunately, in others. That is why we have invited you here. We need you Marin, we need you very much."

Matija patted me on the shoulder a little awkwardly and then we rose and walked towards the city center. I was astounded at the date. It was a strange discovery. Around me the world looked much the same as in Hamilton, notwithstanding the old-style architecture. The one big difference was that apart from blue streetcars there were no vehicles on the streets. When I asked Matija about this I could hear the pride and excitement in his voice.

"The year 2324 had many issues, many problems. Pollution, floods, droughts, no end of environmental catastrophes that were to grow even worse, much worse. Much has been rectified, though not completely. Many parts of the planet are still devastated despite our actions. You will soon see.

But in the more than three centuries that have passed since your time we have done much to make things cleaner and more natural. We progressed from individually owned hybrid vehicles to on-demand hover vans, at least here in Retro Zagreb. You will experience that transport soon enough."

2.2

Just as we were about to cross the road to get to the main square, a group of young men, about six of them, all dressed in smart gray athletic uniforms, walked towards us, clearly expecting us to move out of their way as they approached. I was surprised at how pallid their complexions were. Matija pulled me over to one side so as not to oppose them.

"Who are they?" I asked as they passed by.

Matija waited until they were out of earshot. We stood just under the great clock of the main square.

"That, dear Marin, is why you are here," he said, as he looked towards them and followed their progress down the street. I noticed that other pedestrians moved out of the way as they passed. "Those are the usurpers, if I may use that term. It fits the context. The latest in a long line of alien invaders, only these are truly alien, from the far reaches of the Milky Way."

"I don't understand."

"The officers of those proud young men desire us to vacate the premises, the country, our country. They want us out of here, and so are offering gold to each and everyone. Imagine that. That's what they say, and I've come to believe they are great liars, truly gifted liars. I find our people like to believe in sudden, spectacular riches. If we agree, we will be resettled in border lands that will be cleared of their present citizenry, EU citizenry. I was told our emissaries explained this to you when they met you in Canada, did they not?"

"Yes, I remember now. I remember, but not everything. So, what is to happen?"

"Since our emissaries spoke to you in Canada a great rift has developed between the Browns and the Blues, our main political parties. The military has not committed itself, and is waiting in the wings for direction. The Browns want to take up the offer of becoming rich and then offering their services as watchdogs on the periphery of our country. They believe if they appease the aliens they can secure riches, a new homeland, and the best possible outcome. Both parties know that our technology is inferior to theirs. The Blues want to fight with whatever we have. I must tell you that there are many developments that the Browns are not aware of at this point, the Blue Mist technology for one. With your help and the help of people like you, we will defend ourselves. Meanwhile, our military stands on the sidelines and waits."

2.3

The instructions given to me by the hotel concierge were clear. I was to meet a woman named Vesna in the Upper Town, at noon, by the medieval Tower of Lotrščak. It was a sunny, cloudless day and there seemed to be a festive mood among the people walking leisurely about. My morning was free so I lost myself in wandering about the Lower Town. I noticed there were no cars or motorcycles on the streets. The roads were wide and inviting. I was enchanted by the nineteenth century architecture, and then I turned a corner and came across the golden gem of the Croatian National Theatre, something I'd seen only in my grandfather's picture books. The reconstruction of Zagreb was marvellous. Every detail was captured, even to the group of bronze figures huddled around a well in front of the theater. A plaque indicated the sculpture was entitled *The Well of Life* by Ivan Meštrović. I wasn't aware of who he was and his importance at the time. That came later. An old photo showed a mound of rubble after the devastation of the earthquake. People stopped to touch and rub the heads of the bronze figures with respect, and for good luck. The heads became bright and shiny from countless touching and rubbing to a brassy gold colour. From there I made my way roughly northeast to the main street of Ilica where I took the funicular to the Upper Town. There, I began to look around for a woman wearing a blue polka dot dress and a red carnation.

I spotted her immediately, and just as I did so I was shocked momentarily by the sound of a cannon thundering in the air above me. It came from the Tower and marked the twelfth hour. An attractive woman approached me, introduced herself, and smiled broadly. I was immediately struck by her beauty. She was tall and lithe with silky, shoulder length brown hair that had an auburn sheen to it. She had a sculpted angular face that resembled paintings of young Roman beauties. Perhaps she thought I was shaken by the loud burst of cannon fire, so she took me by the hand and guided me towards a walking path called Strossmayer Promenade. She chatted easily about the charms of Zagreb and the difficulties encountered in restoring it to its former glories. And then, rather abruptly and in a much more serious tone, she began to speak about what she called our mission. She spoke as we walked, every now and then stopping to look at me to see if I understood. She had a delightful habit of raising her eyebrows every now and then as if she had just asked me a question and was waiting for an answer.

"It took us several generations to refine our thinking models. The Blue Mist model didn't come easily, I can tell you that. Initially, we developed our models by a team, a committee of scientists, but it was just no good. There was no consistency or coherence. It just wouldn't fly. We found in the end that we needed to begin with an imaginative model developed by a single physicist, someone who had the mind of a scientific genius and the sensibility of a poet."

"Yes," I said, "Matija had mentioned Tesla's ability to imagine working models and to adapt them as necessary in his engineering work."

"That is where it all started from. Tesla's brilliance. He gave us the concept, an idea about how to proceed, and we took it from there. As Einstein said, imagination is greater than knowledge, always has been."

I stopped for a moment to take in the beauty of the city around us. Then I turned to her with a question. "When will I be able to see the Blue Mist model? I can understand a thing better when I can see it in operation in front of me."

"Soon," she said. "But first the concepts behind the model. That's what's needed to accelerate your learning. You have a number of tutors, all of whom want to ensure you're ready. The next few months will be very busy for you."

"OK," I said, just as a plump, brown sparrow alighted atop a house chimney below the steep hill on which we stood. For a fleeting second it reminded me of home, and I felt a sharp pang of homesickness that left me as quickly as it had come.

"The lead scientist on the Blue Mist project was Toma Radičev. Unfortunately, you will not get to meet him. He is gone from us, deceased. But he left us a great legacy. He said that if you understood the nature of lines, of vertical and horizontal lines, then the principles behind the model would be easy to understand."

"I don't get it. What did he mean?"

"He suggested that the horizontal line represented space, and the vertical line stood for time. He wanted our team to play with the concepts, to have fun with them the way a child would. He said that a line has a beginning and an end, but you can join the beginning and the end to form a circle, and then what you started with is something else entirely."

"I'm sorry I won't get a chance to talk with him. He sounds like an interesting guy."

"Yes, he was. Anything can happen, and happen it did. Just as the prototype design phase was completed, we celebrated with a great feast at the Esplanade Hotel, here in Retro Zagreb, near the train station, and he was the guest of honour. There were speeches and jokes and no end of merriment. Toma and his wife Kristina and their two-year old daughter Bela were the center of all attention. Mid way through the evening Kristina left with Bela to take the child home to bed. As she was crossing the street, with Bela in her arms, they were struck by a tram. It happened just like that. They died instantly. I remember seeing Toma's face when he heard the devastating news. It was as if a powerful light had been extinguished. The brilliance in his blue eyes was gone forever. He carried himself very well through the funeral and the activities that followed. Indeed, throughout all of the condolences and heartfelt sympathies offered, he was stalwart and seemed more concerned with the grief of others than his own. After everyone had gone, he went home to their apartment and put a bullet through his head. He didn't leave a note. That was unnecessary. A thousand tamburitza musicians played farewell music at his graveside. It was tragic."

Vesna's expression looked suddenly distraught, as she recalled the memory for a moment, holding it like a dark feather drawn across her mind for a painful second or two. She stepped away from me for a private moment, and then she returned with a bright smile to the spot where we stood overlooking the city.

"So," she said, "you are interested in Blue Time Mist. Toma had perfected the Blue Time Mist model in his imagination. It took him several months to design. Time compression, time expansion, time distortion, all facets of time were explored and manipulated in the miniature model he had crafted both technically and imaginatively. Toma was standing on Tesla's shoulders and creating bridges to the past. What was impossible became possible. What was proved was once only imagined. Our physicists can provide you with the data and the algorithms if you wish. It's important to play with the concept of time, to shake free of its linearity and supposed irreversibility. The mist is actual mist, fine, incredibly fine droplets of water, of moisture sprayed into the air. Infinitely tiny circles of moisture that are non-linear and that expedite time travel. It has to be calibrated, of course, to a specific time and place in one of our nodal areas, but once executed, the results are access to a new reality, a past reality and time. All of these concepts will be explained to you in detail."

We found a park bench and she continued to give informal lectures on a variety of topics including miniaturization, period objects or things as silent witnesses to history, and ancient Croatian dialects. I was beginning to think in Croatian as well as to speak it fluently. I've always enjoyed feeling the words take shape on my tongue, and now especially the ancient variants of the language. Finally, she raised her eyebrows momentarily and I could tell we were finished for the day. I certainly was. I was getting hungry and needed a break from instruction. She left me with an odd tablet that she said contained my itinerary for the next week. Just as she was about to leave, I asked her if she wanted to join me for a bite to eat. It was nearing the dinner hour. An odd look flashed across her face as if she recognized something personal between us for the first time. She said she had plans already made, but that I was free to join her and some friends for old style drinks later that evening. She said that I might find the old club interesting and that I could inform her if it was historically accurate, as I came from the same time era that the club theme was based on. She said something to the tablet she had given me, and then we departed.

As I walked back to my hotel, I crossed the main square where I saw several foreign looking men dressed in gray athletic outfits, similar to the ones worn by the group I had encountered earlier with Matija. They appeared to be on a tour. Blue trams glided by as I stopped for a moment. The guide was speaking a language I had never heard before and as he spoke, he pointed to the equestrian statue, and said something in a kind of whisper. Immediately upon hearing what he had said, the group erupted into fits of laughter and stood shaking their heads in disbelief.

That evening I was at the club before Vesna and her friends arrived. The place was boisterous and dark within a cavernous basement that had a vaulted ceiling. Graffiti covered the walls. There was a heavy techno beat that throbbed and shook the place. I had to shout my order to the waiter. When they entered the bar, I could see that a trio of beauties caught everyone's attention. They were dressed in tight-fitting leathers, period dress, that accentuated their figures on the dance floor. Soon, we were drinking shots of plum brandy and shouting loudly at the top of our lungs and enjoying every minute of it. It was raucous and authentic and the same hypnotic, powerful beat carried us through the evening.

I had hoped to spend some time alone with Vesna but that was not to be. Not at all. It was clear to me within the first hour that Vesna and one of her leathered companions, Ivanka, were a couple. I could see the small tender ways they touched each other as they danced and looked at each other in ways that signalled their love. It was obvious, and I was happy to see their mutual affection. The third woman, Danica, and I smiled at each other a lot, but the place was too loud to try to attempt any kind of conversation. Danica and I did dance with each other but there was no connection, no spark between us, no ignition. At the end of the evening we all walked together for a while in the cool Retro Zagreb night, a bit tired and happily drunk. Then we embraced, kissed each other twice on the cheeks, and then parted ways.

2.4

The following day I was ushered into a large room with floor to ceiling dark blue curtains covering the walls. I touched one, grabbed a fold of it, and felt its heaviness in my grasp. The lighting was minimal but in the center of the room there appeared to be a large table, about the size of a billiard table, covered with a light blue sheet. Without a word, my guide motioned me to follow him and, in an instant, we stood next to each other beside the table. Whatever was under the cover sheet was irregular with one side considerably higher than the other. That much at least I could make out despite the poor lighting.

And then, with a sudden, abrupt movement, the guide whipped the sheet away from the tabletop. The sheet was very light and floated down to the floor. Then he touched an electronic device of some kind that was positioned on the edge of the tabletop. Immediately, the center of the room and the table were brightly illuminated. There, in front of us, at waist level, was what appeared to be a scale model of the terrain and territory of the state of Croatia. I saw plenty of limestone and darkened areas resembling forests. I have to say I was somewhat puzzled over the dramatic manner with which my guide had brought me to this display. The expression on his face was one of awe. He stood there and gazed down upon the model in rapt fixation. For me, it was nothing special. Certainly, an interesting miniature, painstakingly crafted, but I had seen other models similar to it before, back home in Canada. Train hobbyists and artists had created models just as captivating. And then I remembered the bronze model of old Zagreb near the main square. Interesting, but little more than that. I guess I'd expected something more impressive from the future.

2.5

Odd to me how a lacklustre day has the potential to change the game dramatically and suddenly. I glanced to my left as I was entering one of the retro stores that lined Jelačić Square, and there she was. It couldn't have been more than a few seconds as our eyes met and then broke away from each other as she was leaving the store exit next to the entrance where I was standing. I captured the image immediately, storing it in my memory. How could I have done otherwise? She was beautiful. She was proud, perhaps with a trace of arrogance. She was tall, statuesque, but somehow threatening too. Her luxuriant hair was cropped short, the colour of copper and tarnished gold. Her olive skin was tan and radiant with rosy health. I thought I detected the trace of a wry smile as she looked at me, but the image of her was passing so quickly that I may have just imagined it. What I didn't imagine were the tattoos artfully drawn along her bare shoulders and arms.

She may have caught me looking in admiration, and I tried for an instant to look away, but I hung suspended for a second or two, and then she was gone. What lingered in my mind were her wide green eyes that seemed to assess me, to take my measure. A door closed, another opened, and she was gone. I wondered if I would ever see her again.

2.6

What intrigued me as I met with my several tutors over the following weeks was the concept of Blue Time Mist and how it could enable access to different historical periods to the century, to the decade, to the year, to the month and day, and incredibly to the very hour and minute and second. I had a favourite bench close to the magnificent equestrian statue of the first Croatian king, King Tomislav. I'd sit on the bench watching the flow of tourists as they ambled by, and I'd speculate about how things worked. I allowed myself to drift into a self-hypnotic state as Matija had taught me, and I just let myself go, following along with things. Under the clear blue skies of the rebuilt Zagreb I'd imagine great airships floating high above the country of Croatia, high above the miniature world below. I'd suddenly see a single airship and within it, the figure of someone in a control room calibrating destined time, a past long gone but accessible. And then beneath the great retro airship the release of the special blue mist that was essential to success, the same mist that had brought me such a short time ago from Hamilton to a future Zagreb, time and distance eclipsed by human genius, by Toma Radičev and his team of scientists. And then as the aircraft descended, the landmass grew greater and greater until it hovered over one of the nodal areas spread across the country. The descent entailed fantastic factors of compression until the door opened and I stepped out gingerly, miraculously, onto the ground, the welcoming earth firm beneath my feet.

And always close by, I imagined, an underground kiosk area, usually within a cave, hidden and secret from prying eyes. Nodal kiosks that held the treasured objects of the past and certain human resonances from that past, all within the ambit of the spirit of the place. I paused for a moment feeling the warmth of the noon sun on my arms as tourists passed by my bench sharing the blessing of a radiant sun. A small black and white shih tzu puppy strained on its leash and sniffed at my pant leg before being pulled away by a young girl in a soccer jersey with the number 10 emblazoned on it.

I remembered suddenly that Matija had once said that I would be able to see things within the kiosks that reflected what had actually happened there in the past, experiences and events that had taken place exactly there but in a different time. The nodal areas were spectacularly rich in what he called deposits from the past that were evocative of life lived there or, just as meaningfully, he said, of death encountered there.

I didn't know quite what to make of that when he said it, and he had sensed my confusion. He seemed a bit amused by my discomfort, and said that since I had arrived my sensibility had developed immensely. I was a different man from the one who had left Hamilton. I was experiencing growing pains he said. I remembered his words so clearly.

Just then I felt a pang of hunger, and I rose from the bench, and joined a throng of tourists heading to the northern expanse of park where I knew I could find a sausage and maybe a light dessert.

We were in a café just above and next to the Stone Gate in the old town. It was early afternoon. Karlo was sipping on a double espresso while I enjoyed a cappuccino. He was a thick-bodied muscular man with curly, sandy hair and an easy manner about him. He smiled at everyone. Below us people were passing through the Stone Gate in a steady flow. The Stone

Gate was a kind of shrine where people could light votive candles for the dead or request help through prayer when they needed it. Across from us I noticed a ginger cat sitting contentedly on a windowsill across from us. The ambience of the place felt as warm as the sun on my forearms. Karlo was quiet for the longest time as if he were thinking about how best to begin. His eyes brightened, and he smiled warmly before he spoke.

"Certain places have a lingering hold on us. They have a kind of spiritual resonance that corresponds with something within us. The spirit of place underpins everything we do. Having said that, it's essential, of course, to find the right individual or facilitator who can connect with a place and time and enter it proactively as a potential change agent. That's why you're here. That's why you've been selected. Your DNA allows you to physically travel to the past, and not merely as an observer, a three-dimensional image projection. We can observe, but we can't physically be there as you can. We don't know why you have this ability and we do not, but there you have it. What helps the process greatly are objects from the past, things from a specific time and place, what we call silent witnesses. These objects contain non-animate sensitivities that are remarkable in determining historical truth or collective social memories. If this all seems a bit nebulous to the layman, then that's as it should be. We're dealing with different realities, different potentialities, and nothing less than the evolution of consciousness in human beings. It's going to be quite a ride for you. You're going to find yourself on the very edge of things."

As he spoke I noticed that Karlo sat bolt upright in his chair and his words seemed to build in a momentum that grew richer and stronger with each of the ideas that he presented. His eyes were as blue as a happy dream recalled. A waiter passed our table with a silver tray of wonderful looking pastries that I sorely wanted to try, but I could see it was not the time. I swallowed involuntarily and waited for him to continue.

"You've seen the miniature model of Croatia. Miniaturization helps us to gain a certain perspective, a horizontal spatial location. It helps us to pinpoint special places, but it is useless without a vertical perspective, a time orientation. Space and time are the coordinates we use and apply. Our modern holy cross of sorts. The tiny blue lights that you saw on the simple

Croatia model are representative of nodes across the country. Think of them as special places that contain layered accretions of memory and history. Just as a geological point on the earth can be composed of various accumulations of sedimentary strata, so too do they contain time strata, different historical periods where memory is concentrated. The human brain has layers similar to sedimentary strata. The history of a people can be found to resonate in certain places like the fortress at Klis or the reconstructed Stone Gate below us here in Retro Zagreb, or the small cathedral at Nin. There are many others across the country and you will get to know them. These are power points, nodes at the very center of the Croatian spirit of place. Human memory and living history, despite its fallibility and arbitrariness, is the golden road to accessing the past. You look confused. Don't worry. Everything will become clear in time.

You, my friend, under Brujo's guidance, can help us identify nodal transmitters from each special place, individuals who represent the best qualities of a particular period, our spiritual DNA. After almost two millennia there are certain qualities of spirit that mark the Croatian character. I am not speaking about physical DNA. The best of the Croatian people, indeed, the best of humanity, are found in positive ethical traits, moral predispositions that inform our actions."

I marvelled at the intensity of expression on his face. It was glowing and radiant. Karlo had such a belief in me that I was charged up and ready to go to the very mouth of hell to prove him right. His enthusiasm was contagious.

"I know these terms will seem a bit strange or unusual to you at first, but give it time. You must be patient. Nodes and nodal transmitters will soon be part of your mindset. Human history, Croatian history, is never completely finished. History is fluid and in constant flux with what comes after. The future continues to inform the past and vice versa. For example, new archaeological findings from digs, often dispute what we hold as truth. What we held to be accurate was based on old evidence, old theories. What further complicates our understanding of the past is the abuse of history by individuals who rewrite it to fill their own political agenda. They reinterpret history and arbitrarily change it to fit with their own notion of truth.

In your own time, look at the way museums changed. In the early days artefacts were ripped from the places where they originated and held in distant museums as curios and trophies and the stolen treasure of empires. The Elgin marbles were spirited away from Greece and deposited in the British Museum, held captive for their own protection, it was said, in climate-controlled chambers and under the black British umbrella of a stable democracy. Some of those imperialistic Brits even believed their own lies. But things changed.

In time, many museums around the world were emptied of their loot and their objects repatriated to the places where they came from, the silent witnesses of a different time. Eco museums developed and the spirit of a particular place was gifted again with the items and objects that gave it meaning and nuanced articulation. We refer to these as nodal areas. The tiny blue lights on the Croatia terrestrial model show a network of nodes where history and memory are concentrated. Within these nodes are the nodal transmitters, the leaders from a special time and place that have been identified. Indeed, they are representative of the spirit of the place and the time. Couple that with the objects or tools they loved and used, and you have an incredible power source.

We've created kiosks in special places that we can access at will. We call them kiosks but they're not like the newsstand kiosks you see around Retro Zagreb. For one thing they're much bigger. For us, they are places of learning that allow us to understand where we came from, how our ancestors lived and thought and had their being. Technology wasn't enough. It never is. Weapons are merely things that can be easily duplicated at will, but the spirit, the special human qualities of a nodal transmitter cannot. We discovered we needed a kind of medium that could realign us with the best of our past, with the ethical qualities that we need now to defeat the alien invader. These nodes have been planted across the Croatian landscape, often in limestone caves. Kiosks within these nodes contain the tools and information needed to connect up with the past, with its leaders and the special qualities they possessed and the personal objects that were significant to them. Remember, the different periods of history contained in these nodes are superimposed on each other, like geological strata. Within each of the strata are nodes and the identification of nodal transmitters that are potentially accessible and ready to be used. That is where you come in. You're the medium, the special outlier from the Croatian diaspora that can make things happen.

Are you with me?" For a moment he studied my face intently. He wanted me to follow him every step of the way. To be truthful, I was exhausted mentally, at the very limits of my understanding, and I knew I couldn't take much more. I sorely craved something sweet. But Karlo was so intense and keen to continue.

I nodded. I glanced away from him for a moment to process the information he was giving me. I could hear the din from the pathway below us of dozens of people talking and walking up the hill to see the sights. Then I asked him to continue.

"I'm glad you're with us. I want to tell you that we visited several potential candidates from your time and from the diaspora to solicit their help. Usually, we scared the hell out of them as we did you at first. Some had extraordinary abilities but neither the requisite physical DNA nor the temperament. It helped too that we could encourage you with a financial incentive."

At that he smiled like he'd just told the greatest joke. I could see that he was beginning to enjoy teasing me.

"Don't worry. If you stay with us you can continue to win lotteries. It costs us nothing as you know. Living in your future, we know the results of many such matters. Our Republic is on the verge of insolvency, and that is why the Aliens' offer of immense wealth for every citizen in exchange for our departure and compliance as military guardians is very attractive to some but not to all. But enough of that. Very soon we'll be showing you how we travel to these nodes and access the kiosks throughout the land. But for now I want to take you to someplace special where you'll meet someone from your past. I doubt you'll even remember the gentleman, but no matter. I'm sure he'll be able to refresh your memory. Let's go."

We walked a short distance west and then turned north past a church with a steeply pitched roof decorated with brilliant multi-coloured tiles. Karlo stopped for a moment to let me admire it, saying that it was perhaps the most famous Croatian church of all. St. Mark's. It was an exact replica to the centimeter he said, of the original, before the earthquake of 2205. And then he pointed to a sculptured face on one of the corner buildings of the Square and muttered in a low voice something about a peasant king martyred for his beliefs. Later I discovered his name was Matija Gubec, and that I was a descendant of his, according to one of my tutors.

A moment later we were standing in the interior courtyard of Ivan Meštrović's studio.

"Our restoration wasn't perfect, but we believe we captured the essence of the place. Some things can never be duplicated except by the artist's own hand."

Around us were ranged the monumental and powerful forms of the master artist. I strolled about basking in the sunny ambience of the place until a vision from the past broke into my thoughts. The vision, or what I thought was a vision, was smiling in the very center of the courtyard.

"Ah, the boy from the diaspora, from Canada, now grown to be a man. Welcome again."

It was the strange, little old man with the wizened face whom I had met in the caves near Gospić when I was a small boy. The very same man whom my grandfather had called Brujo. He looked the same though dressed a bit differently. He wore the same white peasant blouse and baggy pants, but on his head, a brimless red cap with black trim and a black tassle on the back. A red and white checkerboard crest adorned the top. I remembered my grandfather having the same kind of cap, one that he wore with great pride on special occasions. It was a fine cap. A crimson sash was tied snugly around his waist.

"I remember you," I said. "You look exactly the same."

"So, are you saying I was prematurely aged the last time we met then?" He laughed uproariously at what he had said, enjoying the wordplay and the joking. And then, on a new tack of thought, and with a gracious wave of his arm that encompassed the sky above and the ground below, he spoke in a resonant voice.

"This courtyard is an ancient and beautiful place. I believe there is what I would call blood memory in our people as you will learn. You, especially dear boy. That is why the stories you will hear are so rich with mysteries within mysteries, like the whorled petals of the rose. The language on our tongue guides us through the mysteries and we come to know the place as never before."

Karlo murmured something about the diaspora that I couldn't quite make out and then the strange little man said to him softly, and with a generous, beguiling smile.

"Our diaspora around the world is like a bunch of grapes. They are all on the same stem. The taste is roughly the same in each grape, but slightly different, and we treasure that difference."

2.7

Karlo nodded graciously and then took his leave. The little man walked about the courtyard, stopping every now and then to admire the sculptures that graced the small enclosure. He turned to me, his face shining, and touched my elbow.

"Sometimes acts of imagination are acts of love. Around us, Marin, are one man's acts of love rendered in stone."

I stood with him in silence for a moment, joyful that we were here together and that he had said my name. It was the first time that he had addressed me by name since I was a small child.

We left the atelier and walked to the central square, towards the equestrian statue that was really the center of the city. We stopped at the Stone Gate, in the semi darkness of it, where he lit a candle and then sat on the first pew beside the table of glowing, melted candles that others had left. I sat next to him and felt strangely elated, being in his presence and in this special place rescued twice from earthquakes.

At a café on the edge of the square behind the statue, Brujo ordered a bottle of white wine and another of sparkling water. It was late afternoon and the shadows of people walking by were lengthening. We sat in agreeable silence and sipped at our drinks under a large sun umbrella. A small group of Asian tourists approached our table and asked if they could take a few pictures with him. His peasant garb had attracted attention throughout the day as we had strolled about. In keeping with the ancient theme of the rebuilt city they used antique iPhones purchased for the occasion. They were as surprised as I was when he addressed them in fluid Mandarin. Later, when I asked him how he knew they were Chinese as opposed to other Asian nationalities, he simply laughed and said that it was intuition aided by the t-shirts they wore that identified them as being from Shanghai.

"Is your training progressing well Marin?"

"Yes."

"And questions. Do you have questions?"

"Not yet. My tutors are thorough and keep me on my toes. It's been almost three months of instruction, pretty intense instruction, with lots of surprises. I just want to get started and do things. I haven't been to a nodal area or kiosk yet. I need to see one."

"You will soon enough, and more, much more."

Brujo then poured a second glass of white wine followed by sparkling water for each of us, and for several moments we sat and drank in contented silence, looking out at the people traversing the famous Square, watching the blue trams passing by, and thinking our own thoughts. High above us in the azure skies there were three airships heading south towards the coast.

"You're not afraid, are you?"

He broke the silence abruptly with his statement and a piercing blue-eyed gaze that surprised me with its frankness. "There are very real dangers that you will encounter. When they happen, things are going to take place and move very quickly, of that you can be sure."

"I don't know what to expect. It's unknown to me, so no, I'm not afraid just now. Maybe I don't have the sense to be afraid. Rather, I feel excitement. I remember talking with my grandfather about that, about fear and excitement. So long ago."

"Oh, Marin, I know you have courage and the sense to know the difference between excitement and fear. And there may come a time when you need to access the courage you're feeling right now in this moment by the Square with the taste of Istrian wine on your lips."

Just as he said those words, he reached over across the glass table and held my elbow for a fleeting moment, pressing my arm ever so lightly, anchoring the event in my mind. It was no sooner done than he said it was time to go. He paid the waiter and left a handsome tip. He wanted to show me something he said, something unusual.

We walked the short distance to Tkalčićeva Street with its many restaurants and bars beginning to fill with early evening customers. A few waiters were standing outside restaurants soliciting customers to come in as they did in bygone times. We'd only gone a little way before he turned left along a side street and stopped in the middle of it.

"Marin, there was a bridge here once. And beneath us, beneath this very street where we stand now, there was a stream that flowed under that bridge. Indeed, that stream still flows underground and has since the beginning of time. I want you to know that, to know that things change but remain the same. Battles were fought here, pitched battles, right here, at this very spot. It's called Bloody Bridge."

We stood there for a moment, in silence, and then Brujo nodded to me and left. From there I wandered through the busy streets and returned to my hotel, curious about what the next day's instruction would bring.

I enjoyed walking through the streets of Retro Zagreb. Often I would simply wander the streets aimlessly, so unlike my outings in Hamilton that were so deliberate and fixed. There were times though that I missed home and my little basement apartment in Hamilton. But then Peter was the only close friend I had there. Mind you, I had many acquaintances from Mohawk College and several girlfriends but not on the same level as my friendship with Peter. But here in Croatia, I was beginning to have many, many friends as a result of my training.

The Croatian outlier in me had come home, to his ancestral home, and it was quite a different feeling I had. I realized in one of those rare flashes of insight one receives out of the blue that what made a Croat a true Croat were the values and outlook that are unique to his people. After more than a millennium of life in this place, and despite the privations and hardships, the Croat nation was here to stay.

Retro Zagreb and even the other places of modern Croatia I had seen had a lived-in feel, as it should have from well over a millennium of Croatian living experience. And beyond that the connection to the Illyrians, Romans,

Franks, Ottomans, and countless others. I felt in my heart that the Croatians would never leave the place, not for gold, not for anything. I knew that the Croatian state was not so much a nation as a huge extended family, a family descended from seven brothers and sisters as legend would have it. It was a storied family that fought off aggressors of all stripes. The Croats had created a mythology of arrival in this place, this Croatia. Yes, it was a family that was well experienced in defending its territory and people from aggressors. The Croats may not be a distinct race of people, but blood memory runs long.

2.8

I'd been told that Josip was to be my principal guide and tutor, but I found it odd and somewhat disconcerting that from the first time we met in the heart of Retro Zagreb in Jelačić Square under the tall clock, he seemed to be far more interested in drink and merriment than guidance or learning. He was a short, heavyset man, thickly moustached, and dressed like a peasant farmer. He wore loose fitting white pants, high leather boots, and a white peasant blouse with fine blue stitching embroidered down the front. His hair was long and the colour of dark straw.

He took me by the arm and led me across the street, seemingly oblivious to the trams moving in both directions. One of the trams bearing down upon us screeched to a halt, the driver shouting and swearing at us as we made our way to the sidewalk and promenade on the other side of the street. Josip simply waved at the man in good spirits. We walked to an outdoor bar on Bogovićeva Street where he said the draught beer was particularly cold and delicious. His face was constantly smiling even as he spoke.

"We must continue your instruction here," he said. "Here, in this little world crafted by memory and desire. Here, where Zagreb tells us its tale through its architecture and the magic of barley." As soon as the waitress had placed the pints of beer on our table, Josip clinked my glass, hoisted his beer on high, muttered salutations to my good health, and then downed his pint in several swift gulps. It reminded me of my student days at Mohawk

College back home in Hamilton where chugging back a pint of brew was a blissful reward for the rigors of study. He immediately signalled for another round, and winked at me. I knew then the kind of evening we were going to have.

After three pints he suggested a move to what he called the glories of Tkalčićeva Street where he said an underground stream, the Medveščak, still ran beneath the surface, like an artery beneath the skin. I guessed he was referring to the same covered-over stream that Brujo had talked about the day before. Indeed we were very close to the same spot where Brujo and I had stood. Josip insisted on paying the tab, and the waitress was exceedingly happy with her tip. It was a short walk and within a few moments we were strolling by pastel-painted 18th and 19th century houses, many of them converted to restaurants, boutiques, galleries and bars. It was busy and vibrant and just beginning to hum. If this was instruction, I was becoming a fast learner.

After two more pints, Josip looked at me earnestly and then suddenly began laughing, a hearty, full-throated laugh from the very depths of his belly and being. He laughed uproariously. His paunch shook and rolled with merriment. People at tables on either side of us looked at us in surprise and unmitigated delight. His laughter was infectious. They couldn't help themselves but laugh as well, and then look away. All of us were tourists in this fantastical city and we were together, free in this re-imagined space that had become real once again.

I learned the most from Josip not within the confines of the classroom, but when we went out for a night of drinking. That's when he was at his best as a tutor, totally forthright, unabashed, and uninhibited. That's when I pushed and probed him. With all of the discoveries that had been made in the future since my time in the past, of what use could there possibly be in having me revisit ancient times even more distant and deluded than my own? Once in his cups, Josip's eyes sparked alive and he became a visionary. Josip talked about spiritual DNA, about somehow accessing the very best of the Croatian character variants, meaning Croatian qualities of character that had been developed because of their steadfast resistance to aggressors. Before we became a nation we were Croats, he said, a people who survived by sticking together against all odds. He emphasized that Croatia was on the crossroads of Europe, a Slavic people who developed unique qualities of character because of the very real terror and oppression they had faced from invaders. Josip always insisted on reminding me that the Croats were never imperialists, never conquerors who laid claim to foreign territory, to lands and treasures that did not belong to them. Indeed, he said repeatedly, despite their courage and military skill proven on Habsburg and Ottoman battlefields, they only wanted to defend and keep what was theirs. But still I pressed him. I asked him to give me a sample of this vaunted spiritual DNA. And after eight drinks that's just what he did.

He leaned forward and pushed his glass away for a moment, reflecting on what he was going to say and then choosing his words carefully. "Throughout our history, over centuries, and beset by foreign imperialists, rapists, and thieves, there developed a negative attitude toward any and all kinds of political authority. This is natural and as it should be, but when the time came for us to back our true leaders, we did not always do so. We did something different."

As he spoke he became at turns softly emotional and quiet, and then angry, causing people at adjoining tables to look at us with concern and a little trepidation. Josip was oblivious to them all. He was in the moment. He was reliving history. Despite all that he had to drink he didn't slur his words. There was no way I could keep up to him. I stopped after five drinks.

"You see, Marin. You need to see that what our people gave their leaders was love and faith. God bless them. They gave them high ideals, hopes, banquets and parades, fine, but they turned away from offering what was really needed, disciplined, unrelenting support." His eyes were moist and he looked away for a moment, trying to reconcile something in his mind.

"But I will not belabour the point with bad examples from our history. It's far more important for me to show you historical moral examples that demonstrate the power of discipline and love. Yes, discipline and love together. And about that I will tell you of the Uskoks.

But look, Marin, my glass is empty. How can I tell you of the wonderful Uskoks of Senj with dry lips." I signalled to our waiter for one more draught beer and then waited to hear the tale. Josip was now in his cups and smiling broadly. The waiter brought two large mugs of beer to our table and when I told him we only wanted one, Josip protested and said that the second beer would not go to waste. I shrugged, marvelling at the man's capacity for drink. The pub was growing noisy with merry shouts and laughter and so I moved my chair a bit closer to Josip. I wanted to hear everything.

"Let us go back then, far back in your mind's eye, until we are in Uskok lands by the shining silver sea. In the sixteenth and seventeenth centuries. Are you with me, Marin?"

"I'm hanging on every word."

"Good. The Uskoks were forced from inland regions by the Turks and driven out as fugitives. And so they were organized as frontier guards and served under the Habsburg flag at Senj, and nearby ports. But their pay and supplies were irregular and caused much privation. No man, and particularly an Uskok, can stand by while their children are hungry and with bulging eyes and bellies sip at thin soup. So, they adapted. They raided the Turks on land, but that was not enough. They needed more if they were to thrive. And so they looked out to the sea.

They were led by brilliant, cunning leaders who looked to the waters and determined that they must adapt further and master the sea. Desperation drives innovation, Marin. The Uskok people learned the maritime disciplines from the people of Senj and other Dalmatian settlements along the coast, and they served their leaders well. They became feared pirates and then there was more than enough meat and bread and wine to set on oaken tables. Their children could play games once again and follow their fathers to the sea and plunder Turkish and Venetian ships. Those empires tried and tried again to eliminate them but failed. Ah Marin, can you believe that the Uskoks, facing these threats, barely had more than 1500 men and 30 ships? Against empires! Ah Marin, that is what I meant by the people giving disciplined, continuous support to their leaders. That is the example that shows the mettle of the people. Enough, let us go home now and sleep. Perhaps we will dream of Uskoks sailing on silver seas. Come Marin, my gifted mercenary, let us go. Tomorrow is another day."

2.9

That I was considered a mercenary bothered me. I don't know why. Josip's statement was true but still, it stung me. I had been given ten million in lottery winnings in compensation for several months work in the future. About a year's work, more or less, I was told. Not a bad return on my time investment. The money was in the bank back home, back in my past. I've never thought of myself as particularly brave but fortune is certainly a great motivator. The money meant nothing to them. A small selection of numbers and it was done. It didn't cost them a dime. From their end, they believed I possessed strange, shamanic powers embedded in my DNA that could be harnessed somehow and used to defeat an alien invader. They cautioned me, however, that there was risk involved, though they couldn't specify exactly what form that risk would take. I needed to think and walk.

So here I was in this reconstructed city of Retro Zagreb of the future, a city destroyed for a second time by an earthquake and then painstakingly rebuilt out of memory and desire and broken pieces of stone. I hadn't yet seen what the future really looked like, the future beyond the charmed circle of old Retro Zagreb. I made my way to Flower Square, to one of the cafes there. I found a table, ordered a coffee and a cinnamon pastry, and gazed at the statue of the soldier-poet standing on a plinth in the square. A white dove descended from the clear blue sky and settled proprietarily on the bronze head. A single feather floated down to the gray flagstones. Somehow it reminded me of a snowflake from home.

I was curious about the future. I didn't know what to expect. Any thoughts I may have had about a peaceful future were gone. I was here, after all, to give assistance in a war effort. My grandfather would have been proud. An old time Croatian transplanted to Canada. His heart was always in the Old Country though he lived in Canada for most of his life. His identity was bedrock Croatian, whereas mine was as a hyphenated Croatian-Canadian. What did it mean? Most European nations were born in the mid-nineteenth century, and I thought nationalism was beginning to die out. Indeed, people talked about nationalism as a relic of the past. But that wasn't the case, at least not yet. My own identity was Canadian, the country where I was born and nurtured. My first allegiance was there, certainly, but just behind that was the storied land of my grandfather and of my ancestors, lines stretching back into dim antiquity. I was a Croatian outlier. Double loyalties, to old and new, and double identity as well. Of course ten million in the bank helped in my decision-making to join them. I looked down at my dessert plate and savoured the last bit of the pastry, the taste of the cinnamon powder still on my palate.

There was no doubt in my mind that the money was important to me, but there was also the growing awareness of new friends and exciting adventures. I'd been promised a tour outside the city proper where I could get my first look at the future. The city of Makarska was mentioned in this regard. I paid my bill and left a tip from money in the billfold I'd been given by Matija, and then walked the short distance to the main square dominated by the resolute man on a horse.

As I stood in the Square and looked up at the gray statue I became entranced at being here, here in the historical heart of the ancient city. I wasn't aware of time or the fact that I was in a future that celebrated the past. I just stood there with people passing by on all sides while I was only half aware of their presence. A light wind ruffled my hair and it reminded me of the affectionate touch of my grandfather from another time and another world. I felt the spirit of the place and let it take hold in me. It was nearing dusk and a few street lights blinked around me.

I knew I'd be travelling soon to places far and wide in terms of Croatian history. Blue Mist and airships would take me there. The memory of Hamilton was already receding. I'd given myself over to a new reality, and as improbable as it was, I meant to see it through. Improbability was the central fact in my new life and I remembered with a smile the way I had run down the football field back home to catch the airship hovering in the blue mist. Kindred spirits, Canadian spirits, had guided me on that field and carried me to my destiny. Youthful spirits from a great world war that had robbed them of their own destiny. I meant to make the most of my own.

I reached up and touched the great plinth beneath the statue. It was smooth to the touch. I felt a sudden jolt pass through me, for a second only, not longer. Random thoughts coursed through my consciousness as I brought my arm down. Images in my mind flowed like precious flotsam on turbulent rivers to the sea. Images of Slavic migrations moving south from snowy mountains. Shadowy images of peoples from before, of Illyrians, Celts, Greeks, Romans, all of them and more, coalescing into one, into a fusion of diversity and strength on the crossroads of Europe. And then flashing images of war and strife, of terror and misery, of servitude and sorrow. All of these images grew bright and then faded leaving me adrift on a broad sea of imagination, memory, and history. Suddenly, I heard a shout behind me and there was a vendor asking if I wanted roasted chestnuts. The man extended his arm and offered me a small paper cone filled with chestnuts. For a moment I was not sure what he wanted. I looked at him, baffled. The images had been so powerful, and then a swiping transition to a new reality. I declined and shook my head and then hastened to my hotel, surprised and excited by my experience.

I slept well that night. It was as if something had become very clear to me. At breakfast, just as I was putting great dollops of marmalade on my croissant, I got it. I knew in a flash what made Croatians special and why they had survived and prospered despite being beset by overwhelming military power and imperial forces through the ages. They always stuck together and came to each other's aid. Other nations, it could be argued, do the same thing but with the Croatians it's a quality that is stronger than DNA and that they seem to possess in far greater measure than others. They always go the distance for each other. I remembered the old adage. A single straw or twig is easily broken but not a handful of straws or twigs. Not at all. That trait is strong and true and pure. It makes them who they are. Their kings and warriors and peasants and pirates have always known that.

After breakfast I went for a long walk and ended up sitting on a bench very near to the equestrian statue of King Tomislav. The day was bright and sunny without a cloud in the sky. There were a few tourists ambling about. A small group of them was enjoying a simple breakfast picnic on the grass. I was beginning to feel I belonged here, here in this place that was simultaneously the past and the future. Back home in Canada we were a nation of many nations and ethnicities, and I loved that central fact. I remembered again people saying that the nation state was dying and that one day the idea of nationhood itself would be outmoded and left behind as new universal realities emerged in the human experience. But here in the future, the nation state of Croatia was alive and well, and grounded not in race but in mutual respect and a grand sense of belonging. That's what Josip was trying to tell me. And now, just now, given the threat of an alien invasion, nothing was more important than that feeling of belonging and common identity. Here, at the crossroads of old Europe, old Croatia raised her head and readied herself for war once again. King Tomislav's statue glistened in the sun and I knew I was a part of it all. Despite being an outlier from the Croatian diaspora, I was now woven into the warp and woof of the Croatian experience. I was both Canadian and Croatian simultaneously. Suddenly, I spied a small red and white checkered airship sailing high above the park. I stood up and let out a great whoop of untrammelled delight. The tourists sitting on the grass looked at me in momentary surprise and then laughed aloud. I waved to them and they waved back. It felt so good to be a part of all this, a part of everything.

2.10

It didn't take me long to walk from the Palace Hotel to the beer garden that was located at the base of the funicular, just off the main street, the Ilica. It was around ten in the evening on a cool summer's night with just the sliver of a moon showing above. I was told the entire venue had been booked by the military as a reward night for participants in the war games that had recently been completed in Slavonia, in Osijek. It was a huge beer hall inside with vaulted ceilings like a church. The moment I walked in my senses were assaulted by the cigarette smoke that hung in the air. Military personnel of all stripes were enjoying themselves with loud laughter and much, much coughing. The smoking was in keeping, I was told later, with celebrating the habits of the ancient citizens of Zagreb.

Most everyone was in uniform and looked smart. I felt somewhat out of place wearing blue jeans and a black cashmere sweater, but I had thought it was to be an informal social gathering. I made my way to the polished mahogany bar to order a draught beer. Throngs of happy drinkers barred the way. The moment I took my first sip of the lager I saw her.

At once I realized she was the same tattooed woman I had seen exiting one of the retro malls a few days earlier. She was easily over six feet tall, lean but curvaceous, with short dark silky hair, and a face that was more handsome than beautiful. She was standing amid a group of men and women who were examining an extensive model that I took to be related to the war games recently concluded. There were hundreds of tiny figurines and small airships converging over the tabletop at various heights and angles, and actually moving. I noticed the miniature troops were also moving by themselves, programmed in some way, and with a digital timer above the action similar to the time and score marker above the rink at hockey games back home. It was quite remarkable and I pushed through the crowds by the bar to get closer to the scale military model, and of course, to the attractive woman who seemed to be holding court and commenting on the action and display.

Soon, I was standing next to her with my half empty stein in hand. Somehow I wanted to introduce myself to her, but she was far too engaged in her conversation with the others to take any notice of me. I stood there with a silly grin on my face hoping for an opening, an entry of some kind, if there was a lull in the conversation. I didn't have to wait long. Suddenly, she turned towards me, and with a vicious swing of her arm, knocked the glass of beer I was holding to the floor.

"Don't crowd me, fool!" she spat out. And with that, she dismissed me, to the surprise and glee of her companions. For a moment I stood there immobile, frozen with humiliation. Then I retreated with my tail between my legs like a scorned, wet dog. Looking back, I saw her re-join the conversation with her friends with no more thought of me than you would a passing annoyance in a crowd of strangers.

I struggled through the crowd to get to the stand-up bar where I could order a second beer and nurse my wounds. Within a minute I was drinking a cold lager and savouring the taste. I looked around and spotted a familiar face smiling at me. It was Goran, the very first of the emissaries I had met in my Hamilton basement apartment, the soldier I thought I had hallucinated. He pushed his way towards me, elbowing others out of the way, and carved out a place next to me. He clinked my glass with his and toasted to my health. I noticed the peach fuzz under his nose was covered in foam from his beer. He had a mischievous look on his face. He moved closer to me so that I could hear him over the din of the bar.

"Ah, Marin, so sorry your encounter with our Beserka ended in defeat. I watched as you made your move, or perhaps I should say attempted to make your move."

"Have you been following me?" It occurred to me that it wasn't a chance meeting,

"One of my duties, and only occasionally, is to ensure your safety."

"But what have I to fear from anyone here? These soldiers and cadets are celebrating the end of war games. An invitation was extended to me by one of my tutors. How did you know I would be here?" I was a little angry at being monitored, especially when I had been shot down in flames after trying to meet a beautiful woman. Public humiliation is not something I enjoy.

"Marin, Retro Zagreb is a small town, especially in military circles. Everyone knows the business of everyone else. But, more to the point, and to your personal safety, I must caution you to be careful in whom you approach. We need you to be focused on your mission here. We would prefer that you not engage in activities of a romantic nature until after successful completion of our mission. OK? Besides, Beserka is a renowned destroyer of men. Back in your time she would be called a ball buster. She has a reputation for making mincemeat of men, the stronger the better. She enjoys it. In Beserka you have the essence of the modern Croatian woman. Truly gifted professionally, but a holy terror outside of her work.

There is an incident that I wish to tell you about, an incident that is typical of her behaviour. As a captain in our elite military police squad, she was approached by a senior military man, an advisor to the President, a man with impeccable credentials and a taste for beautiful women. She was told by this gentleman that her advancement was contingent upon her 'malleability,' as he put it. The story goes that she smiled lasciviously at him, whetting his desire with lewd remarks and light suggestive touches. And then she quietly asked him to meet with her at midnight in the nearby Grič tunnel. He did. Perhaps ten minutes passed, certainly not longer. When he exited he was not quite the same man who entered the tunnel. Shall we say he was a little less of a man than before, and leave it at that. Senior officials tried to hush the incident. Details were not given, of course, but the adviser soon departed. Beserka never spoke about it, and no details surfaced regarding the incident. However, it enhanced her reputation, and there was never again any harassment issues ever reported."

The next morning Goran informed me that Josip had been involved in an altercation with several Karstians, and that he was in the hospital.

2.11

"What the hell happened to you?" I had just entered the hospital room and Josip's face was a bloody mess. Obviously, he had been in some skirmish with his wounds treated but still fresh. The bed next to his was empty.

"I learned you were here for a broken leg. Did you have a fall or were you in some sort of scrape?" Josip shook his head from side to side. The expression on his face was one of surprise and disbelief.

"An encounter with some Karstians, near the top of the funicular stairs. I was walking up and a few of them were coming down. They wanted me to give way, and I wouldn't so we fought and they pushed me down.

But the real action happened here. I have difficulty believing what happened myself. Yesterday there was a man in the bed next to mine suffering from a broken collar bone. I was sitting up on the bed just as I am now. A soft purple light covered us both, and I could feel the healing taking place. Quite pleasant.

His wife or girlfriend came to visit. She sat next to him, close to him. She was a massive woman wearing the tightest bodysuit I had ever seen. I smiled at the couple and then just stared into space thinking about our work and what needed to be done. And then she reached for something on the counter on the far side of his bed. She bent over, and I couldn't believe the size of her bottom. She turned her neck, saw me looking, and that's when it started. I must have unconsciously said something about her bottom. It was barely contained by the special fabric that compressed it. It was colossal.

She accused me of ogling her and looking at her lasciviously. I tell you I just couldn't believe the woman. Well, she said to her mate that if he were a man he would defend her honour. She kept on and on in this way until the poor devil leapt out of his bed and into mine and began pummeling me in the face. I tried desperately to protect my leg, and screamed in pain but the fool wouldn't stop. So I used what energy I had and put him in a headlock and increased the pressure. Just as I did so, she jumped on my bed and my broken leg was pinned under her knee. The pain was sheer torture. Having heard the commotion two male nurses entered the room and managed to pull us apart. The couple left screaming and kicking, saying how I had insulted the woman and that I had hurled abuse at her. But, Marin, I had only defended myself after they attacked me. They were gone just a moment when the woman returned like a mad hornet and threw a filthy bedpan at me. It took all of the strength of the two nurses to pull her away. I swear I didn't mean to insult her. I tell you, Marin, she was wild with anger. Even when they locked the door I heard her screaming like a devil and trying to get back into the room. I heard the man with the broken collar bone moaning and crying outside in the corridor. I'm sure I almost broke his neck when I had him in the headlock. The pain in my leg was incredible and it was a full quarter hour before I was given a painkiller. And all that over an unintended insult. Whatever I said was in sheer wonder at the size of the woman's backside."

2.12

I had a day free of training so I did what I love to do best. I slept in. When I awoke, I was staring up at the high ceiling of my hotel room and wondering what to do with my free day. Doing nothing seemed about right. I just wanted to chill. I thought about what had happened since I arrived in Retro Zagreb. My days had been filled with training and best of all, I wasn't bored. Back home in Hamilton that's what I hated most, being bored, being an unemployed student, and being stagnant. But I had ten million waiting for me there. Canadian dollars. I just had to get through a few months, do what they asked of me, and then head back home with a song in my heart and money in my pocket. I was learning things here, strange things about the spirit of place, magical objects, and preparations for war. I was sympathetic to their cause but in the final analysis it wasn't my war. I'd never thought of myself as a mercenary, but I guess that's what I was. Ten million in the Bank of Montreal on the corner of Bay and Main in Hamilton proved that. I stretched, wriggled my toes and got out of bed. I wanted breakfast and a long walk about town. Within half an hour I was out and walking along the Illica, the busiest street in this rebuilt city.

I stopped for a moment by the merry statue of Stjepan Radić and rubbed the bronze foot for luck. Josip had told me Radić was one of the greatest of Croatian patriots, a Croatian Lincoln he had called him. I realized this was the biggest adventure of my life.

Physically I was quicker, stronger, and more resilient than ever before. Franjo, my physical skills tutor and a surgeon by profession, had made sure of that. He had put me through a rigorous body analysis and what he called a primary augmentation process. What that meant, as I understood it, was that he had manipulated my kinesthetic muscle memory to such an extent that I was athletically enhanced and able to perform at a professional level in several sports and martial arts. It had taken several hours of non-invasive surgery over three days that left me feeling quite wonderful.

But initially I was more than a little apprehensive when he told me that I was to have my boxing debut. I remembered my anxiety when he had taken me to a boxing club and ushered me into a ring and there, opposite me, was the biggest, most savage looking pugilist I had ever seen. He had a build like a hairy Neanderthal hunter with a sloping forehead and heavy muscles everywhere. A bell rang and we were at it. But to my surprise I had the advantage of a full half-second in response time to anything he threw at me and quick-twinge jabs that wore him down quickly. I was hardly winded after three vigorous rounds. He had a serious cut over his left eye that stopped the fight. The blood on the canvas mat was his, not mine. Future medicine had made immense strides in developing the athletic prowess of healthy human beings. On the way home from the match to my hotel, I sprinted like an Olympic athlete for the sheer joy of it.

Once back in my room I sat in one of the leather club chairs and reviewed what was being drilled into me, my purpose in this strange mission. I closed my eyes and rubbed for a moment the comfortable armrests that supported my arms and hands. I felt as if I was sitting on a throne.

Each of my instructors reiterated the plan that I was to follow. Initially, I would be transported by airship to a specific time and place in the past. I would be monitored by select personnel who would provide on-ground support from one of the resource kiosks located adjacent to the targeted area, should I need it. The small airship would land and a Blue Time Mist canister would be released immediately prior to landing to ensure pinpoint accuracy in entering the requisite time zone.

The resource personnel situated in the kiosk area would not accompany me into the past. They would die if they did.

For each mission, prior preparations would have been made for my ready acceptance in the local community. Those preparations would include the planting and nurturing of trusting and familial relationships in the past that would make my sudden appearance plausible and welcome. I understood that I was part of a clan, and my relations were of the utmost importance. I would only be accepted if my hosts knew my background. That connection was essential. My grandfather's friend, Brujo, was pivotal in this regard. His work had been to facilitate my entry into the local community.

Once situated within the context of a time and place of interest, I would then endeavour to identify those individuals who manifested the desired trait for emulation. This character trait, as I understood it, would be linked to an object. This object could be of any shape or function. It was a kind of working depository that contained within itself the very nucleus of the sought-after character trait. The object could be anything. It might be a musical instrument or a weapon or a piece of art. Essentially, it was a witness to the past, and once duly identified, it was to be claimed and brought forward for military use against the Karstians. The difficulty would be in obtaining it, for it must be voluntary. It could not be a theft for it was intimately connected to the ethical trait wanted and as such it had to be freely given as a gift or reward. They hinted that a minimum of three such objects from different eras would be necessary, but I was not given any further details about the matter.

I took a deep breath as I remembered these elements, and my eyelids flickered open. Around me my Retro Zagreb hotel suite offered comfort and security, something that would not be readily accessible in the past. I walked over to the desk and scanned the menu. I had a sudden craving for the hotel's famous dessert, a generous block of vanilla custard between layers of flaky pastry that was served warm. Life was good, and dessert was even better.

Everything was so odd to me. In a way people were looking to me as some kind of potential saviour from the past. Imagine that. Here I was, an outlier from the Croatian diaspora from centuries earlier, and they seemed to think I had special powers, that I was some sort of hero. The training I was given by experts in their respective fields was incredible. And all of this was in preparation to do battle with the Karstians. The trust they had in me was beginning to change me a little. How could it not? Some part of me wanted to be the man they wanted me to be. Certainly the money was an incentive, how could it not be, but when you have people looking at you in ways that you've never experienced before, you begin to feel it, and it makes a difference.

I wanted to know more about the aliens. Josip had pointed out some of them to me. The ones I had seen walking about Retro Zagreb looked to me like very pale Europeans on vacation, Austrians perhaps, in desperate need of the sun. They walked about the city in groups of a dozen or so, like visiting soccer players enjoying the sights between matches. Not what I'd imagined aliens from the Milky Way to look like. But then so much of what I'd experienced was improbable, but not impossible. Ever since I'd left Hamilton I'd realized that anything can happen, and did. Blue Time Mist travel, retro airships, miniaturizations, secret caves, things of the imagination, had become real. I was in future time and I was in a period of adjustment. Everything was different and I had to adapt.

Josip had told me that negotiations were underway with the Karstians and had been for weeks. There seemed to be a real sense of urgency at play.

He told me that in their talks at the Sabor, the government building in St. Mark's Square, the aliens repeatedly said they wanted a peaceful solution. That raised eyebrows as many questioned why there shouldn't be anything but a peaceful resolution to the ongoing diplomatic discussions. As always, the negotiating aliens were excessively polite and diplomatic in speech and manner, but the bottom line was that they had to have it. They had to have Croatia, all of it. What that entailed amounted to massive population clearances from Croatia to border areas. In addition, they were insistent that all adjacent mountain ranges would be included in the transaction and be viewed as part of Croatia proper. When it was pointed out that these mountain ranges belonged to other sovereign nations, distinct from Croatia, they dismissed the problem and said that it was a minor detail and would be dealt with by a frontier force that would be duly compensated. It soon became abundantly clear that, in return for treasure and foreign land, the Croatian state would also act as a perimeter of defense, and safeguard Karstian sovereignty.

What wasn't discussed was what would happen if Croatia refused to submit to their terms. The Karstian spaceship at the Retro Zagreb airport resembled a gigantic TicTac in shape, and was heavily guarded by several hundred of their troops. The Karstian negotiators brought exotic gifts for the Croatian leaders and smiled benevolent smiles. They hoped and prayed, they said, that the great Croatian nation would recognize its valued, supportive place in a reconfigured world of perpetual peace founded on Karstian hegemony. That was how they spoke, in high-sounding phrases and honeyed words. It was puzzling at first to hear their demands. They shook hands all around. They kissed us on both cheeks. They bowed ceremoniously and spoke softly, and then withdrew for executive sightseeing tours of the retro city and its environs, particularly the mountainous Karstian regions.

One evening Josip and I were drinking craft beer at a pub on Tkalčićeva Street. There were a few tourists about, but they were sitting outside in the patio area while we were the only patrons inside. He leaned forward across the scarred oak table and confided in me with a whisper.

"I tell you Marin, cracks are starting to appear on the ship of the Croatian state. The party of the Browns, the far-right politicos, are ready and willing to take the money. They claim that fighting is not an option. We wouldn't have a ghostly chance, they said, against the superior technology of the Karstians. They've supposedly seen it in action. But I have no details of that, none. Not yet." He leaned back and stared at the vaulted ceiling for a moment and then continued, still speaking softly and quietly.

"And the Blues want to fight, regardless. They think we have a chance, a fighting chance, if we can be ready soon, very soon. We know it's a long shot but what else do we have? Nothing but spirit."

"And how about the military? Who are they with? Will they support the Blues, or the Browns?"

"Both."

"What do you mean both?"

"Just that. The military is divided. It'll be a civil war if it comes down to it. Nothing less."

"But that's absurd."

"Tell me something I don't know. It's happened before."

For a moment we just sat there, staring at each other and drinking, contemplating civil war, absurdity, and the destiny of nations. I didn't know what to say or do. But I knew there was urgency in the air, and I had to act, and act soon.

2.13

Vesna was an exceptional trainer. She would use analogies and metaphors to get her points across. She told stories that stuck with me and made the learning easy. I remember when she was trying to impress upon me the similarities and differences between a knife blade and contractual negotiations.

"The thing is, Marin, if you touch the very tip of a knife blade, it's like a period on a page, simple punctuation. But, so, so different. The period on a page is nothing but the conceptual representation of a stop in thought. But the tip of a blade is something other. What's behind the tip of the blade? And even if you've ascertained that, you have to ask yourself if there is the potential of force and mass and heft behind it, behind the tip of the blade.

The period on a page of a contract, the simple punctuation of it, is different of course, but no less dangerous. It is even more dangerous, but perhaps not recognized as such, at first. After all, it's abstract and the tip of the blade of a knife is not, especially as it slides into the destined, surprised flesh."

Josip had once told me that Vesna was the leading practitioner of the Tesla retina scanner technique and that she had a photographic memory. The inventor, Tesla, had posited that a person's ideas could be read in images on their retinas if you had a device whereupon they could be projected and received. Vesna was gifted with a rare talent whereby she could read what a person was thinking by steadily looking into their eyes and discerning the images that were there. She didn't need an intermediary device to see the images and ideas on a subject's retinas. It was a remarkable skill, and one day it was put to an even more remarkable use. Josip recounted what had taken place when Vesna had been introduced to the leader of the Karstian negotiating team.

"Everyone had left the Sabor after the discussions, and most had returned to their apartments in the lower city, but Vesna, myself, the political head of the Brown Party and the alien diplomat, a man named Fortin, made our way to a small quiet bar near the Stone Gate. After a few drinks everyone was relaxed and happy that the negotiations seemed to be moving ahead without any significant problems. But then something happened that was most unusual. I remember clearly the shocked look on Vesna's face immediately after she had posed a question to Fortin, the most important of the Karstian negotiators. It was an innocuous question, hardly significant.

"Mr. Fortin," Vesna asked, "can you share with us what you most treasure in Croatia, what will bring you and your people the greatest joy?"

"Fortin had smiled warmly at Vesna and uttered some platitude about the variety and beauty of the landscape. His response was diplomatic and self-assured, just what you would expect. However, the very moment he made his remarks Vesna almost fell out of her chair. She recovered quickly of course but I had seen it, and I knew it had something to do with her ability to read retinal images. Despite what he had said, Fortin's idea or thought, by a kind of reflex action, had produced a corresponding image on his retinas that Vesna was able to see, and to understand. She was alarmed. I could hardly wait to leave the bar and talk with her, but I had to make small talk and exercise the greatest patience. Fortin seemed to be enjoying himself and ordered yet another round of drinks. Finally, the night drew to a close and we shook hands and left the bar. I walked alongside Vesna and could see that she was staring straight ahead, still in shock at the images she had beheld in Fortin's eyes. I asked if I could talk with her for a moment when we arrived in front of her apartment door. She nodded and invited me in where her partner was waiting. Vesna hugged her affectionately, and then asked her to leave us for a moment. Once we were alone, she turned to me and shook her head in a look of disbelief mingled with horror."

"They mean to kill us. I saw the images clearly. Images of war and then bodies, hundreds, perhaps thousands of them."

"You read Fortin's mind, didn't you?"

"Yes, he couldn't help himself. He answered my questions superficially but his retinal images, he couldn't conceal. I believe the negotiations are a charade meant to pacify us until they are ready to dispense with us once and for all. Talk of fortunes for everyone and new lands on the periphery are nothing but pipedreams. And we believed it, like innocent, deluded fools. Can you imagine that? We believed it."

Three weeks had passed, and still I hadn't been beyond the confines of Retro Zagreb. I didn't know what the real future looked like. I was in a great living reproduction of a city from the past, my own era. Fantastic. Great. But I wanted to see the real thing. What had changed? I was getting impatient, very impatient, to see new things, new sights, new everything. One of my instructors had mentioned Makarska, and I was eager to see it, or any other city for that matter. And I guess I wanted a break from all of the training I was getting. So, I resolved to press the issue with Matija the first chance I got. It happened sooner than I thought. Just three days after my resolve to bring a departure date forward, I met with him briefly, and the deed was done. I'd been cleared for a Blue Mist journey to the past, but no date was given.

2.14

I hadn't been able to sleep very well for a few nights. I thought perhaps it might be the growing imminence of my first-time flight to the past. It was looming, and I was getting a tad anxious. It's one thing to think about something that doesn't have a deadline or departure date. It's quite another to have a set time and place for leaving. I'd accepted the money. And it was making great interest in my bank account. Excellent profits. I was a rich man, but you can't spend money if you're incapacitated, or if you're dead. I tossed and turned until I felt myself falling into a deep sleep.

At the edge of my consciousness, I felt a rustling, a movement beside me that pulled me abruptly out of sleep. Suddenly, I was fully alert and conscious. Someone or something, was there in the bed with me and lying on top of me. I was just about to scream when I felt a hand over my mouth, and a split second later, the tip of a blade at my throat. I could feel its sharp point. I was paralyzed with fear. I didn't move. I didn't dare take a breath.

Within a second, I knew who it was. Beserka gently withdrew the knife and placed it on the side table. It made the slightest sound of metal on wood. She removed her hand from my mouth and kissed me then, very lightly at first, and then more deeply and passionately. The weight of her body was fully atop me. She was naked. She whipped away the light sheet that covered me and then took a deep breath. I thought I heard a chuckle escape the back of her throat as her body moved over me. The surprise of her after the dread of the unknown shocked me to the quick. In the numb darkness my world had changed.

My senses were sharpened to such a high degree that I felt surges of power extending throughout my body on swollen currents, as if on flooded rivers rampaging to the sea. The night was hot with rapacious caresses, heavy with the feeling of displaced fear. My fingertips moved across her in hungry circles of pent-up desire, and I heard her shudder with pleasure as we probed each other and then parted, and then probed again. It was more a savage encounter than anything else, brutish and strange. Just before dawn I saw the dark shadow of her slip away, and I was left with a dry metallic taste in my mouth, and the remnants of a dream spawned from a nightmare. I wasn't sure whether it had happened or not. I fell back again into a deep sleep that covered my exhaustion with coils of satisfied desire.

2.15

We were at an upscale café opposite the national theatre. Matija had just given me a brief history lesson regarding the first Croatian dukes and kings, and the importance of Nin and Zadar in the medieval period. I found it quite fascinating just as I was enjoying the last sip of my double espresso and the delicious dark chocolate that came with it. Just as he was about to move into the renaissance period, I made my move.

"Matija," I said, simultaneously motioning to our waiter for a second cup of coffee. "I need a counterpoint to all of the history tutorials I've been given. When do I get a chance to see other areas of Croatia? Hopefully that will happen before my official work starts. What do you say?"

Matija's face dropped with disappointment. "I thought you would have found the old city of interest before your journeys begin. It's one of the top-most tourist attractions in the world. You don't find it exciting, being here?"

"I do, but I'm more curious than ever to see new places." The waiter came by, removed my empty cup and chocolate wrapping, and left a fresh espresso on a tray for me. On the silver tray there was also a new chocolate for me in a light gold coloured wrapper. Matija was still sipping on his cappuccino. Every now and then he would cough violently into his hand-kerchief. I noticed his chocolate was untouched.

I unwrapped my chocolate and put it in my mouth and followed that with a sip of espresso. The taste sensation was marvellous. I savoured the hazelnut chocolate on my tongue for a moment as it melted with the hot coffee.

"Before we continue with our lesson, Marin, let me brag for a brief moment about some of our modern accomplishments, developments that have taken place since your time. Let's begin with health, with medical advances. Something you'll be experiencing yourself as you prepare physi-cally for your assignments. The clothes you wear here in the future monitor your health. They preserve your good health."

"I don't understand. What have clothes got to do with it, with my health?"

"You'll notice, once we leave the city, that people wear form-fitting garments and attractive headgear, wonderfully feathered hats. It isn't just for style. It's much more than that. But for now, let's continue with our history lesson. Rest assured, you'll soon have a date and place for your first mission. But for now you will have a taste of the old Croatia at Makarska. It's been arranged. I know you are eager for that experience."

2.16

The journey to Makarska took place the very next day. Josip and I boarded an airship at the Retro Zagreb aerodrome and within an hour we were sitting on a bench overlooking the Makarska harbour. Behind us, Makarska with its brooding majesty stood in watch. The day was dismal and overcast, and the threat of rain was imminent. Josip was playing with his keychain, tossing it up into the air and then catching it as it fell, repeating the motion again and again. I was feeling blue and out of sorts. Here I was, grounded in the future and about to go on missions to the past that were as incredible to me as they were questionable. I knew I was being paid well for what I was doing, but that didn't make it any easier to understand.

"Josip, sometimes I wonder about all the time and effort expended on me to seek out and return with things associated with the right kinds of values and ethical traits and military prowess from the past, the Croatian past. I mean that's a bit of a stretch, isn't it? Other countries have their own values and objects that are also worthy of emulation, don't they? What's so special about Croatia?"

Josip put away his keychain and with an amused look on his face turned to me. Above us, gray clouds scudded menacingly across the sky.

"Think about it. For well over a thousand years tiny Croatia has managed to survive against all odds, and a turbulent history to say the least. Imagine how it was when they came here in the seventh century. They found themselves among people of mixed origins and wide-ranging ethnic makeup.

There were the native Illyrians, and then of course the descendants of Celts, and Greeks, and others. Naturally, these groups intermingled and added new strains and elements to the Croatian identity. But the one thing that was pure was the Croatian spirit with its values and harmony and resilience.

How could such a small people continue to exist and thrive given the forces arrayed against them from every direction? Marin, I know you must think that I am some kind of proselytizing zealot, but that is not the case. Listen to me. Listen. The people had to stick together, at all times, and throughout all kinds of adversities and setbacks. That takes heart and collective courage. Whatever crisis happened to one of us happened to all of us. Whenever it was needed, there we were together as one. There has always been this immense feeling of togetherness that has supported us all and that everyone could feel. We were knit together through empathy and compassion and love. This attitude of mind and soul existed from the start and is with us today. It is rooted in our identity. It is rooted in yours. It's our spiritual DNA. Perhaps you could call it our moral inheritance. Other countries, no doubt, have their own ways and means, but for us, it is a heartfelt passion, and one that flows through our veins as surely as our rivers flow to the sea. That is what you must know and never forget. OK?" He was silent for a moment and then took a pen from his breast pocket. He drew a large circle on a sheet of paper. "This is the kolo circle Marin. It is defensive in nature." He looked across at me to make sure I was listening and then drew arrows pointing outward on the circumference of the circle. "Together the people can fend off aggressors and feel the might and power of unity. Now watch this." Josip drew another larger circle and drew arrows on the inside of the circle pointing inwards. "This second circle is the kolo dance circle. You see, there are two circles, one defensive and the other celebratory, social. That is the key to our identity. That shows who we are."

I could feel the raw conviction in his voice as he spoke, and as he finished, the first drops of rain began to fall. The two of us hurried to a nearby café and just managed to escape the heavy downpour that followed us. We didn't speak any more about a people and togetherness, but I knew what he meant. We each ordered a double espresso. I heaped three large teaspoons of brown sugar into mine and savoured the sweet bitterness of the drink.

The rain abated quickly and soon we were walking in a north-westerly direction towards the modern new town. I marvelled at the wonderful architecture of the place with its colours of luminous pearl that changed in intensity as the winds blew over it. It was as if the buildings themselves had been created by nature rather than man. The old part of the city was charming with its limestone buildings, and in some way the two styles of architecture, ancient and modern, complemented each other. I was happy to have seen it. Josip mentioned that I would be returning soon to Makarska for a closer look. I wasn't sure what he meant but looked forward to it. That very day we returned to Retro Zagreb

2.17

Josip left a message with the concierge at my hotel. I was to meet him at a wine bar in the upper city. He said that it was urgent. When I arrived, I caught sight of him sitting alone in a rough wooden booth. His head was bowed, and he seemed to be staring blankly at the tabletop. He was distraught and obviously drunk. He looked up at me with a broken smile. His eyes were swollen and rimmed with red.

"Ah, Marin. The ten-million-dollar man of destiny. Well, we will need you more than ever now, more than you can know. Sit, sit, and drink, drink." He waved at the bartender to bring another glass and another bottle. An empty liter bottle of wine was beside him. I slid into the booth seat opposite him and waited for him to begin.

"The team is down one, down a precious one, dear fellow. Our Vesna is gone, no more. Yes, our Vesna and her partner have been murdered." For a moment he rested his head on his forearm, wiping his nose on his sleeve, and then slowly he looked up at me. His nose was bright purple and wet.

"But how?"

"A knife."

"Who?"

"Who else? The Karstians, of course. We don't need a forensic detective for that. It is plain to see or not to see in this case."

"What do you mean?"

"Marin, they took their eyes. They ripped their eyes out, leaving dark holes where beauty had nestled. Both of them. Vesna and her beloved. Somehow the Karstians had found out that Vesna could read and see the images on their retinas. She had perfected the ancient Tesla skill. Despite what they said around the negotiating table, the tell-tale images on their retinas could not deceive. They had given their word. But what the tongue allowed the eyes could not. Vesna had told us what Fortin's retinal images revealed. That very night after we had gone for drinks after our discussions with the Karstians, she had told us. Do you remember I told you about that?

And then, in the middle of the night they had come, surprising them in their sleep. The attack was brutal. Thieves and cutthroats. And do you know what they said? They have offered to lead the investigation. Superior technology and all that. The audacity of swine. They took their eyes."

Josip began to weep then with his face buried in his hands. He wept quietly, almost inaudibly, but the sound of it was terrible. I placed my hand on his shoulder and held it there for a few moments. I had heard him laugh many, many times, but I had never heard the man cry. Never. Something caught at the back of my throat, and I felt the emotion rise within me and then spill over in sorrow that I had not felt for a long, long time. I said in a strange, muffled voice that I didn't recognize in myself, that I must go. He nodded, his face still covered with his hands, and then I left. The night air was moist with the threat of rain. The stars were shrouded in torn pockets of deep gray cloud that were moving slowly. The streets were almost deserted.

2.18

A week passed. Matija met me in the lobby of my hotel, and we spoke of the beauty of Makarska. He was coughing quite a bit as he spoke. The conversation was short. "Now that you're near to becoming a blue mist traveller, you will have an uncommon understanding of the vagaries of time. You can, with help of course, enter and exit different eras and periods with comparative ease. The work of Tesla, Toma, and countless others supports the wherewithal behind your travels. As early as the nineteenth century, with the advent of photography, we had a pronounced precision in witnessing the way people actually looked. That was just the beginning, and it had little to do with time travel.

It started simply enough. An old photograph would spark reveries and encourage people to wonder what it would have been like to be there, actually there, at that exact time, a time that was captured by the lens of a camera. Behind a group picture, for example of two or three hundred people, there were the countless stories of the individuals who were captured on the film. We couldn't delve into those stories. But there was a world there too, a different world, and one that we wanted to explore. And that we have accomplished, thanks to genius, and courage and resolve, and maybe a little luck."

2.19

Josip and I were standing in the small garden of the Archeological Museum near the center of Retro Zagreb. His face was slightly flushed from a night of drinking. Fortunately, I had decided not to join him. He never lacked for drinking friends. It was a bright sunny morning that promised a fine day. A sparrow flew nearby, then bounced twice and settled for a moment atop an iron gate. There wasn't a cloud in the sky.

"Marin, where we stand was once covered with fragments of Roman column stone taken from Zadar and since returned. It took us a long, long time to realize the importance of repatriating the artifacts to the places where they belonged. Retro Zagreb was once filled with things that didn't belong there. Museum pieces. Things speak truth to history, to real life as it was lived. Now, across the country, you'll see kiosks, big and small, replete with the objects that belong there. There are displays, three-dimensional action events, that are as close as possible to the life once lived there. Different kinds of events. Battles certainly, but also people going about their daily business. Perhaps wine-making or crafting tools and carving figures and the like. And this is where you come in. With your help we can develop real images, real scenarios, that were true to life based on your actual experience of them. One day I will take you to my mother's garden near Karlovac and show you wondrous things."

I could see the fire in Josip's eyes as he spoke. His voice quavered with excitement and emotion as he continued. I had never seen him so intense and passionate.

"We're realizing how porous time is, as porous in its way as our limestone. Time may appear to be strictly chronological, but it is more like a tree, a wonderful tree thrusting its trunk and branches high into the heavens, linking dark roots within the soil and reaching up to the sky, to a commingled reality."

2.20

Two weeks later Goran came to my lodgings bringing an invitation and a gray uniform for me to wear at the military ball being held at the famous Esplanade hotel across from the train station. The place was buzzing with excitement when we arrived. Waiters threaded through the crowd bringing champagne and appetizers on silver trays. Goran introduced me to several of his friends all splendidly attired in dark blue uniforms with gold trim on the sleeves and collar, and a thin red stripe on the trouser legs. We chatted pleasantly for a while and then took our seats for the dinner and awards ceremony. Several of the recipients of the awards were people I had met during my training. It felt good to see them honoured, and then I saw her.

She was sitting at the head table with an expression of amusement on her face. She was wearing a form fitting dark blue uniform with a single gold medal on her bosom. She scanned the crowd and nodded almost imperceptibly when she recognized someone she knew. When our eyes met, she raised her wine glass and tilted it slightly in acknowledgement of me, and then turned abruptly to her left to talk with an older dignitary who seemed enraptured by her presence.

The evening passed by pleasantly enough. I did my best to mix and mingle with the crowd and people I knew, but I've always hated that kind of forced sociability and so I slowly made my way to the exit.

Just as I left the building and turned to walk back to my hotel, I felt the pressure of a hand on my shoulder.

"Why the early departure, Marin?"

I felt my heart race as I heard her unmistakeable voice, slightly husky and inviting. I couldn't conceal my excitement as I turned to see her in a fluster of surprise and delight. "Beserka!"

She took my hand lightly for a moment and then dropped it. It was exciting to be walking with her. She was such a handsome woman and dangerous. We crossed the street towards the King Tomislav statue and then made our way northward through the park. The dark, crooked finger of a scudding cloud moved across what was left of a crescent moon.

I couldn't think of anything to say, and she was smiling, clearly enjoying my discomfort. She could read me so easily, and I didn't like that. It made me too vulnerable.

"What about a race, Marin?" she said.

"What?"

"A race, a sprint, say one hundred meters?"

"Why?"

"Why not?" she countered.

"OK, where and when?"

"Right here, right now," she said, stopping to pull her pantlegs up and adjust her clothing.

I tightened my shoe laces and made ready.

"OK," she said. "Now let's go!"

She sprinted off, and I raced to catch up. The cement walkway offered good traction and within a few meters we were head-to-head in an even race. Just as I was gaining distance on her, she kicked out at my leg violently, and I fell hard on the ground, scraping my hands and forehead. I was a little bloodied. For a moment I was stunned at what she had done. I looked up at her in surprise. She extended her arm towards me and helped me to my feet.

"Are you OK?" she asked in a petulant tone.

"My ankle feels a bit tender. Why did you do that?"

"I wanted to win," she said simply, as if that was enough of an argument.

"But that wasn't fair. You were losing, and so you cheated."

"We didn't establish any rules, Marin. Not at all. You're a bit upset. I can see that. So, let me make it up to you," she said in a suddenly, sultry voice.

"How? Another silly contest? My ankle may be sprained. I can't race on it," I replied, massaging my ankle.

"I have an idea. Much more fun than a footrace. Your hotel is nearby. We can put some ice on your ankle, and I can give you some tender care. What do you say?"

I shook my head in wonder and disbelief at this crazy, magnificent, green-eyed woman standing in front of me. But, my god, she was beautiful. She leaned forward and kissed my bloodied forehead as I winced from the pain in my ankle. I noticed that there was just the slightest trace of my blood on her lips. She stared at me for a moment, her tongue flicking at the drop of blood and absorbing it, and then she smiled.

She insisted on leaving the drapes open, for the moon glow she said, with an enigmatic smile. There was a slight silver sheen on the gray bedspread that appeared cold and icy. Part of me wanted to stop what was going to happen, to ask her politely to leave, and to end it there. The other part was sliding into an embrace that was as pleasurable as it was tinged with regret. I shuddered at the feel of her perfect breast upon my hand. I heard her gurgle at the back of her throat and then laugh as she swept me under her, reversing our positions with a speed and a power that surprised me. The sensual touch of her and the twists and turns of our bodies pulled me further and further down a slope from which there would be no return and no retreat. In the silvery edged darkness of the room our two bodies engaged, and the pleasure of the encounter slowly and strangely transformed into a kind of contest, a struggle of passionate wills, a match. Neither of us would give in, neither of us would allow even the possibility of dominance in the other. Random images flashed through my mind. I loathed myself for the pleasure I was taking, but I continued. Nothing else mattered but this carnal opposition and the thundering power of our limbs and lust.

2.21

A few days later I returned to Makarska and waited at the small market for my contact to arrive. I was soon met and escorted by a lean, middle-aged man named Antonio to a vantage point high above the city. From atop Biokovo Mountain we could see the islands of Brač and Hvar, resplendent in the mid-morning sun, the Adriatic Sea a brilliant blue with silver highlights dazzling in the near distance like shook aluminum foil. Antonio motioned for me to follow him, and we walked across an abandoned potato field towards some decrepit looking farm buildings that had seen better days.

The two of us entered a crumbling stone ruin of a house in a forgotten village of four similar ancient structures, all of them rundown and unused. I didn't quite know what to expect but simply followed along. There was no door. We sat on a cold stone floor in what must have been a kitchen at one time. Light streamed in from an old glassless window. Antonio had an air of expectancy about him. Suddenly, there was a soft swishing sound and the floor beneath us functioned as an elevator and dropped slowly into a cavern below. Antonio gently placed his hand on my arm to reassure me that everything was safe. In a moment we were at the base of a huge cavern that was bright and spacious and several stories high.

What struck me immediately were the great shapes of airships or dirigibles high above us in the huge cavern. They were moored to stalactites. I couldn't make out the names upon the sides of the airships. An older woman in her late thirties, stout but attractive, with short dark hair, smiled briefly, said something to Antonio in a dialect that I couldn't make out, and bid us follow her with a wave of her arm. She walked very briskly ahead of me with purpose in her step. She had very shapely legs. Antonio had introduced her as Manda Frankopan, the lead scientist on the Blue Mist Project.

She led us to an adjoining cavern that was very well hidden from view behind a stone wall. It was much smaller than the first and not very well lit. There, we ascended a narrow metal staircase and then on to a walkway. We continued a short distance until we stood on a steel platform where she went to a control panel and turned on some very powerful overhead lights. I was struck by what I was seeing. It was a large-scale model of the country of Croatia that was about the size of a football field. It seemed to be suspended in the air above the cavern floor.

Manda literally took me by the hand and showed me various points of interest such as the blue-lit nodes and hidden kiosk areas. She spoke very slowly as if she were talking to a small child or an idiot. When I tried to remove my hand from her grasp, she simply tightened her grip on me and continued with her lecture. Every few moments she would stop and simply look at me rather oddly, her eyes running over my body. I could see Antonio smiling at my discomfort. Still, I focused hard on what she was saying.

She explained to me, speaking rather too loudly I thought, that the virtual model of Croatia could change to show actual population densities, migrations over time, invasions, historical periods by precise date, all of that and more. Tiny blue lights blinked on and off over nodes on the model. Indeed, what really struck me was the highlighting and pinpointing of all major nodal areas that I had learned about in Retro Zagreb and their respective pivot points of entry. The degree of miniaturization accomplished was superb. From high above I could see what looked to be miniature versions of the large airships that were tethered to stalactites and stalagmites in the adjoining cavern. Remarkable optical lenses stored beneath the table could be accessed by a tabletop control system. Only through the powerful magnifying lenses could an observer take in the full scope and detail of the masterwork.

When I asked her if I could somehow take a look from above the model with one of the optical lenses, she nodded curtly and sent Antonio to fetch a drone. In a moment I found myself lying face first on a two-seater drone, or rather a two-cot drone, with the stout lady lying beside me, manipulating some controls. As she was quite tall and needed more physical space, she muttered a wet apology in my ear, and then threw one of her legs over my backside. I turned my head to see Antonio biting his arm to stave off laughing uproariously at the strange couple on the drone. As she needed even more space to adjust the controls and optical lenses, she further positioned herself over my backside until she was literally on top of me, pressing down. I could feel her lips on the nape of my neck, and her breathing was labored. I was very uncomfortable with her weight on my back. What was happening was absurd. I glanced across to Antonio once again to see him running down the metal staircase, beside himself with merriment at my predicament. The sound of his steps as he retreated echoed through the cavern.

As I made my way out of the cavernous hall I was terribly excited. Despite having had Manda literally riding on my back, I was impressed with the technology or magic of the place or whatever you want to call it, that was at play. A miniature model of Croatia, a living model that was so much more than that. All across the country, in different cities and towns, I had noticed bronze models depicting the buildings and underlying landforms of a certain city. But this was far different and beguiled thought. It transformed a conceptual model into a reality.

I tried to piece together what I knew. The model I saw was real. Somehow, it was an exact living replica of Croatia, only miniaturized, and about the size of a football field. In terms of geography and space it was totally accurate because it was the real thing. It wasn't a copy. Later, in the control room, Manda showed me how different periods of time were accessible. It was incredible.

I remembered that at one point in our flight together, Manda had deftly manipulated some controls that allowed us to descend through the clouds, and as we did so, the country below us grew larger and larger until we hovered over Jelačić Square in Zagreb. It was amazing. We were close enough to see people walking about though it seemed they could not see us. I saw a blue tram stop to pick up passengers and then we shifted our position slightly to hover above nearby Dolac Market. There, one of the vendors, an elderly woman, was stacking bright red apples into a pyramid formation as she merrily spoke with another vendor in a nearby stall. It was absolutely masterful. It was wonderful.

Within a few moments we were back in the offices of the Makarska Aerodrome. Once there I was briefed by three junior scientists on the relation between blue mist time travel and the miniaturized model of Croatia. The two were interdependent. They were eager to show me how things worked and they tried their best to keep things simple, but it was difficult for me to follow them. I could see by the expressions on their faces that they believed they had lost me. I smiled politely, nodded my head in thanks, and left. Manda and Antonio were nowhere to be seen.

My thoughts raced as I made my way to the crumbling stone house above the underground mountain aerodrome where the blimps were tethered. I sat on the ancient kitchen floor, pushed a stone to activate the descent mechanism Antonio had shown me, and within a moment I was on the ground floor of the adjacent underground aerodrome. I was relieved to see Antonio there, and I looked around anxiously, but mercifully Manda was nowhere in sight. Truly she was a gifted scientist but utterly obsessive as a human being. At least to me.

Antonio was standing in the entranceway of a small dirigible. Ausania was the name written on the airship's hull. He was waving his arms about madly, urging me to hurry aboard. The roof of the mountain aerodrome was opening and I could see a canopy of stars in the night sky. It reminded me of the sports domes back home, only far more sophisticated in its operation.

"Hurry Marin," Antonio shouted as he entered the aircraft. I was with him in an instant as the door slid into place and our seats were secured. Once the Ausania cleared the mountain peak, I could see the lights of Makarska below, and beyond that the dark, hulking shapes of the islands, Brač and Hvar. It felt good to be returning to Retro Zagreb after all that I had seen. It had become my reference point, my pivot on this strange new world that I had opted for.

"The flight over the model was exhilarating," I said to him. "Magical."

2.22

A meeting was scheduled for the following morning. However, I was beginning to experience real doubts, doubts about my role in this venture, and doubts about things in general. I looked around the conference table. Besides myself there were six of us in the room.

"In the final analysis things are just things. Sure, they have provenance if they're special historically somehow, but they're not alive in any real sense."

I was frustrated and showed it. It seemed to me that all the hopes and dreams of this future Croatia besieged by enemies, from within and from without, was nothing but folly as in the old days when the churches contained the relics of saints among their many tax-free treasures. Perhaps a toe or the desiccated ear of a martyred soul. Enough or too much I thought.

I could tell my outburst had struck home. The pained expressions on their faces lingered for a moment until Matija spoke.

"We have all felt that way, Marin. But we have witnessed the power of things and the power of their provenance. Spirits select and inhabit inanimate things by day, and then may take on different forms come nightfall. Not always, but it happens. You can see these shapeshifters if you allow yourself to." His words droned on and I tried hard to concentrate but to no avail.

My mind drifted away from the sound of his words. I was tired and sorely needed sleep. Behind him there was a three-dimensional painting depicting the arrival of the Croats on the coast. I had seen a much smaller version in Retro Zagreb. My eyes were involuntarily drawn to the battle axe held by a warrior on the left side of the artwork. It was familiar. I knew I had seen it before because of the tattoo-like incisions on the shaft of the axe. Suddenly, Matija's words broke through my reveries and I was listening to his words once again. "Have patience," he said, "things will become clearer once your work begins."

2.23

Josip and I were sitting on a curved stone bench at a vantage point overlooking the Church of St. Mary's and behind that, the Cathedral. It was quite beautiful and photogenic with two old style lampposts to our left, the stuff of old postcards. I was always amazed at the precise reconstruction of old Zagreb. Perfect. It was a brilliant morning with not a cloud in the sky, but cool. A perfect time for reflecting on things. We sat in silence for a moment and then I posed a question.

"Why do you think the Karstians chose Croatia to invade? After all, it's not the richest of countries. You would have thought Germany or France would have been the better choice."

Josip turned to me, scanning me with his bloodshot eyes. "Simple," he said. "A question of geology. First and foremost, they need caves for their wellbeing and perhaps for their very survival. They need lots of them and we have that in abundance. I don't know why, but that much we've learned about them. Secondly, the Croatian character fits into their plans nicely."

"What does the Croatian character have to do with anything?" I asked, incredulous at his comment. "Surely character has nothing to do with it. I can understand their obsession with caves. For them it's a question of staying alive. That's been clear from the start. But character! That's a stretch."

"That's where you're wrong. They want protection on the borders of the state. Study your history Marin. What better guardians than the Croats, who for well over a millennium have defended the country against all sorts of invading empires. We pose a stubborn resistance to foreign powers. The great Napoleon is reported to have said that if he had one hundred thousand Croat warriors, he could take over the world. It's been bred into our collective, spiritual DNA. We're not a separate race from others, but our consciousness is different. We're a small nation of warriors who don't take kindly to being attacked. Not at all. That is the nature of our people. That's where character comes in. We thrive on adversity. Always have and always will. There's a saying amongst us that it is better to be in the grave than to be a slave. The Karstians did their research well. They know us. So, they offer great wealth for all and a role to play on the periphery.

And you Marin. You're here because you're one of us, but from away. We too did our research, and you're proof positive of the results. You passed all the tests, ones that even we in the old country cannot. You're the Man as they say from your part of the world. You're the outlier come to your ancestral home to save the day. Things will happen because of you."

Just then a fat ginger cat ran in front of us, startling both of us. Oddly, it reminded me momentarily of home and a normal world.

"Even if I accept your premise about the warrior character of the Croats, many other small nations can boast the same. It's one character trait among many. Croatians possess bad characteristics as well, wouldn't you agree?"

"Certainly. We are good, and we are bad. Indeed, we are better than most and we are also worse than most. I won't argue that. We have our saints and sinners, like other nations. There is a natural correspondence between good and evil. One can't exist without the other. And when that correspondence no longer holds, then the space between one and the other carries us on. The space contains both."

"Well, you've lost me on that one."

"Our capacity for goodness dissipates over time. Gradually. So too, our capacity for evil grows smaller and smaller until there is nothing. Is that better?"

"No."

Josip had a tendency to become very abstract especially after a night of drinking which was often. And this was one of those days. He looked at me with what I thought was an expression of deep compassion, then he shook his head violently from side to side.

"But our character issues from values of honour, hospitality, and tight, family bonds. We love a good joke, but our sense of humour can turn quickly and become deadly in a moment. We suffer from the vice of envy. If someone is doing well, we become spiteful and mean, even to close friends. But I tell you Marin, our world view is rooted on a naive innocence, like our primitive art, an innocence that binds us together as one. Sometimes, however, we suffer from an insular world view. We are compassionate, but not on a global scale, and that can lead to a collective bias against other races, creeds, and nations. Unfortunate but true. In the final analysis we Croats cherish some values more than others, and those values have become ingrained in our spirit and our way of life. Welcome my brother." Suddenly he looked at me and placed a powerful arm on my shoulder.

"Enough of this. We need coffee and lots of it right now. Let's go, Marin."

The very next day I was given a definite destination and a time for my first Blue Mist Travel assignment. Sometimes it is disconcerting to get what you want. It was to be Nin, but a few days before I was to begin my work, Josip wanted to take me to Karlovac on public transport and he said, a special place nearby.

2.24

Josip met me at my hotel and we walked a short distance to what he called a public shuttle station. We boarded a streamlined, driverless vehicle that resembled a van in size, but one without wheels. It hovered over the ground about a half-foot. I kept looking around in amazement while Josip settled into one of four seats and closed his eyes. We were the only passengers. There were some blinking blue and green lights on a small control panel located beneath one of the side windows, but other than that there was no sign of how the vehicle operated. Fifteen minutes later we were at the Retro Zagreb Aerodrome. I was staring up at several airships, large and small, and of different colours, tethered to mooring cranes and separated by huge fenders similar to the ones you see separating yachts in a harbour but much, much larger. There was an air of excitement in the air as groups of tourists boarded their respective ships. Josip explained that, apart from cargo airships transporting goods, the national tourism industry depended on airships for conveying tourists throughout the country. Later he was to tell me that these aircraft had nothing to do with the military's use of airships, and actually provided a convenient cover for clandestine uses. He said that we could have taken a shuttle all the way from Retro Zagreb to Karlovac, but he wanted me to experience as many modes of transportation as possible.

At last I was leaving Retro Zagreb and I was finally getting a taste of the future. Very soon we were up and away in one of the smaller airships. Below me were the spires of the churches and the squares of the city. It looked like a miniature city from the air. I could see the green horseshoe of parks in the lower city, resplendent in the morning sunshine. Retro Zagreb was a great city but it had been recreated from artifacts of the past, from pictures and movies, from documents, from memories. It wasn't a living city. It was a kind of Disney world, a city for tourists to visit and experience the past. But it wasn't real. It was like those insects captured in pine resin. It looked similar to the city that once existed, but the living pulse wasn't there. That was long gone. But everyone I talked to was so proud of it, so taken by its retro charm but it wasn't the real thing. It could never be. I kept these thoughts to myself as I looked down at the passing landscape from my window seat in the airship. I glanced at Josip sitting with his eyes closed in the seat next to me. He was snoring lightly. Before we left the aerodrome he had quaffed a pint in the airship lounge, telling me it was a necessary pre-flight habit that calmed him.

I leaned to my side and forward to look out the window. There were no traces of industry or paved roads or transmission lines. The only things I could see were fields and dense pockets of green forest with blue hills in the far distance. Nothing like the future I had imagined, at least not yet. Josip began to snore loudly, and then I felt his head fall against my shoulder. I tried to quietly extricate myself without waking him, but that proved futile. A minute passed and then he made several loud snorting sounds with his head bobbing violently in front of him before he woke. His bloodshot eyes stared at me in shocked wonder. It took him a blank moment to realize where he was. Then he smiled, grunted in a kind of greeting, rolled his shoulder for privacy, and closed his eyes again. When we landed a few minutes later, I had to poke him gently in the ribs to get him going.

We stood with a small group of passengers in front of the airship terminal for no longer than five minutes before a vehicle arrived to take us to the center of Karlovac. The transport to our hotel was quite remarkable and different from the vehicle that had carried Josip and I from the shuttle station in Retro Zagreb to the aerodrome. It hovered above the ground making no sound, but there the similarity ended. The coach seemed to be made of a transparent plastic material or something similar to that. When the door opened I noticed that the seating arrangement was reconfigured automatically to comfortably seat the fifteen of us that entered. I saw Josip smile at me, sensing my wonder, and then give me a thumbs-up sign, an anachronism from Canada I had taught him. The journey to Karlovac was smooth and short. It couldn't have been more than five minutes before we were in front of the Karlovac Hotel.

2.25

"Marin, Josip, so you've come to join the party."

The voice was familiar and resonant, and everyone turned to see the handsome woman standing on the stairs leading to the lobby of the hotel. Beserka was dressed in a form-fitting tan pantsuit that accentuated her curvaceous beauty. I could hear the chuckle in the back of her throat as she caught me looking at her. She came down the stairs to greet us, gently but firmly pushing away several people who were trying to enter the hotel. She gave me a welcoming hug that lingered a moment longer than it needed to, and then a peck on both cheeks. I noticed her lips were very soft against my skin. She nodded to Josip curtly but in a welcoming way.

"What party?" Josip asked. I could see he was surprised at seeing Beserka here in Karlovac.

"Why, the LGBTQ convention of course. The celebrations originated in Karlovac. They've taken place in the city every year for decades. It's become part of the history of the place. Three days of partying and fun like nothing you've seen."

"Ah, now I remember. Of course, it is the famous and storied rainbow coloured regiment, the most decorated of all. Such a proud military history, the envy of the forces. Yes, indeed, but we have come here by chance. Still, we can celebrate with you. Certainly. But Beserka, I did not know you were in the LGBTQ regiment. I thought you were in the Uskok Special Forces regiment. Are you not?"

"Yes, I am, but I have many friends across the forces, and I am welcome here and have a standing invitation. I am an honorary member and am privileged to wear the regimental tattoo. I have a few errands to complete but let's meet this evening in the Stoplite lounge here in the hotel, shall we? I think you'll enjoy it."

Beserka joined us later that day for a drink in the spacious hotel lounge. It was crowded, colourful, and boisterous. I was amazed at what I was seeing. The colours of the rainbow moved in undulating waves like silken scarves floating above tables on what I assumed were draughts of air. Beneath the din of the partiers, strange haunting music filled my ears. But what most surprised me was a three-dimensional painting on a rotating dais at the far end of the lounge. Small palm trees and mango trees laden with ripe fruit framed what was happening. Green parrots and tiny blue hummingbirds issued from a curved white duct shown in the artwork and suddenly they became real or so I thought, and flew through the air. They came forth and flew in flashes of blue and green and gold, surprising and delighting the entranced viewers who reached out to try to capture them in their flight.

But they were illusions only and their hands grasped out at nothing. Several people came to our table to pay their respects to Beserka. I could see she was held in high esteem. Suddenly, she shifted her gaze and looked directly at Josip. A turquoise parrot with a golden-coloured beak and an orange stripe under its wing nestled on her left shoulder and then disappeared before she spoke.

"I learned only this morning that I am to be redeployed from Retro Zagreb to assist in your work when required. I am to act as lead officer. I trust, Josip, that you do not have any difficulties with that."

"Of course not. It's always a delight to work with you. But I'm curious as to your role."

There was just a hint of irritation, and perhaps resentment in Josip's voice. He signalled to a waiter to bring another round just as a splendid silver-blue hummingbird hovered over his finger.

"Oh no, not for me. I've had enough to drink," Berserka said. "I must make some time for old friends here that I have not seen in many a day. But as to your question regarding my role, I am to reconnoitre the caverns, both public and private, and determine how they can best be used should engagement with an enemy be necessary. I'll be conducting a kind of inventory, and I'll need your input. But we can talk of that in more detail at another time. Ciao." At that she stood, flashed a cryptic smile, and left.

"That woman is a holy terror, but I'm glad she's on our side," Josip said. He insisted that we have another round of their potent rainbow specials, drinks that contained several bands of differently coloured liquids and densities, and then we left just as the noise level was rising and green phantom parrots filled the air. I ducked to avoid one, but I needn't have done so. It flew through me. It was a grand illusion.

Perhaps for reasons of economy Josip and I were sharing the hotel room suite. I had hoped for my own room but that was not to be. I was ready for sleep, but I could tell that Josip was not. He poured himself a brandy from the bar counter and then sat on a large club chair that appeared to conform to his body shape and movements as if it had been programmed to do so. The future had its creature comforts to be sure.

"So, Marin, what did you think of the festivities? Similar to partying back home for you?" he asked, as he twirled the amber liquid in his glass. He savoured its aroma before he drank.

"From where I sat, everyone looked to be having a great time."

"But my understanding is that in your time LGBTQ people were not afforded the same freedoms that we celebrate in our time, here in Karlovac and across the country. Am I right?"

"Yes, that is true. We're not there yet."

"Please explain what you mean."

"Well, some people had a hard time accepting the nature and freedom of others. In fact, some people hated them for who they were, the LGBTQ community I mean. I guess they didn't conform to their ideas on sexual orientation and wouldn't let them be. They harassed them in direct and indirect ways. They didn't respect them as fellow human beings."

"Yes," Josip said, his voice rising in anger. "In our history books we have records of gay couples being beaten, and of acid thrown in their faces, of suicides. So many horrible stories of physical and emotional terrorism. All so stupid, so inhuman. It was right for the LGBTQ community to challenge the moral ugliness of those times and fight back. Perhaps because of that oppression they became the elite force in our military and have been for centuries." He rose from his chair to pour himself yet another brandy. I was constantly amazed at his capacity for drink. We were both silent for a while and then I remembered what I had experienced in the lounge.

"Yes, and tonight in the lounge, for me to see a community celebrating their diversity and difference, that was an incredible privilege."

"Well, over the many decades they not only won respect, but demanded it. Lovers and warriors became their motto, and they have proven it over the centuries. Now no one dares insult them. Or if they do, they do so at their peril. But enough, I can see you are tired and need sleep. Go ahead, I will stay up for a bit and think about things. It's been a good day and a better evening."

I decided to take a shower before bed. I undressed in the dark and then groped about for the light. The very moment I turned on the switch in the bathroom, the place was transformed. I was suddenly in a tropical rainforest at sunset. I stood in a small clearing amid vines and orchids and a rain shower fell upon me. Strange sounds came from the dense foliage surrounding me. I was startled when a golden snake with black diamond marks on its skin slithered to one side of where I stood and disappeared into the bushes. I followed a path that led to a nearby river glistening in the last light of day. As I walked the rain shower continued to fall upon me within a diameter around me of about eight feet. It simply fell from the darkening skies upon my skin, cool and refreshing. I stood for a moment on the bank of the river marvelling over the scene before me, and the artistry of the technology that had created it. The illusion was perfect. I was not confined to the dimensions of a hotel bathroom. The jungle setting around me was vast and keyed to my perceptions in every way. Even the heavy smell of decomposing earth and vegetation was flawless in design and true to the actual experience. A light breeze blew by me carrying the scent of orchids in its wake. I walked back to the small clearing. My feet sank in the jungle soil to just over my ankles. The ground was soft and squishy. The moment I raised my arm the rain forest disappeared and I was in the hotel bathroom once again. I put on a bathrobe from one of the glass shelves and returned to the bedroom where Josip was snoring loudly.

2.26

The next day, out of the blue, Josip suggested that we take a trip. We took public transport and within ten minutes we were we were walking in a small village on the hilly outskirts of Karlovac. Several people nodded to Josip as we walked. It was obvious from the expressions on their faces that he was known to them and well regarded. Soon we walked up a steep incline and he stopped in front of a modest wooden house on the crest of the hill. The architecture of the building and indeed that of the houses we had walked past seemed to me to be modelled after fairy tales, with thatched roofs, and round windows that resembled the portholes of a ship.

Josip tried to open the door, but it was locked. He knocked hard three times and then turned to me.

"Marin, this is my home, my boyhood home. I want you to meet my mother, Ana."

The door opened almost immediately, and there in front of me stood a stout, elderly woman with thinning gray hair and a fiery expression on her face. Her cheeks were bright red as if she had been drinking.

"What? Have you lost your key, or do you need to sharpen your knuckles against my oak door?"

"I want kisses, not criticism, Mother."

She smiled warmly then, kissing him on both cheeks, before turning to me.

"This is Marin, my friend from Canada. I wanted him to see our village."

She welcomed me and then led us along a corridor to a rectangular open garden in the center of her home. As we walked, she was talking non-stop to Josip, admonishing him for being away so often.

A sliding door opened. There, in the middle of the courtyard was a statue of a seated woman holding a book in her lap. It was monumental on a human scale. I found it quite striking and powerful.

"This," Ana said, "is a copy of Meštrović's 'History of the Croatian people.' Have you seen it before, Marin?" she asked, looking at the piece with ardent adoration.

"No," I said, stepping closer to the bronze sculpture. "I've seen many of his pieces at his home in Retro Zagreb where he lived and worked, but I do not recall seeing this work there."

"It is a slightly smaller rendering of the original," Ana said. "You can touch it if you wish."

I did. It felt good to touch it.

"Hah, there's more to it than what you see," she said in a low voice. "Make it dance, Josip."

Josip stepped behind the statue and touched the woman's right elbow. Suddenly, the statue transformed into a three-dimensional hologram with people and animals moving about.

I looked at Ana and Josip with surprise. I had never seen anything like it. It was a moving miniature caravan of sorts. Rugged looking men and women moving across a mountainous landscape in steady progression. The detail was incredible, and was there, just in front of me.

"How is this being done?" I asked. Josip looked at me and then at the model, excited to be sharing it with me. Josip was absorbed in the movement of the figures. He took a step closer to it. There was no sound. There was only the movement of people and animals across a rock-strewn landscape. It couldn't have lasted more than thirty seconds in all. And then, just before the image faded away, a face appeared to be staring curiously at us. It was beguiling and so intense. The face was grizzled and lean with sharp dark eyes and thick gray hair falling to his shoulders. The expression on his face was one of amusement and curiosity. Before the image faded from view completely, the man turned and spoke to those beside him, but I could hear no sound. They appeared to be laughing uproariously as if they had just been told the greatest joke. And then the sculpture was there once again occupying the space where the images had been.

"There, did you see it?" Ana exclaimed. Josip turned to me, excited and energized by the experience. It was all over within a minute.

"This was a gift to me from Toma Radičev. It is from his early work, before he developed his blue mist technology." Josip's face beamed with the memory of it. He went on to tell me about the experiments Toma had conducted in space and time based on Tesla's work. The brief three-dimensional exhibit we had seen was a fragment of living history. Josip explained that it amounted to a bird's eye view of one group of the legendary seven siblings who had migrated to new lands in the eighth century and had settled there, in modern Croatia. Cutting edge technology had visited and captured a few seconds of the past history of a people.

"And Marin, the weathered face that you saw in the last few seconds was, we believe, a shaman or soothsayer. Somehow, perhaps intuitively, he caught on to what we were doing and communicated that. His intuition proved a match for our advanced science. We looked into the past and he reciprocated. He looked into the future and laughed. That foray into the past could never be replicated quite like that. Toma had to try and try again and finally move in a different direction altogether in order to prepare the wherewithal for you to do your present work. Life as it's lived is always stranger than fiction. Toma and I were close friends and he honored me with this gift from the past. Ana nodded her head vigorously and then left us for a moment. The statue of the seated woman was there before us again, solid and unmistakeable. It was a work of priceless art that held more secrets than we could imagine. We sat in silence.

At that moment Ana came into the garden and broke our reveries. She carried a wooden board with coffee and what looked like a loaf of bread upon it. She placed it on a garden table and began to cut the bread into thick slices.

"Ah Marin, now you will taste my mother's walnut roll. She is famous in the village for it."

There was a look of quiet triumph on her face as she heard Josip's words. She served us and in truth it was the most delectable dessert I had tasted in a long time.

"And the show Marin," she asked. "How did you like the show?"

I knew she was referring to the strange and wonderful three-dimensional history hologram. Despite its brevity it was similar to the spectacles from the past I had seen in the kiosks. A kind of living history that was as much a mystery as anything I had encountered in my life.

"Wonderful!" I replied. "There is something about it that is so real, and especially seeing the face, the face of a shaman or soothsayer. Do you remember him? He walked with a staff and wore a bone necklace. It seemed he was looking directly at me as much as I was looking at him. And then it stopped abruptly. I would have liked to have seen more."

And then Josip leaned back in his chair and shook his head in wonder. "I never tire of seeing this living moment from the past, from ancient history, in the way that it actually was. I wanted you to see it, and now you have, Marin."

"It's incredible," I said, sipping at the excellent coffee and then tasting the walnut roll. I could see Ana's face light up as she watched my obvious pleasure in partaking of the dessert she had prepared. She smiled and then left.

Josip became thoughtful and silent for a few moments, and then continued.

"The longer I live, the more the line between life and death becomes blurred. We can actually look into the past and see lives in motion. That's what happened here in this little show of one band of early Croatians entering into the territory that became Croatia. This was the first of its kind and very special. Marin, what you've seen in the kiosks came later, much later, but the continuity is always there and affords us a remarkable glimpse into the past, the true past, as it was experienced. Much, much superior to the scribblings of biased historians."

Josip motioned for me to follow him and we went into the kitchen where Ana was busily preparing a meal. The walls were a luminous white colour that I noticed had a relaxing affect as we sat on comfortable chairs around a heavy oak table.

"Mother, you are making my favourite, bean stew and smoked sausage. Marin, you are in for a treat. This is one of her signature dishes. You will love it. A heavenly feast. Simple and hearty. The kind of meal they would serve in heaven if there was one."

Suddenly, Ana took a long-handled wooden spoon, and without warning, smashed it against Josip's back in a single stroke. It broke in two as Josip cried out, more in surprise than pain.

"What!"

"I've told you often not to speak like that. You blasphemous devil! Be happy that it was just a wooden spoon."

"Ah Marin, you see what I have to put up with. What do we know in this life? Three things, and I am not referring to a trinity. We grow old, we die, and there is no god."

Ana looked positively apoplectic with rage. She stood by the stove and glared at Josip with controlled menace. She was as silent as doom itself. Everything had changed in an instant. The walls that had almost shone with pearly light were now a stark gray tone, obviously in synch with the human emotions close to it.

"Come Marin, let's go, and go quickly. Mother can get like this at times, especially if she's had a drink or two. I could tell by her rosy complexion. I'd forgotten."

We raced out of the house like cursed children and didn't dare look back. As we made our way down the hill Josip began laughing until he had to stop and catch his breath.

"You see what I have to put up with. Ah, but the bean stew. Too bad. Let's go back to Karlovac and find a spot where we can talk. What a warrior she would have made!"

Blue Mist Travel

PART THREE

3.1

I DIDN'T QUITE KNOW WHAT TO expect, about where I was going, about Nin. Josip had told me that it was the old royal Croatia, the birthplace and seat of princes and kings and bishops and all manner of royals, but I knew little else about the history of the place. To be sure there wasn't a wealth of information about ancient Croatia. Brujo had told me to expect that when we were at the museums in Retro Zagreb. He shrugged his shoulders when he told me that history was patchy at the best of times. The history of the early Croatian royals fades in and out of clarity, sharply focused at times and then momentarily gone from sight, like driving down a country road under brilliant sun alternating with the overarching shade of trees. But my very ignorance intrigued me. It meant that I would have to figure out things for myself. I'd take whatever clues I was given or found and work from there. That's what I was being paid handsomely to do.

There was a heavy blue mist surrounding me when I disembarked. The sleek, ultra-modern airship was similar to the one I had taken when I left Hamilton for Retro Zagreb. It was early morning, pre- dawn, and no one was about. Birds were starting to sing. As soon as my feet touched the ground the airship ascended soundlessly and disappeared within the cloud of blue mist. I felt a trace of moisture on my face as if there had been a light, delicate rain. I walked directly to the Church of the Holy Cross of Nin as Josip had instructed me. It was close by. I could hear the sound of my footsteps as I walked. I stopped for a moment and stood on the foundation stones of what appeared to be an old Roman temple. The Church itself was quite tiny, like a small house, and occupied little space within the much larger perimeter of ancient temple stones. A light, early morning fog was beginning to dissipate as I crossed the threshold of the Church. I noticed some plait work above the doorway that looked Celtic to me. Inside, a huge, bearded, middle-aged man stood waiting for me just as Josip had said. He was quite massive in stature and wore a blue linen tunic with a red sash tied tightly about his waist. My own clothes, the ones left for me in the airship, matched his own. He didn't say a word. As instructed by his gestures, I dipped my fingers into the basin of holy water, knelt, and crossed myself. I was quite surprised at how small and intimate the Church was, about nine meters by nine meters. The interior was painted in brilliant colours of red and blue and gold. There were narrow, rectangular window openings on the walls. I slowly approached the big man and then reached within my lambskin vest and withdrew an elaborate silver buckle from an inside pocket as I had been told to do. The man studied it for a long moment running his thick fingers across the incised, curved designs. He looked at me with just the trace of a smile and nodded, tucking the buckle into his sash as he did so. The buckle was proof of my lineage with an Istrian clan and the ticket to a meeting with royals. Brujo had prepared the necessary groundwork of relationships, including a Pula uncle. So far, so good.

When I said "good morning" my words reverberated in the tiny space around us. The acoustics were excellent. The quiet giant standing in front of me did not answer my greeting. He simply motioned for me to follow him with a brusque gesture, and I did so. I had to quicken my steps to keep up with him. The hem of his tunic fell to just above his knees. I marvelled at the size of his calves. His lower legs were the most powerfully muscled I had ever seen. They were pistons of flesh anchored in heavy leather sandals.

A slight breeze was coming from the sea. The air was fresh and invigorating. Daybreak was becoming morning quickly. The blue mist that had brought me to Nin was completely gone. High above me a golden falcon soared high in the heavens and described a great arc in its flight. Immediately I sensed that something felt different about the place. There were mudflats in the near distance, and beyond them I could see mountains on the mainland. There were several large buildings, some of them timbered, fronting both sides of the roadway we walked upon. A white kitten scampered in front of me, looked at me quizzically with an abrupt turn of its head, and then darted away. I heard the creaking of heavy hinges as a massive gate opened allowing us entry into a very large courtyard. An old grizzled porter with only one eye squinted at us and then disappeared. The three-story U-shaped building around us was constructed of white stone with rows of green wooden shutters on the second and third floors. The giant motioned for me to sit on a stone bench while he entered one of the side-doors surrounding the courtyard. At the far end of the courtyard I saw several guards positioned in front of barred doors. They were armed with spears and swords, but their manner was relaxed and easy. They paid no attention to me after they had seen me enter the compound with the giant. They were practicing with their weapons. I sat against a wall and watched them.

About an hour passed before the giant returned. As he approached me I thought I saw someone peering from behind a slightly opened shutter on the upper story but could not be certain. My companion still said nothing, and I was beginning to think he was mute. Not a word had come from his lips in all the time we had been together. I noticed the silver buckle I had given him was still tucked into the sash he wore. He motioned for me to follow him as before, and I did so.

He was walking briskly, and soon I was almost jogging to keep up. The terrain was flat and we were walking towards the sea. It was a glorious morning, and to one side, in the far distance, I could see a range of mountains shining like a golden boundary gifted by some generous god. Soon we passed salt flats, swampy areas, and irregular sandy beaches. I could taste the salt air on my lips. I saw several sandpipers moving contentedly along the edge of a beach. There were also other smaller birds that I had never seen before flying about. They were emerald coloured and blue with flashes of red, like the birds of paradise.

We walked and walked until at last I could see human figures in the distance, though they were blurred and indistinct. Beyond them there were several large tents that shone a brilliant white under the sun. There were several horses too, corralled near the tents. Suddenly there were shouts of alarm and dozens of the figures ran towards us. As they drew closer I could see they were naked and covered from head to toe with dark mud. They spread out and began to encircle us. Some held spears while others brandished short swords and long-handled, single and double-bladed axes. The giant held his arms up and shouted a word, a code word of some kind I thought. It was the first time I had heard him speak. His voice was low and resonant. But still the menace of the attacking warriors was there before us and motioning us away, urging us into the sea with their weapons. They looked like long-haired morning devils, mad with hate and fury, and caked with reddish-black mud. I noticed their circular formations as they moved towards us.

The first circle was the largest, meant to keep us at bay, and after that, smaller, concentric circles, each of them running in turn, clockwise, and then counter clockwise until in the very center only two figures stood, a male and a female, both dressed in white linen garments that were soaked through, almost transparent. A grand silence ensued, covering everything in an airy blanket that held for a long moment.

And then laughter, sudden, raucous laughter, erupted from the inner-most circle. Colourful banners were being raised high. At last I realized what was happening. A Royal and his lady were bathing in the sunshine of early morning, while retainers and soldiers stood guard nearby. The royal couple were enjoying themselves in the health-giving mud of an ancient sea. I watched them as they dipped into the sea and then, fresh-bodied and invigorated, they walked to their tent, laughing and joyful, a resplendent couple in a seaside paradise.

Several of their followers studied us closely. Their nakedness was as natural to them as the sunshine that fell upon them. That surprised me. I'd have thought that they would feel vulnerable and race to put on their clothes. Instead, they stood on the sands and waited, their weapons held firmly, but we posed no threat and they quickly realized it. A few commands were shouted and the warriors dispersed. I watched as they turned slowly and jogged towards the tents. Once there, they put down their weapons in orderly spots around the perimeter of the tents and then ran into the sea to remove the mud from their bodies. They ran with their knees high, shouting with the vigour and elation of strong bodies striding in a shallow sea. They swam and splashed and laughed and then entered the tents to dress.

We stood there and waited to be called forward. Suddenly three men approached us, and one of them spoke to my companion in a rapid-fire dialect I did not understand. They didn't look as if they had been among the swimmers in the mud. The trio was well dressed in light tunics and leggings, and I took them to be courtiers of some kind. They were very serious in their mien and looked at me with some degree of mistrust, or maybe it was just caution. My friend responded to them slowly and methodically using the same dialect, and he showed them the silver buckle I had given to him, and then he pointed to me. I heard the words Pula and uncle and assumed he had explained who I was and why I had come. One of the men took the buckle in hand and returned to one of the tents, the one the Royal and his lady had entered. The others waited to hear what I had to say.

My giant friend turned to me and spoke to me for the first time in full sentences. He spoke in a low voice, slowly and carefully, and I guessed he wanted to make sure I understood every word.

"They want to know how you came to be here. I told them you are from Pula and that your uncle is a close friend of our Duke. They explained to me that there are several cordons of troops surrounding the island and its environs. Hundreds of troops. Somehow you penetrated our defenses, and they want to know how you did that. I told them we met at the Church, but I did not know how you had arrived on the island."

As rehearsed with my Retro Zagreb handlers, I told them that a boat from Pula had put me ashore on the island, and that I had walked through the pre-dawn night until I came to Nin and the Holy Cross Church. I did see a few campfires on the beach, but I avoided these as I did not know if they were friendly or not. I also told them that the Duke had been advised of my visit.

They spoke again using the dialect I was not familiar with. It seemed to me they were chiefly concerned with how I had managed to get past their defensive rings around Nin. My giant friend shrugged his shoulders and grinned. He said I was lucky to be a shadow in the night. The other two men said nothing but were clearly angry at the defensive breach. The third man who had left earlier with the silver buckle returned and welcomed me to Nin. He said the Duke would see me that evening and sent thanks for the gift from my dear uncle. I breathed a sigh of relief at hearing that, nodded and smiled, and then I was taken to my quarters in one of the rooms above where I had seen the soldiers practicing with their swords and spears. I had arrived safely, and now my work could begin.

3.2

That same evening I was summoned to a celebratory dinner adjacent to the building where I was staying. There were crowds of people everywhere, cheerful and excited at the latest news. Children were running about play-ing tag and laughing uproariously. I learned that Duke Branimir had been recognized as a ruler from Pope John VIII. As I entered the great banquet hall I heard cheers and laughter and no end of merriment. I was ushered to a table very near to the Duke's own, and I sat contentedly drinking a fine white wine. When the Duke entered the hall, there was a great hush and then tremendous cheers resounded through the air for several minutes. He was a full head taller than most of those in the hall, and lean, with long dark hair and grand moustaches. I observed that he was wearing a blue tunic with the silver buckle I had brought for him cinching the leather belt around his waist. An elegant gold crown with three small crosses rested atop his head. There were pearls over his ears, and his curls fell gracefully to his chest.

He strode to a raised dais and then sprawled more than sat upon his throne. Behind him there was a cross and a sceptre. I noticed that the hem of his robe appeared to be weighted with round plates sewn into the garment. He was surrounded by several courtiers who whispered in his ear as gifts were brought before him and piled to one side. His handsome face was a ruddy gold colour charged with confidence and power and excitement. Every now and then he would lean on his broad sword and stretch one of his long legs out before him. On his left side stood a tall noble attired in the style of a Byzantine. Another gift giver in Frankish dress handed a jewelled scabbard and sword to a courtier and then prostrated himself, face down, on the floor at the Duke's feet. The Duke placed his boot on the back of the gift-giver's head and looked about at the crowd below him. He raised his sword in acknowledgement to them, and they cheered wildly. He truly was their beloved Duke. And I could see by the set of his smile that he knew it.

For several days I simply kept to myself as I was given no instruction to do anything else. The big man, the one I had first met in the Church of the Holy Cross, looked after me, and made sure I had food and lodging, but for the most part I was left to my own resources. I could tell he was very busy and spent much time in the Duke's quarters.

I walked along the beaches and through the small town, looking for something to do. One day I noticed a group of about a dozen warriors axe throwing. I stood to one side and watched as they threw long handled axes at a target thirty feet away. There was much laughter and joking as some of the contestants missed the target completely. It looked like great fun, and I couldn't help but move to the center of the group. A tall, lanky youth with long blonde hair offered an axe to me, by way of invitation to join them.

The target was a star-shaped yellow-orange gourd suspended from a horizontal pole that was attached to a post. I steadied myself, raised my arms high above my head, and focused on the center of the star. I took a deep breath as I shifted my arms back and then threw the axe, keeping my eyes on target all the while. My throw was perfect and the axe blade cleaved the gourd in half. I thought it might have been the training I received in Retro Zagreb. The blonde youth cheered and patted me vigorously on the back. I believed I was lucky more than anything else. An axe was offered to me again amid much laughter and some teasing, but just then the big man stood in front of me with a broad smile and steered me away from the good-spirited group.

"The Duke wants to meet you. You've been given a short audience as he exercises his horse. He is very fond of your uncle and holds him in great esteem. We must hurry now or we will miss the opportunity."

The two of us jogged towards the beach and soon I could see several mounted warriors in the shallows, the Duke among them, his face beaming with delight. He was dressed simply in a light blue cape, shorts, and sandals, ready for exercise. His horse was a grey-dappled stallion that was chafing at the bit to get started. Everyone was in high spirits. The Duke motioned to a spot beside him where I should stand, and the other horsemen fell back behind us. The big man, whom the Duke called Marko, told me to remove my shoes. He said he would take care of them. I did so just as the Duke began to walk his horse slowly in the shallows of the sea. I walked beside him in a few inches of water. His horse snorted with anticipation but the Duke held him firmly with his reins.

"Your uncle is well?" he asked, glancing down at me.

"Yes, my lord, he is. He said he hopes that you are in the best of health."

The Duke laughed. "I am keeping well in that special charmed place between the Franks and the Byzantines though it sometimes gets a little too close for comfort. I have to match their cunning with that of my own." After he said that, he immediately allowed his horse to move into a slow trot and I had to run alongside him to keep up. The water splashed silver filaments across me as I ran.

"Your Uncle has had his share of Frankish hospitality has he not?"

"Yes, my liege. He has indeed." Behind us, his guard had left some distance between us. I glanced up at the Duke and his face was bright with the mid-morning sun. His dark eyes shone with a sharp focused intensity. I could see he was amused as I kept up the pace he had set. His horse snorted loudly, straining to move into a gallop. The Duke held him back, not allowing any quickening of pace. With just a few deft touches, the Duke's fingers kept the great power of his stallion in check.

"Your Uncle has asked that I keep you with us for a short time to learn our ways. I have agreed, and I have charged Marko with the task of guiding you along. Just keep your wits about you, and watch and listen. You can join us as we move about our kingdom. But you must be aware that we are positioned between great powers that would have us be subject to their whims and expectations and greed. Great things are afoot and you are one of us. Now I must allow Max his head. Good luck."

The Duke and his steed broke into a gallop leaving me behind in an instant. I moved to one side as his horse guard followed him in a rush of splashing water and eager, joyful horses. I turned to see Marko waving to me from the far end of the beach. That afternoon my instruction began in earnest. And I was surprised at how it all started.

What struck me was how fresh everything felt. Here I was, in the distant past, in ancient medieval times, and yet things were new and surcharged with wonder and great potential and possibility. It felt to me as if I was in another country, and not the past. The very air I breathed was pure and fresh. Nothing in my training in the reconstructed Zagreb had prepared me for the feeling state I was in. I didn't know what to expect, but by God I was ready. I didn't feel fear. Maybe that would come later, but it meant nothing to me now, not in this moment. I was about to embark on a daring adventure and felt alive from the top of my head to the tips of my fingers and toes.

What struck me, in due course, was the fact that there was no one palace or fortress that was the center of his wealth and power. Branimir's kingdom was a peripatetic holding. An advance party of several hundred souls was always sent out ahead of the royal party to ensure safety and adequate preparations for his visit. We moved from place to place in a royal caravan that was well met by loyal followers who provided food and lodging for the Duke and his retinue. Even when I could not see the cohorts of warriors that accompanied us, I always knew they were about. There was always a happy excitement in the air when we arrived, and a festive atmosphere. I remember the procession from Nin to Zadar. The Duke would meet and confer with local nobles who ruled the area. We would stay as guests for a few weeks and then move on. The palace fortress of Klis, the royal lodgings, was our next stop, after Zadar.

Marko would spend a few hours with me each day, and together with a group of grizzled veterans, demonstrate military techniques covering swordplay, archery, spear and pike use, axe throwing, and all manner of weaponry. I could see he was training me as a trainer who could bring military skills back to Pula. But that was not my mission. The technology and trappings of war were not what I was after. I asked Marko if I could be present at some of the meetings between the Duke and the nobility. At first he cursed me in a stream of obscenities that surprised me with its virtuosity. He was a man of few words and communicated largely through a series of grunts and vigorous arm gestures. I could tell he was incredulous at my presumption to be in the presence of the Duke during his negotiations and meetings. He appeared to tremble with rage and his broad face was mottled pink and purple with strong emotion. But I persisted. I needed to get a sense of the qualities of leadership that were at play, and hopefully, an object of some sort that I could bring back with me.

A day later I found myself in the presence of the Duke in the vaulted council chambers of Zadar. He dismissed a dozen courtiers with a curt wave of his arm. Only two extremely large bodyguards remained. He embraced me warmly and said, with the trace of a smile, that he understood what I was about and he would grant my request. I could attend two of the sessions with visiting diplomats, one Frankish, and the other Byzantine. Marko stood beside the Duke, mute and stolid. I noticed the Duke's bodyguards held Marko in great regard.

I was not disappointed. Seeing and hearing the Duke in discussions with the diplomats at the separate meetings was revelatory. Both foreign men were the esteemed representatives of great and sovereign empires, many times the size and strength and military power of the Croats. The Duke stood on a raised dais with the sun streaming in from a high open window at his back. He displayed a range of emotion and vocal inflection that was quite remarkable. At times he was placating. At others he fell into a towering rage. He strode about on the dais, his boots striking loudly against the polished oak floor. He paced across the stage like a lion in a cage. He mentioned incidents and slights that he could not forget or forgive. Indeed, his anguished face seemed to burn with rage at the remembrance of certain events. I noticed that he would often pause for emphasis mid-sentence, and say, for example, that in the interests of peace and prosperity and mutual sovereignty, he would forget such behaviour. He had a habit of slowly pulling at his long, drooping moustaches signalling when the meeting was over.

After each of the sessions with the diplomats, and only when everyone had left the meeting hall after the Duke's dismissal, he would stride up to me, clap me hard on the back, and ask me what I thought of his performance. That was the word he used. Performance. He laughed when he said it. I could readily see it was a game for him, an elaborate, absorbing game. His face was flushed with power, and a sense of destiny.

"Marin, in discussions such as these, manipulation is inherent in the interactions. For a small dukedom such as ours, diplomacy is essential. What can one do but play the game with the things one has got? We are caught in the middle between great empires that push and shove and expect the bending of a dutiful knee as their God-given right. Hah!"

He stood before me and looked up at the high vaulted ceiling, as if he was reading something there that intrigued him. He could only have been a few years older than me, perhaps in his late twenties or early thirties, but the difference between us was immense. I couldn't help but compare myself to him, and really, there was no comparison, none at all. His eyes fell on mine once again, and he continued, in a thoughtful, considerate, confiding manner, given that I was a visitor from an old friend, my Pula Uncle. He stepped off the dais and approached me.

"The thing is, my Marin, one must always strike a balance with outside forces. Play them against each other. Be bold, but never reckless. Be prepared, through stealth, or cunning, or even marriage, to even the odds of warriors on the field. I have at my beck and call the finest troops, and the ones I value most are the ones who are beyond false bravado. They are past shouts and loud curses. The silence of the best and the bravest makes for successful diplomacy. They stand behind it. Here, take this, as a memento of our time together. It will, if you are worthy of it, stand you in good stead."

He undid a leather strap from his waistband and extended his arm. The gift dazzled me. it was a Byzantine dagger that looked to be of great value. The Duke withdrew it completely from the scabbard, holding it high, admiring the handsome blade for a moment, and then he replaced it in its case with a satisfying click. As I took it and held the precious gift with both of my trembling hands, the Duke smiled and nodded. When I thanked him he said that the finest instruments and weapons of war are ceremonial in nature. It would take me a while to realize what he meant.

15 July 03:30 881

3.3

S EVERAL DAYS LATER I WAS in the palace fortress at Klis.
Marko and I shared a small bedroom with two small beds in it. He
was a big man and the mass of him spilled over the edges of the narrow
bed. The very moment his head touched the pillow he fell fast asleep.

With my hands cradling the back of my head I thought about the
dagger. Why was it so important? After all, it was only a thing, an object
that could be manipulated. It didn't have consciousness. It wasn't animate.
At best it had symbolic value, a thing given to me by a Duke. It had value
and some provenance I suppose, but little else. I turned and twisted on my
rough bed until I'd had enough.

I rose and walked over to the narrow rectangular opening overlooking
the courtyard below. I pushed the heavy curtain to one side. A few torches
were burning there, and I could hear sentries talking to each other, but I
couldn't make out what they were saying. A dog was barking ferociously
at the very bottom of the tiered fortress hill. I returned to my bed and lay
down in the darkened room. Still sleepless and somewhat bored, I retrieved
the dagger from beneath the mattress where I had stored it and pulled it
from its scabbard. It made a rich, metallic sound, quite loud against the
silence of the room, but Marko didn't stir. He lay face first with his huge
arms outstretched around the bed and dropping to the floor.

I held the dagger carefully by its blade and raised it high in front of me.
Suddenly, it seemed to glow a light greenish blue colour that surprised me

by its growing intensity. The light was emanating from the blade and lit the space surrounding it. I was mesmerized by it, by the steady, sharpening colour that dispelled the darkness around my bed. Then, I felt a tingling in my hand as I gripped the hilt of the dagger. It wasn't a numbness. It was altogether different from that. As I grasped the handle I felt an accelerating strength growing in my hand that was quite remarkable. It was as if the dagger was becoming an extension of my arm and hand, a part of it. My body seemed to be pulled up from the bed until I was standing up and making circular motions with the tip of the blade, greenish-blue circular motions that lingered for a moment in the darkness and then fell away. After a few moments a very fine red mist appeared at the very tip of the blade. I stood transfixed by the development. In an instant the red colour disappeared and there, hovering high in the center of the room was a three-pointed golden crown. It shone brightly for several seconds and then was gone. I didn't know what to make of it.

I heard Marko snoring heavily and then suddenly stop. Afraid that he should wake suddenly and see what was happening, I grasped the dagger by its hilt and shoved it into the scabbard in one quick movement. It made the same sharp metallic clicking sound that I had heard when I had first withdrawn the dagger from its sheath. It was as if a circuit had been completed, an adjustment of some kind. I stuck it under the mattress and all was dark and silent once again. Marko was snoring softly in his tiny bed, oblivious to the light show that had just occurred.

I was restless and excited from what I had experienced, so I rose quietly from the bed and made my way on tiptoes to the predawn courtyard below. No one was about. Only a small torch was burning against the stone wall. I could just make out a few guards standing about at the lower levels of the fort where a small fire blazed in the darkness.

From where I stood I could see the flickering fires of Solin and far beyond them the harbour fires of the distant port. All was quiet. I stood for a few moments and then sat down against a cold stonewall, my senses heightened in the darkness. Suddenly, I heard a rustling sound and then silence once again. I buttoned my tunic against the cold and made myself as comfortable as I could. My backside was already chilled. I smiled at the tender memory of my grandmother who cautioned me against sitting on stone. A future past that was still with me. I pulled part of my tunic under me. Ah, how I missed her and my grandfather. The memory of their sun-bright kitchen was with me for a moment, the laughter within the home, and the aromas of food. And then the image of it drifted off and away until I was left with only the heavy darkness of the courtyard where I sat.

I needed time to think. It seemed to me I had completed my mission. I had an object, the Byzantine dagger, the gift of Branimir. What more did I need to do here? I had what I needed. My instructions from Retro Zagreb were simple. Gain the confidence of a leader and somehow secure something special from him or her, an object with provenance. My Pula credentials had served me well. An uncle who had the confidence of Duke Branimir himself. Brujo had done his preparatory work well in creating that uncle, and I had done mine. During my training I had asked if it was possible to alter the past, to change it in any way. After all I was living in the past. It seemed as if I had simply entered another country, as easy as that. The instructor said that my being there was no more than a few undulations of the ether. The past was flexible and mutable. And that was how I was experiencing it.

There was something special about this place. So much had happened here. I felt so many waves of emotion in this courtyard, here, in this pre-dawn darkness that had witnessed so much, so many different eras. I felt strange, new feelings course through me, feelings of triumph and feelings of dread. I huddled myself against the cold and darkness. Again I heard a rustling sound, but this time it was very distinct. It was followed by shouting and raucous laughter as at a merry party. I moved to one side quickly and as I did so, a clear image formed, a bubble of light within the darkness. There, before me, as if I was peering into a large circular window about six feet in diameter, was a hall, a festive hall, with much drinking and merriment.

There, seated at heavy banquet tables were Romans and Illyrians. I recognized them as such from pictures and dioramas I had seen in Retro Zagreb museums. The dress and costumes were the same. There were women among the Illyrians, and their faces too were flushed ruddy with wine. They sat alongside the men. There were great trays of meat and fruit upon the tables. The Illyrian men wore loose cloth belts around their bellies, and I noticed that as they drank, they pulled the belts tighter and tighter. Their arms were covered with tattoos, some of which looked Celtic in design. It was wonderful to see them. Here I was in the past, a medieval past, the past of Branimir, and looking into an even more distant time, Roman and Illyrian time. Nothing in my training had prepared me for this. How to explain it? What to make of it? It was not something I was trained to do. It was instinctive to me and came as naturally as breathing. I was sure my instructors would be amazed at the sight if they could monitor me. And then just as suddenly the circular window before me began to fade until I could not see the bright hall within the charmed circle. Another moment and there was nothing there. The sights and sounds had vanished completely. All was gone.

The next evening a banquet was held for visiting dignitaries from Byzantium and the Frankish lands. The hall was packed with long tables for the feast. Marko and I sat near the entrance. I noticed he was extremely vigilant and watched the movement of personnel into the hall very closely. Just outside the entrance six soldiers collected weapons from those entering the hall and placed them on numbered tables behind them. A smiling Branimir, in a green and silver cloak, was sitting in the center of the raised head table. His eyes were looking out at the world with a burning intensity. His long drooping moustaches glistened with robust health. I noticed he was wearing the silver buckle I had brought for him. It was pinned at his shoulder. To his immediate left and right were the visiting nobles and beside them soldiers of the royal guard, his bodyguard. Oddly, I could see that beneath the royal table where Branimir sat, there were two large canvas sacks, both dark brown in colour and rough. I wasn't certain but there appeared to be movement within them. I asked Marko what they were, if there was anything inside, and he simply smiled, glanced indifferently at the sacks, and continued eating.

After the dinner, the tables were cleared and more pitchers of wine were served. Branimir, still seated, spoke in his great stentorian voice, welcoming his guests, and thanking them for the lavish gifts they had brought with them. While he was still speaking, from the back of the hall a tall foreign looking man with long blonde hair stood and cheered, interrupting Branimir's speech. The man held a wineskin in his hand and looked to be drunk. Within seconds, a bald, jowly guard leapt up unto the tabletop like a great jungle cat and scrambled on all fours from tabletop to tabletop until he reached the man, grabbed him by his golden hair and dragged him from the hall as if he were a rabid dog. Branimir took no notice. He smiled broadly, made a few remarks pertaining to the visitors and then, with the slightest finger movement, barely discernible, indicated that the visitors could stand and speak. Each of them spoke in soft, honeyed voices praising Branimir and his ducal kingdom. Each of them, in turn, raised a cup and toasted him and his health and his good fortune. Branimir nodded and called for more wine.

Later that night Marko took me to a small wooden structure at the very base of the hill leading up to the palace. Several men were positioning ropes across a beam running the length of the building. Then two canvas sacks were hauled in on the backs of two very big men. They looked to be the same sacks I had seen beneath Branimir's table in the banquet hall. The sacks were opened and within each of them was a man, gagged and bound hand and foot. I could see that one was dressed in Byzantine garb while the other was in Frankish attire. But they were not the nobles I had seen at Branimir's table. They were terrified and on their knees, dreading what was to happen.

A rope was tied around their bound wrists from the back, and then they were hauled up towards the beam, forcing their arms to bear the weight of their bodies. Both of them were still gagged so there were no screams. But their eyes expressed great pain. Each of the men was pulled up a few meters, in sudden jerks, and then the rope was let go. Their shoulders were dislocated. After several times of being hauled up and dropped down, they were raised to the rafters and then dropped one last time. Finally, when the two men lay crumpled and broken at the end of loose ropes, Marko signalled me to follow him.

The first light of dawn cut the darkness around us as we entered our room. I shuttered the window and fell upon my bed exhausted from the events of the night, but curious too about the men I had seen. The morning came quickly.

"Marko, why were the men in the sacks tortured? What had they done?"

"Torture? Hah, that is not torture, my boy. They are being prepared for interrogation It is believed one of them knew about an attempt to assassinate our Branimir. That is why the preparation was gentle. Tomorrow we will enter the discussion more fervently, and have the details we seek. Of that you can be sure."

At that, Marko bid me good night and was asleep as soon as he lay on the bed.

The following afternoon I was summoned to the Duke's quarters. He was sitting on his throne and wearing a red and gold tunic that accentuated his lean muscularity. His dark hair was tied back in a bun. I fell to one knee as I had been told to when in an audience with the Duke. He bade me rise.

"Ah Marin, I have a lesson for you, one that you can carry home to your Uncle for me. Will you do that?"

"Anything, my lord. Anything at all."

"Yesterday you saw the Frankish and Byzantine emissaries at my table, did you not?"

"Yes, I did. They sat on either side of you, and made speeches."

"But what about the others?"

'I am sorry but what others? I only saw the two nobles."

"Ah, but surely you saw the ones in the sacks at my feet."

"I didn't know about them then. I wondered what was in the sacks."

The Duke smiled at my discomfort. Then he stood up and walked over to me and placed his hand on my shoulder. It felt heavy. After a moment he began to speak.

"One sack contained a Frank. The other sack held a Byzantine. Each of them was bound and gagged within his sack. And at my table was still another Frank, and yet another Byzantine. I drank and ate with them and we exchanged courtesies and pleasantries. Did you see that?"

"Yes, I did."

"What I want to tell you is that the Frank and the Byzantine at my table were thinking the same thing about me as the Frank and the Byzantine in the sacks beneath my table. Do you understand?"

I stood stock still trying to process the information. After a long moment I spoke, but hesitantly.

"Yes, my lord, I think I do. An attempted assassination, by one of them. Marko confided that to me."

"Exactly, and as of this morning, it is known that the Byzantines are owed a special gift, and one which we will repay shortly, and in full. But that is another matter and one that doesn't concern you. However, I want you to tell your uncle that he must secure even greater ties with the Franks, but nevertheless, he must be most careful as the Franks will no doubt be feeling in the ascendant once news of our repaid gift becomes common knowledge. Understood?"

"Yes, my liege. Understood."

"Ah, excellent. And now my dear Marin, it is time for lunch and I have some freshly caught sea bass for our table. Come, join me."

The following days and nights passed quickly. I even had another audience with the Duke where he emphasized once again that my uncle must be wary of the Franks. He said they must always be embraced, but with a dagger at ready. The same was truer of the Byzantines who had crossed a line he said. Then, after a few sundry remarks, he embraced me with a strong hug and nodded. I bowed and left his presence. I knew I would sorely miss him.

I made my preparations to leave, and was saddened to depart. I felt that the people were friends and kinsmen. Marko advised me on the route to take for the return journey to Nin. He even offered a small escort of three warriors, but I politely refused. I told him it was best that I travel alone. He nodded but cautioned me, saying that there were traitors even here in the royal seat. I must keep my wits about me, and my weapon handy. Anything can happen, he said, and it was best to be ready for it.

The escape field in Klis was waiting. That very night the airship would be there, in the middle of the night. Once I saw the blue mist I must leave immediately. The dagger the Duke had given me was tucked into a belt and sheath that I wore at the small of my back.

Marko and I shared several cups of wine the night of my departure. The two of us were alone in our bedroom. There was a small oak table between us as we sat on our beds. He said very little but his eyes were moist, and we toasted each other. And then, suddenly, he lay back on the cot in his majestic sprawl and fell asleep instantly. I noticed with a smile that his feet dangled over the edge of the bed. He had become a friend whom I dearly loved.

I was not sleepy so I decided to rejoin the festivities. Midnight had passed. After a time, I left the party and wandered towards the high eastern side of the fortress. The night air was crisp and cool. Great dark clouds shrouded the moon. Only a few brave stars pierced the darkness. There, kneeling by the stone walls that resembled the prow of a ship was a soldier dressed in black garments and a great hood. He nodded at my arrival by way of welcoming me to his silent vigil.

"You are alone," I said.

"It's best for a guard to be alone. There are no distractions. Concentration is easier."

"But you can still hear the partygoers."

"I block them out. Besides, I don't need to hear anyone. I left off listening some time back. There's a better way to determine if an intruder is nearby."

"I don't understand."

"I grew up knowing that I was to be a guardian. It is a family tradition, and a proud one. My training began with confusion."

"What do you mean?"

"My mother would confuse me. When she wanted me to listen, she would use the word smell in place of listen. I used to get very angry with her for doing that to me, for confusing different verbs. It wasn't her fault. She was a guardian too. I learned that during wartime, you listen hard for the enemy, but you can listen so hard that you hear nothing. Nothing at all. At a certain point the listening falls away, and though you can't hear the enemy, you can smell them. And then you know they are near. Most useful during war. It takes a great deal of training to change senses, and to go from listening to smelling."

At that he started laughing as if someone had played a great joke on him. I began laughing too and bade him good night. He nodded again, pulled his hood up, and then sat with his back against the wall.

Slowly, I walked down the hill, past the few palace guards, until there were no buildings, and darkness seemed to envelop everything. I made my way to the distant escape field more by instinct than anything else. Suddenly, the skin on the nape of my neck pricked up, and I was instantly on the alert. I looked behind me, but I could see nothing. And then, a deeper shadow of darkness against the darkness showed itself. An image formed. A woman's face, unaccountably wild and savage. The very whites of her eyes appeared to illuminate the black pitch of the night. I knew I must escape from her. I ran like a demon desperate to get away. She pursued me in a mad, fierce race, almost at my heels.

Ahead, I could barely discern the blue mist of the airship, so close, but so far away from the madness behind me. I stopped and ducked to one side to steer clear of her. She turned abruptly, and her looming presence was now in front of me. The moment was frozen. I could see her clearly, her face cast in blue from the illuminating mist close by. And then the stillness was broken. She swung an axe that barely missed my left shoulder, tearing the cloth. She uttered a wild scream, barely human. I reached behind for the Byzantine dagger, drew it from its sheath, and then held it high for a split second. The dagger plunged downwards in its fatal trajectory and stopped at the very root of a piercing unearthly sound. A fine red mist now coloured the darkness, illuminating it brightly for a few seconds before the blue mist gained ascendancy once again. Her body fell in a heap at my feet. I wiped the blood from the dagger across her bloodied cloak and sheathed it. Then, I turned and ran towards the blue mist and the safety of the airship. I threw myself into the seat just as the door closed shut with a gratifying click. I felt the airship rise high into the sky, away from the deranged woman, away from the palace at Klis, away from an ancient death.

3.4

My heart was still pounding as I looked out the circular window of the airship. The earth was as dark as a closed vault beneath me. I was moving into the future, to Makarska, my mission achieved, but at great risk and danger. I had the Byzantine dagger, the gift of Branimir himself. The provenance was assured. I would bring forward with me a treasure of inestimable value, an object that could contribute to the strength and safety of a nation. I felt nothing in having killed the woman, whoever she was, in self-defence. Had I not done so her axe would have finished me. Of that I was certain.

The airship ran silent in its flight. The blue mist within the cabin had dissipated and was entirely gone. I was moving in time, following along with what I had been taught, but confused by it too. I grew pensive. I remembered seeing the Romans and the Illyrians drinking wine at the palace in Klis. My Retro Zagreb handlers hadn't anticipated that or anything like it. How had I seen that? I pondered mightily over time and its distortions. Is all the time we experience contemporaneous? Is everything that is happening now, happening always? Is there a simultaneity to human events? There I had been, in medieval Klis, in the ancient world, standing mutely in the pre-dawn, in a palatial courtyard peering into the lives of an even older world, that of the Romans and the Illyrians. The notion of it baffled thought.

If it was true, that everything on earth was happening simultaneously, then history itself could be subject to verification by a gifted or trained observer. Nothing that happened could be erased, ever. The traces of human events were always there. I grew excited at the thought, clutching the armrests of my seat tightly, and peering into the night, into the very heart of a living dark mystery. What did it mean?

In very ancient times, history was dependent on memory. But memory itself is so fragile, and so easily distorted. People remember what they want to remember, and not necessarily what actually happened. Memory is as evanescent as a snowball falling on burning desert sands. What we remember is subjective and cursed with the deforming nature of that very subjectivity. People die off and so do their memories, so thus there is a vanishing point to anything recalled in the days of pre-recorded history. And even with recorded history, the stuff found in libraries, museums, and laptops, getting to the past as it really was is impossible. There are many versions of the past, more or less credible, depending on the given time and point of view. I took a long swallow from a flask of water beside me and steadied myself. If memory was defective, unreliable, and illusory, then what could be counted on as true? I was in a new world now, one that was light years away from old tales around the fire of what came before. I heard the hissing sound of a canister opening automatically. Blue mist began to fill the cabin once again, and I looked out into the future. And there, in front of me, in the distant horizon, were the lights of modern Makarska, beckoning me to the aerodrome.

3.5

As soon as I had disembarked, Josip was eager to hear of my experiences. He was particularly curious about my having seen the Romans and the Illyrians. He puzzled over that for the longest time. He dismissed my killing of the madwoman as unfortunate collateral damage as he put it. He said he thought it was a random occurrence. And then he asked to see the dagger, and held it in his trembling fingers as reverently as if it had been the Holy Grail. He placed it in a golden box and gave it to a subordinate to put safely away.

We were seated in one of the aerodrome's offices situated on the periphery of the aerodrome with its great cavernous space before us. We could see the tethered airships well lit up by the intricate web of lighting under the closed karst roof high above us.

"Marin, what I'm confused about is your observation of the Roman and Illyrian banquet. We hadn't accounted for that when planning your mission. Tell me more about that. Tell me in detail. Leave nothing out."

I began by stating where I was standing, alone in Klis Palace in the predawn darkness, after a night of heavy drinking with Marko. It had been cold and dark. All around me were the artifacts and architecture of bygone eras and it had stimulated my imagination. I remember walking back into the banquet hall to see who was still there, curious as to who had lasted through the night of debauchery. Josip hung on my every word. His mouth was slightly open.

In my memory of the event, one who caught my attention was a very inebriated lute player. He was a man of middle height and build with curly, shoulder length blonde hair. He was in his mid to late twenties and sat against the rough stone wall, cradling his lute in his arms. I had heard him playing earlier in the small banquet hall, and he was quite wonderful. Later,

I remember seeing a beautiful young woman in a playful and teasing mood who had drawn her silk scarf slowly about his neck and then given him a haughty, dismissive look as she left the room with a wave of her splendid blue and silver cloak. What struck me as I looked at him now was that he appeared to be talking softly to his lute. I moved closer to where he sat so that I could hear what he was saying. His words were slurred and soft and plaintive, but it sounded to me as if he desired his lute to play for his lady, to win her heart as he had been unable to. Despite his drunkenness he carefully placed his lute on a small oak table and then fell into a drunken, snoring sleep beneath the solid legs of the table. Josip smiled at the incident, and then nodded at me to continue.

"It all began with a sound, a rustling sound. And then the sounds of a gay party, people drinking and laughing. I changed my position and then I saw it… a great bubble of light emerging from the darkness, from the cold stone walls in front of me. It was absolutely brilliant. Suddenly, I was peering through a large circular window about six feet wide into a grand banquet hall at the Romans and the Illyrians."

I tried to remember every detail and spent some time recounting the event until I exhausted all traces of what remained in my memory. I stopped and waited for Josip to say something. The silence in the room was charged with a powerful undercurrent of something new and unexpected that had been unearthed.

There was a look of awe on Josip's face. He made a sharp whistling sound, and then smiled warmly at me.

"Hah," he said, "all these decades and centuries of technological progress, of great feats of engineering and intellect, all of that bested by the sensitive imagination of an artist from the diaspora peering into the darkness of the past and recreating what took place in that spot, that very spot where men and women drank and made merry. Hah!"

11 Sept. 06:15 1602

3.6 Senj

The three of us were sitting comfortably in the undercarriage of the airship Aurania Minor as it sailed majestically through the cloudless skies south of Zagreb.We were on our way to Senj. The overhanging windows enabled me to fully see the green countryside passing slowly below. It was an idyllic landscape, an agricultural one, with fields of various crops, some golden, some green, some blue, and most of them separated by low stonewalls. There was no sign whatsoever of asphalt roads, or industry or electrical grid networks beneath us. The undercarriage was spacious and bright within, and I thought I could detect the slightest scent of lavender in the air. I was dressed in the same dark blue uniform as my companions, Josip and Beserka. The material seemed to be an odd combination of light wool and rubber of some kind, but it felt extremely comfortable and form fitting as if it had been expertly tailored to my individual specifications.

Josip stood and walked over to one of the cabinets below the starboard windows and poured himself a drink of a clear, faintly blue liquid. With a nod of his head he seemed to inquire if I wanted one, as well. It was too early in the morning for me and I shook my head. Beserka scowled from one side of her mouth and muttered something that appeared to be derogatory under her breath. She loathed Josip. She smiled at me briefly and then looked away as if I was a stranger. I couldn't understand the woman.

The contrast between my two companions, despite the common uniform they wore, couldn't have been sharper. Josip, short and stout, with his straw-coloured hair tied in a ponytail, exuded a cheerful, devil may care attitude about him, while Beserka was very serious, tall and voluptuous, with olive skin and short, silky dark hair. I found her incredibly attractive, but somewhat sharp and brusque in her manner. Her beauty had drawn me to her from the first time I had seen her. She was a hard woman with a reputation that was fearful. She seemed not to remember our sexual encounter and that puzzled me. I watched her as she rose from the contoured seat that regained its original shape as she stood and then walked to the front window of the undercarriage. She said we were nearing Senj and set about preparing for our descent. From one of the storage cabinets she removed an apparatus about the size of a small portable air conditioner and placed it effortlessly in the center of the room. It appeared to be very light in weight. She manipulated a number of switches on the surface of it and then took her seat. Josip quickly poured himself another drink, swallowed it in a single gulp, and then sat down once again.

Within seconds there was the hissing sound of escaping vapour and then I saw a fine blue mist forming in the air above the apparatus that soon engulfed the entire cabin. The effect it had was instantaneous. As I inhaled the mist my eyelids closed and I felt a great sense of comfort and wellbeing and joy as if I was returning to a home that I had forgotten about but suddenly remembered. Sometime later I felt a hand upon my shoulder and opened my eyes to see Josip standing in front of me and smiling. We had arrived.

"Welcome, brother. Welcome to Senj! Welcome to the home of the Uskoks."

"What?"

Beserka leaned over me, a vision of green-eyed beauty, as she studied the surprised look on my face. She spoke gently, compassionately, encouragingly. "Everything is fine Marin. You have learned much in a short time, but experience is far superior to knowledge. Soon you will experience Senj. Welcome."

When we disembarked it was late in the morning. We were in a flat scrub area about half the size of a football field. The small airship hung suspended in the air and was stable, just a foot from the ground. The camouflage of the airship's covering blended in perfectly with the rocky outcrops, shrubbery and woods surrounding us. I noticed with some surprise that the covering of the airship, the skin of it, appeared at times to be transparent and reflective, constantly changing, mirroring the landscape. The terrain beyond the field where we stood was hilly, and I could see mountains in the far distance.

Beserka carried a small kit bag with her that she adjusted across her shoulders. After a short fifteen-minute walk we were beside the steep slope of a rocky hill. Beserka removed a small device from her bag, about the size of an iPhone, and manipulated several buttons. Suddenly, part of the rock wall slid easily to one side and there before us, was the mouth of a large cavern. I followed them inside to find a well-lit and spacious hall the size of a gymnasium. Around our room, along a rough circular periphery, were several large stalactites and stalagmites, with shadows and darkness beyond them.

What caught my interest was a large kiosk about thirty feet in diameter in the very center of the hall. It resembled a kind of open theatre with its stage floor raised several feet above the ground. The roof of the kiosk was transparent and circular with strange looking projections attached to the rim. A luxurious seating area was positioned to one side. Josip guided me to an impressive looking chair larger than all of the others with a small table in front of it. As I sat, the chair conformed automatically to my shape. It was similar to the one in the airship.

Beserka stepped in front of me and looked down at me, her face confident and encouraging. "Now Marin, it's your turn. I am going to place an object in front of you, one that will assist in re-creating, in re-living events from the distant past. The object is from early times. Do you remember the time you spent with Brujo in the Retro Zagreb City Museum? It was significant to us. That time, and your reaction to it confirmed your worth to us. Through your sensitiveness to certain objects, to objects invested with the hopes and dreams and powers of past leaders, we will be able to connect up with new alignments and understandings vital to our interests and survival. We can only go so far. So much is left to you. We remain in future time and cannot travel with you to ancient places."

As she said that, she walked away for a moment and returned with what looked to my eyes like a walking stick. She removed a dark leather sheath from the handle by loosening a small piece of bone attached to strips of leather. Then she laid it carefully upon the table directly before me. The shaft was a golden-brown colour with incised designs upon it that looked similar to tattoos. Some of them looked like the structures you see embedded in snowflakes. What I had thought was the handle, the grip of the piece, was actually a blade of steel that reflected brilliant silver light when you looked upon it. There were small scratches and marks upon the surface of the blade. It was a long-handled field axe.

The moment I held the shaft of the axe in my hands I felt a bolt of energy surge through my body. It almost slipped from my grasp but I held on to it firmly and looked up to the stage in front of me. Suddenly there were flashes of brilliant light and beneath the light, strong turbulence that shook the kiosk roughly from top to bottom. It lasted for several seconds and then stopped all at once, the light and sound disappearing in the heavy, silent darkness.

I turned to look at Josip and Berserka whom I thought were directly behind me. but they were nowhere to be seen. There was nothing but darkness all around me. I waited with some fear not knowing what to expect. I couldn't see anything at all, and strained to see something, anything, and then the tiniest shard of light pierced the impenetrable gloom on the stage.

An image came to me then, but it was more than an image. I was there, right there, one of several men sitting in a dining room. Somehow, I knew these people. I was one of them. Brujo had done his preparatory work well. Beserka and Josip were nowhere in sight.

The blonde-haired boy, Niko, couldn't have been more than seven years of age. He was carrying a small bowl of honey for his father Roko. There was a pleasant buzz of voices around the breakfast table. The breakfast was a simple one of polenta mixed with milk, but sufficient. I watched the boy carefully as he set the bowl down on the rough wooden table in front of Roko, very slowly, with his small hands cradling the sides of the bowl, as if an offering to a capricious god. There was love and reverence in his bright blue eyes. His father was beaming with pride and glanced around the table at his companions, about a dozen in all including me. It was as if he wanted everyone to share in the moment. Roko's face was shining. The boy's mother smiled from the kitchen doorway, wiping her hands on her apron, and then continuing with her work. I noticed she had a purple birthmark on her cheek.

Then the father reached down to his side, below the table, and pulled out a knife from its sheath. He dipped the blade into the honeypot and turned it around in the heavy amber liquid, some of the honey dripping back into the pot, and some of it falling on the tabletop. He held the knife high for a moment, lowered it, and then moved the blade slowly, inexorably, towards his son's mouth, offering the honeyed blade to the boy with a nod. The boy opened his mouth and waited as the tip of the blade entered, and then stopped. His father looked deeply into his son's eyes, nodded once, and then moved the blade forward. The boy's mother was standing again in the kitchen doorway, but on her tiptoes now, transfixed by the scene, her mouth agape. The boy turned his head infinitesimally slowly, his eyes still on his father, and then carefully positioned the tip of his small pink tongue against the side of the steel blade and tasted the honey, and swallowed. The boy's eyes were closed as he savoured the honey. His father carefully withdrew the blade then and stood up. He raised his arm high over the table and drove the knife with great force into it, the tip of the blade suddenly embedded deeply into the wood. A collective sigh of relief shattered the tense, heavy silence that hung suspended above the table. And then a great cheer filled the dining room as the boy leapt into his father's arms, the trace of honey still on his lips. The mother coughed awkwardly into her apron, turned away, and fled to the back of her kitchen, wildly grateful to peel some potatoes.

And then another bright image flooded the stage in front of me. It was a maritime scene of ancient ships, of galleys, of soldiers and sailors shouting and cursing, of colourful flags flying under azure skies. I was looking down upon this scene and yet felt intimately connected to it. I was looking at myself standing on a deck on one of the ships with about thirty others cheering along with me. There was a tremendous feeling of triumph and victory in the air.

The image became sharper and sharper. A very large and splendid Venetian ship was surrounded by five much smaller Uskok ships that were escorting and guiding their captured prize to its moorage at Senj. Scores of Venetian soldiers aboard the captured vessel shouted sporadically and then grew quiet as they fully realized their predicament. Uskok sailors on their small ships cheered and cried out in the happiness of victory. Blasts of welcoming cannon fire erupted from the fortress on the hill above Senj. Precious cargo was unloaded from the Venetian ship and each item catalogued except for the casks of wine that were brought to the central square for immediate use. Celebrations had begun that would last several days. Everyone shared in the booty according to the investment they had made in the Uskok venture. The priests were particularly satisfied with the return on their investment and joined in the festivities. There had never been a day like it in Senj and there never would be again. The images swirled above me on the kiosk stage gaining in pace until nothing was distinct or discernible. A flush of rose suddenly filled the space and then darkness engulfed everything before me. Several moments passed and then three-dimensional images began to form once again, slowly gaining clarity and definition. I was surprised at how vivid everything was. I recognized faces in the crowd. I saw the man Ruko and beside him his son Niko. And then more images melding with each other and then separating.

3.7

Once the images settled, it was as if I was actually there with them in the fortress room high on the hill above the town. Dozens of Uskok pirates lined the walls of the meeting hall. They wore feathered caps, loose cotton blouses, tight leggings, and leather slippers. Everyone was armed with a choice of swords, rifles, daggers, or axes. There was an air of expectancy that was almost tangible in the murmuring of voices. I looked out a window and saw hundreds more on the hill below the fortress, and then some wild commotion. The crowd divided to let a number of prisoners through their ranks and into the fortress. The prisoner in front was bloodied and bruised. So too were the other seven men with him who looked grim and fearful.

They were dragged into the stone hall and forced to their knees while around them in a tight dark circle the Uskoks waited. Petar, the new Uskok leader, after a few preliminary remarks, began to speak, with menace in the measured tones of his voice.

"Ah, General and associates, how nice of you to grace us with your presence. My men tell me, General, that you were somewhat surprised to have your sleep disturbed. So, so unfortunate. We do need our sleep, don't we? Not to worry. We will help you with that in abundance. But first, some details are in order.

You know, I have just come back from Graz where I was informed by the Archduke and his staff that you had taken it upon yourself, shall we say, certain liberties with the lives of several of my Uskok brothers, and sadly they are no longer with us. I was told you separated their heads from their bodies. So, alas, they cannot speak. They have moved into the grand silence of death. So unfortunate." For a moment Petar looked away as if in deep thoughtfulness of their fate. He cleared his throat of emotion and studied the prisoners closely.

Outside the fortress I could hear shouts and curses from the hundreds of townspeople of Senj. They were crying out for vengeance. It was a bright sunny day, mid-morning, while inside motes of dust hung suspended in the still air. In a moment the silence was broken as Petar continued.

"So, the eight of you are with us now. And you can help us understand. It is important to us that we understand the reason behind it. Who authorized this action against us? The Archduke clearly did not. So, can you enlighten us?" Just as he finished speaking Petar placed the blade of his dagger under the chin of the kneeling General and with its flat side gently raised the General's chin so that their eyes met.

"Stop this farce and get on with it," the General cried out. "You know all there is to know. These men with me do not deserve to die. They were under strict orders, and it was their sworn duty to follow my command."

Petar lowered his dagger and carefully inserted it into the sheath on his belt. He smiled at the General and then took a deep breath. Just as he did so, an elderly, white-haired woman, thin, spectral, pushed through the crowd surrounding the prisoners and stood before Petar like a gray harbinger of doom. She leaned against her walking cane, breathing heavily, and waited a moment before speaking. There was a purple birthmark on her cheek that stood out against the pallor of her skin. Her voice sounded low and very tired as if she had come to the end of a long and arduous journey. Petar nodded gravely and respectfully before her, and waited for her to speak.

"It is my right to avenge my son and my husband. Both of them gone now and with them any joy I might have had in what remains of a life. So what? An old woman's grief is like rain falling onto the sea. It matters little. Death comes to all, but treachery must be punished. I want the hands of Rabatta, and I want the hands of the men who killed my son and my husband. After that you can do what you want with them as I know you must. I will wait by the stump in the courtyard."

The old woman removed a sheath from the handle of her walking stick, and I was startled at what I saw. It was a long-handled axe with tattoo-like designs upon the shaft of it. It was identical to the axe Beserka had shown me in the kiosk, the one that had ignited my vision of Senj. The men cleared a space for her as she walked out. The General stared directly ahead knowing his fate was sealed. One of his men, kneeling at his side, whimpered like a beaten dog.

Petar conferred quietly with three advisers and then moved General Rabatta and his men to a small room adjacent to the hall where they stood. A few sharp cries were heard coming from the room as the men were interrogated. Within an hour the General and his men were taken to the courtyard to meet with the old woman who stood beside several very large men offering their assistance. There, screams of pain punctuated the tense silence that had curiously prevailed to that point.

The old woman placed all of the severed bloody hands in a straw basket and returned to her home. After a short interval of time the General and all six of his men were beheaded in the same courtyard.

Then a darkness enveloped everything, and I lost consciousness. When I awoke as if from a powerful anesthetic, I was on the airship again with Beserka and Josip. They briefed me and said that the tests within the cavern had gone very well. I was ready they said, for the next phase.

3.8

A few days later I was travelling alone and on an airship bound for Senj once again. When I disembarked in a field, blue mist surrounded me and then dissipated. I felt a slight queasiness in my stomach but that was all. I made my way to the harbour where I was greeted warmly. Brujo had once again prepared the ground well. I was accepted as a friendly visitor from Pula and not a stranger. I was like family. Someone took my arm and bid me join them.

It was to be a night of drinking, heavy drinking. Booty, taken by the sailors, was to be enjoyed well into the morning hours. I had several weeks before I was to be transported back to Retro Zagreb so I wandered about as food was prepared in the fortress high on the hill. I had no idea of the object I was to bring back with me, not yet. What was it to be? Would it be given to me?

The stone houses near the harbour looked laced up and formal as if they were slightly shocked at the riches ripped from the sea. I walked past one of the city's campaniles, away from the bustling harbour and the shouting and crying out of the sailors. They were happy to be home with treasure piled high in the warehouses, the tally yet to be taken of all that had been seized on the sea.

I was a part of all this and yet apart. I knew the history of the place. I knew what would come after the bitter cost of it all. The uncertain future to come, the forced removal of the population from Senj, like a dagger thrust in the back, and finally to permanent exile in the rough hills and mountains of Žumberak. A mangy black dog ran by me with a bloody bone in its mouth, desperate to get away from a yellow mastiff in hot pursuit.

Suddenly, someone shouted my name. I looked to my right and saw a huge man waving his arm in greeting, urging me to join him. He was standing like a colossus under a stretch of canvas and swinging a bottle of wine merrily. From head to foot the man looked the part of a pirate. Great drooping moustaches accentuated a rugged face, and a cloth cap with three long feathers was held in place by a stunning emerald jewel. He wore a long peasant blouse with puffy sleeves at the wrists and a blue embroidered collar topping it off. The slim leather belt held a dagger in front and a sword at the side. A leather bag was strapped across his shoulder. He sported baggy trousers from knees to waist with ribbons keeping his long socks in place. An old-style rifle was leaning against a wine barrel. Rough looking leather shoes, similar to moccasins, completed the picture. Here was the epitome of a man.

It was very strange to hear someone call my name. I didn't recognize the man. He was tall and solidly built with curly hair the colour of chestnuts and a broad open face that appeared to look upon life as one huge amusement. He pulled out a jewelled goblet from a gilded box on the table before him and poured a generous serving of the wine for me. He extended his massive hand and I shook it, and toasted him with a wink and a nod. It was a fine Venetian wine from the markings on the bottle and it was almost done.

"How did you know my name?" I asked, as he pulled a new bottle from a case beneath the table.

"How could I not?" he replied as he deftly used a short sword to sever the neck of the bottle in one fluid motion. Not a drop was spilled. He refilled my goblet and his own, and then looked at me closely.

"The man from Pula," he said. "I was told about you and how you were sent here to learn our ways. I am Nikola." He went on to talk about ships and pirate prizes and the wonders of the sea. A few hours passed quickly and then he gestured to the fort on the hill. "Time for fun now. Let's go."

Not a person passed before us whom he did not greet warmly and ask about their health. Many were struggling under a heavy load of items unloaded from the Venetian ships. Nikola was all smiles and good cheer anchored by square shoulders and a powerful barrel chest.

Six barefoot children stood idly nearby waiting for him to notice them. Suddenly he did.

"Now Marin," Nikola said, making his voice loud and clear, "look at us trudging up this hill and wanting to sit for a moment or two. And not a chair in sight. Surely someone will notice and offer to remedy the situation for a prize."

A thin boy, about ten years old and cross-eyed, shouted out to Nikola. "We can find you chairs, good solid chairs and comfortable for gentlemen like yourselves." He was clearly the leader of the group.

"What is your name?"

"I am Tomica."

"Can you bring us two chairs, with cushions," Nikola said.

"Of course, and what can you offer in return?"

"A handful of gold coins, one for each of you if the chairs are sound."

"Done," the lad said, and then the group of them raced down the hill in haste, narrowly avoiding the men and women struggling up the hill with their loads.

I was to learn much about Nikola over the following days, but the gist of it was that the man had a genius for friendship. Within a few moments we were sitting at his private table at the fortress on the hill. As one of three captains reporting to the Uskok leader, keeping company with him was valued and sought after. I could see that it was also extremely rewarding in terms of treasure and reputation. His table faced the doorway, and dozens of locals approached the table to say hello and congratulate him on a successful mission. He basked in their praise like a spaniel pup, but his expression was always amused and somewhat sad beneath it all. He knew that circumstances can change as surely as the passing of the seasons.

On this particular day I was to learn much. He waved to a group of five gentlemen, foreigners from the rich look of their attire, who entered the banquet hall. Nikola embraced them all heartily and bid them to join us on the oak benches. There was much laughter and good natured teasing and joking. He introduced me as the Pula man who had come to learn seafaring in exchange for providing military information about Pula. And then he slapped me resoundingly on my back and swore his trust in me. As we drank Nikola shared their stories with me, and I could tell by their facial expressions that they were somewhat surprised at his openness and candour.

"Ah, look here Marin. Look at our happy table of friends and foreigners. These are my brothers. They have taught me to speak the finest English, and in turn, I have taught them to speak excellent Croatian. Look at this fine Englishman who goes by the name of Godfrey, a finer corsair cannot be found." A silence ensued as Nikola stared at Godfrey who was a bit uncomfortable with the compliment. "Born a noble, but unfortunately, the second son of a royal, distinguished line. That means he has a title but no gold, no lands, no castles. But look again at this castaway from one of England's finest families. Perhaps you might think from the look of him that he is more monk than mercenary, but perception and reality are often distant cousins. In battle, aboard a burning deck, he has raced from bow to stern ripping the life from the Venetian dogs. This I have seen. He is one of us but wears his own colours, and for his bravery I love him as a brother. And look again at the ginger-headed fellow at his side. Another English castoff here to fill his trunks with booty from our pirate wars and return home a victor despite his birth. Ah yes Marin, you sit at a table of warriors, loyal and foreign, desperate to live like proud men from the pickings of the sea."

I watched in surprise as Nikola stood and walked around his table and planted a great kiss on Godfrey's bald head. Godfrey couldn't help but laugh uproariously.

"Marin, we are all of us second sons in different ways. But this castle fortress is our palace, and more gold and booty moves through this space than anywhere else along this coast. This is our safe harbour and our unassailable fortress, and we respect and love the protection it has given us. And beyond the fortress, this place has bequeathed to us the secrets of its winds, and we guard these secrets beyond our treasure."

Before he could continue there was a sudden, wild commotion as the cross-eyed boy and his motley crew ran into the banquet hall and shouted at Nikola to step outside for a moment. Nikola strode outside and laughed to see the half dozen boys we had encountered earlier, a couple of them sitting like impoverished princes on two wonderfully carved oak chairs.

One of the young lads shouted to their cross-eyed leader to demand the promised gold coins. Nikola laughed like a demon, sat on one of the chairs, and reached deep into his pocket. Then, he stood and pulled out a handful of gold coins which he tossed high into the sky above the young leader and his band of boys.

There must have been a dozen or more gold coins that seemed to hang in the air for a brief moment and then fall upon the wonderstruck boys who dove to the ground to grab what they could, the bigger boys stretching out their arms to haul the coins in. The smaller boys shouted in despair as they were pushed away from where the coins had fallen.

Nikola cried out jokingly, with a wink and an aside to me, that they had tricked him as there were no cushions to be had, just the hard seats and back rests of oak. No sooner had he said that when two small boys, each carrying a gold satin cushion, dropped them on the empty chair next to Nikola. He reached down once again into his voluminous pocket, pulled out a sack of coins, and then gave each of the boys a gold coin in turn, even those who had scooped up the tossed coins earlier.

And then Nikola looked with fondness and pride at the boys. He turned to one of his attentive serving men, whispered something in his ear, and pointed to the bare feet of the ragamuffin group.

"Boys, go with my man, Franjo here. He will take you to my warehouse, and in the green trunk marked by a Venetian lion, there is a large satin sack. Bring it to me as quickly as you can and you will have something more. Now hurry." Within five minutes the boys were back and two of them carried the satin sack. It was not heavy. It was just large and awkward to carry because of its size. They pulled out several pairs of huge Venetian bedroom slippers, made of satin and silk and fine gold trim. The boys slipped them on, but they were far too large. It didn't matter for they were the very stuff of childhood wonder and magnificence. At the end of the day the Venetian slippers would be tattered rags with no trace of their noble provenance, but the giving of the gifts I was certain would never be forgotten.

"Now Marin, let us go back to the hall for more of that excellent Venetian wine. But first help me tighten my belt. Then I can drink another two liters once the belt is pulled and tightened. It's an old Illyrian trick for drinking more." I did as he asked me and then tightened my own cloth belt. Soon we were putting that esoteric Illyrian knowledge to the test.

It was at that stage of the evening when people began shouting to emphasize what they were saying. The wine was flowing freely. I was happy to be there, happy to count myself one of them. I heard one of them refer to me as their cousin from Pula. My chest was swelling with pride and drink.

As he rose from the table, Nikola whispered for me to join him. We walked outside to the courtyard where the first stars were beginning to show themselves. The night air was cool and pleasant after the noise and stuffiness of the hall. We walked through the courtyard and onto the hill where below us were the lights of the harbour and Senj. Nikola turned to me suddenly serious, sober, and businesslike.

"So, my friend, what can you tell us of the defenses at Pula, at how we can best attack the city?"

"There are certain places on the walls that can be breached and with some help from the inside that is not a problem. I have made a map that shows three weak areas that offer the best points of entry."

"Excellent. Tomorrow we'll meet and draw up some plans. Do you need any resources once you return home?"

Nikola was sharp and alert despite his bloodshot eyes.

"Yes. I will need gold to assist matters from my end."

"Done. Time now for a soft bed Marin, and a loose belt."

The days that followed passed quickly, and I learned much, but what I was most curious about had not been addressed. I approached Nikola on the matter once again. "I just want to know what it's like-the piracy, I mean. How do you do what you do? And what do you do? My uncle sent me here to learn from the best he said. I have some time left here before I return to Pula, and I want to know as much as I can about piracy."

Nikola glanced sideways at me, smiled, and then began. "It is how we make a living, and it's a profession of sorts. It has developed over time since we left Klis and came to Senj. We had to learn how to sail and read the winds and the currents. Marin, we were driven to it. I say driven because there was nothing else we could do when the powers that be would not pay for our soldiering."

Then he stopped walking and kicked a stone out of the way. His face was tight, and he seemed to be dredging up memories. His voice was tired and slow when he spoke.

"Our children ate grass and the bark of trees. There was nothing else for us to do but take what the sea offered. Better that than stone soup.

The local people and the ancient ones took us in hand and taught us. They taught us well. Look at our ships. Our ships are cunning in design. We learned how to trim our sails with nimble hands and take an easy refuge in shallow waters because of how our ships were built. You have learned all of this. But piracy demands different levels of skills. Bloody, savage work it is, but rewarding as you know. But more of that tomorrow. Let's hurry to the banquet hall. Tonight, once again, we will drink fine

Venetian wine with golden goblets, and later, our dreams will be Venetian too. Let's go."

I spent a lot of time in Nikola's company over the next several days. He enjoyed walking and talking. I noticed he walked with a swagger and there was nothing he loved more than a good joke. He would laugh uproariously at his own jokes. Once when he was showing a young sailor how to tie a complicated knot that the lad couldn't duplicate, he broke into a gale of laughter and said "You have a head for four legs." The poor boy didn't understand that the comment meant that he thought like a beast and not a human. After his remark, Nikola belly-laughed even more to the point where he couldn't speak.

Nikola spent several days with me sailing about and finding safe harbour in shallow bays that afforded refuge if followed by an enemy whether Venetian or Turk. But I wanted more than details about sailing and winds. I wanted to know what the experience of piracy was like, and so I asked him repeatedly about it, until finally he answered.

"Marin, it is different than you suppose. Here, in Senj, we are different men. We have families and friends and duties. Each of our missions requires extensive preparations and we must secure the resources we need to ensure our ships are seaworthy and very, very fast. We are small in number, perhaps fifteen hundred souls, but everyone contributes, and that is why we are so successful.

The important thing to realize is that we need investors for our work, people who can provide the gold and resources we need. They may be city officials, soldiers, priests or monks, but they want a return on any investment they make. They don't know the details and don't want to know. What they want are profits and results. All of our people have a stake in this business. Just look over there."

Nikola pointed to three priests standing on the deck of an Uskok ship. They were examining some articles within an ornate trunk.

"Have you ever seen happier priests?"

He stated laughing then and slapped his knee hard, as if he had made a wonderful joke. And then he turned to me suddenly and became serious and quiet.

"I've seen your map of Pula. I appreciate the detail and the zones on the wall that we must breach. What kinds of tools are needed for us to gain entry?"

"Iron bars and picks and chisels, with stout hammers. If you have some good men it won't take long, perhaps a half dozen strong men at each of the three zones marked on the map. Ladders, too. At least one of the three places along the wall will fall. Of that you can be sure. I've studied them up close. You will not have any trouble I can assure you."

He nodded his head then and I could almost see a shift in his thinking as he remembered my question about the experience of piracy on the high seas. We were standing atop a steep hill near the fortress. There was not a cloud in the sky.

I watched with dismay as the expression on his face grew hard. It was as if he were recalling memories, painful memories, from the look of him. For a moment he turned his face away as he gazed at the ships in the harbour. There were at least fifteen Uskok ships in the docks. Hundreds of people were milling about, some chatting with sailors, others very business-like and officious in manner as they stood in a queue outside one of several warehouses near the main thoroughfare of the town. Because of the recent maritime successes, there was a festive mood in the air.

"So, Marin, look below at the harbour. Look there. It's a grand time for the citizens of Senj. Everyone is smiling. And listen. Some are even singing of their good fortune. This is why we do what we do. But all of those ships now at rest sport a bloody wake behind them. Just a few days ago our sailors clambered aboard aTurkish ship and whatever stood in their way was cut in two. Heads were chopped off, lives forever changed. That is the other side of what you see before you. The shock of terror, of sudden vicious attack, the chaos, the confusion, and then the bloody victory. That is the other side of the treasure-laden ships resting at harbour that you see before you under a brilliant sun."

"Is it true what they say about the Uskoks eating human hearts and dunking their bread in blood? Did that really happen Nikola?"

Nikola cursed under his breath and then stared at the clear blue skies above us for the longest time.

"Is it true?"

"What is true is that we have as much food as we need and more. What is true is that our stomachs are full and that our children roll on the grass and do not eat it. What is true is that our pockets are filled with gold coins that we can scatter to the winds if we wish it.

If a child starves and dies in a dark corner, is that all right? There is no blood, no violence, yet there is death. So tell me, if a Venetian merchant profits from a child's death, is that all right?"

"You did not answer my question."

I could see the look of disappointment on his face as if I had somehow betrayed him. Suddenly I blurted out what I had been thinking.

"Do you worry about your sins? Are you afraid of Hell?"

"I go to confession. I kneel and pray at the stations of the cross and I am free of sin. I have seen Hell and know that I need to pass through it to win my heaven here in Senj."

"So you admit to barbarism, to depravity, to savage acts of violence and mayhem?"

I tried to speak in a calm voice, but the nervous tremors in my voice were anything but normal.

"My dear cousin," Nikola said, with the tight trace of a scowl on his face, "eating a human heart strikes me as a crude act perpetrated by a madman. But even an act like that, a stand-alone act, can have its uses, to terrorize an enemy, and strike fear in his soul. Surely you must know that."

"I don't know what to think, or how to understand what you're saying. My Uncle has sent me here to learn seamanship, but torture and grisly murder are not what I want to learn."

Nikola slapped his thigh and laughed until I thought tears would come from his eyes.

"Piracy is more than tying knots and hoisting a sail. Look, beyond the harbour is the sea. Once we leave harbour, everything changes. You leave the man of Senj that you were behind and chart a different course from the landsman. You leave your wife and family and townsmen behind with the understanding that what you do as a pirate, is something other than who you are. It is necessary work that is violent and not readily understood by the moral codes of the townspeople, who stay at home in warm beds.

But you must remember, the other side of the piracy coin is business. When we are planning our missions and require resources, we encourage everyone in Senj to contribute, as an investment. They are handsomely repaid upon our return. Of that you can be assured. Everyone, including the clergy looks forward to seeing a tenfold return. Little wonder that the priests absolve us of our sins. We are pirates and take great risks in our profession, and so we expect great rewards.

We would starve if we did not look after ourselves. On one side the accursed Turks. On the other, the clever Venetians. Ah yes, and the Habsburgs playing their shrewd games with us as pawns. So you see Marin, this is who we are. We take from the land and the sea because if we did not, nothing would be given to us. We would die."

At that he grew quiet and suddenly the big man wept. I embraced him and murmured that I understood. He turned away from me then, and looked at the sea before us. I had come from the future and it too was anything but kind. I had not the heart to tell him how his world of piracy would be snuffed out by a little war between the great powers that saw the brave Uskoks pushed out and left penniless once again.

How could I tell him that in a few short years his people would be swept away, swept north to the regions of Žumberak, forgotten and dumped in a mountainous rural world, far from the sea and the vigorous life they knew. How could I say that their homes would be taken from them, that they would be marched north to inhospitable places to eke out a living, as best they could.

My last days in Senj were a blur. Nikola had left on a pirate mission, and I missed him. On the eve of my departure, Franjo, Nikola's factotum, came to my lodgings and gave me a package wrapped tightly in white canvas. He said it was a parting gift from Nikola. Then he embraced me as a kinsman and left.

I unwrapped it. It was the single blade battle-axe, the same one I had seen once before with tattoo like incisions on the shaft of the axe. A gift with grim provenance. I knew that Nikola was smiling somewhere. My mission was complete and successful. On to the next and the last.

27 May 03:10 1530

3.9

A WEEK LATER A SMALL AIRSHIP was waiting for me in the cavernous Makarska aerodrome. I felt a pang of sadness, knowing this was my final assignment. Just before I departed, I glanced up at the control room and saw Manda there. She waved at me with a sudden smile, and then blew me a kiss. I stepped aboard and settled in, and within a moment the familiar fine blue mist filled the cabin. I felt a slight queasiness in my stomach as I had on previous flights, and then fell into a comfortable sleep on a short flight to ancient Omiš.

3.10

It was mid-morning when I entered the timbered hall. At first I was blinded from the sun outside and could not see anything. All was darkness for a moment. My hand shot up and covered my eyes, and I stood where I was, just inside the entrance, so as not to bump into anything. It took a moment for my eyes to adjust in the dim light of the place and then gradually I could see forms taking shape, and slowly, slowly, colours inhabited the shapes. I felt a warm hand take me by the wrist and guide me to a chair beside a great table.

I sat and looked up at the most beautiful face I had ever seen. She had high cheekbones, blue eyes, and a rosy glow to her skin. The barest trace of a smile enlivened her features as she noticed me staring at her. I rubbed my eyes to make sure I wasn't deceived by a trick of perception. But no, the beauty was real and beguiling. I found myself tongue-tied and sat there with my forearms resting on the large oak table, mute and somewhat stunned. I must have muttered something to her because I heard her say that her name was Marta. I stood up and held out my hand. When she took my hand in hers I felt her strength course through me.

That evening Marta and I walked through the streets of Omiš and then along the Cetina River. We didn't talk. High above us, the towering limestone cliffs glowed a golden red colour as the sun struck the mountainsides. I could see why it had been a pirate haven for centuries. From atop the mountains a small force of pirates could rain down arrows and weaponry of all sorts upon Venetian or Turkish ships that were caught in the shallows of the Cetina. I'd heard that the pirates could dart about the river easily with their swift, flat-bottomed boats escaping any pursuing forces, as the enemy ships were much larger. Indeed, I was to learn that they even fastened chains underwater that would ground foreign vessels with their heavier keels. With limited manpower and a taste for fortune and adventure, the cunning corsairs of Omiš owned the Dalmatian coast for centuries. Just before sunset we turned and headed back to the old town. Marta wanted me to see the view from atop the Mirabella tower, and to meet her cousin who was visiting.

I had learned that a great Ottoman force was on its way from the East and my mission was to find someone influential who possessed an object of interest. It had seemed simple enough back in Retro Zagreb but here in Omiš it was anything but.

As Marta and I walked side by side our hands would brush against each other at times. Once I held onto her hand for a moment and I saw her smile and then withdraw it.

The view from the top of the Tower was magnificent. We could look out to the sea and the dark blue islands beyond. The town itself glowed with the falling rays of the sun, and then I heard Marta laugh with delight as someone climbed up the stairs from below.

"Marin, I want you to meet my cousin Mila, from Kostanje. She is staying with us tonight."

There, in front of me, stood a young auburn-haired beauty with the fresh and open countenance of a goddess. She was in that precious zone between girlhood and womanhood that is as fleeting as a butterfly's flight. She had a self-assured manner about her and the most wonderful smile, with a single dimple on her left cheek. She was lithe, and tall, and her carmel-coloured skin glowed with radiant health.

She and Marta were excited to see each other and shared stories of people and places they knew as we made our way to Marta's home where a number of related families lived together. My reason for being there, a visitor from Pula, had been seeded long before by Brujo. I was accepted easily as a distant cousin from the North who had come to learn the ways of pirates and warriors.

For the next few days life was joyful and idyllic. The three of us would go on long walks, and sometimes we would climb to the mountaintops above the town. From a vantage point there we could see far out to the sea. Mila sang as we hiked, and I marveled at the ease with which she moved up the steep paths before us. Marta teased her, calling her a mountain goat. High above us a golden eagle soared majestically across the pale grey sky. I said it was a good omen of things to come.

Mila laughed, saying the good things were here now, and not to be deferred to the future. She picked up two round stones and tossed them to me, one at a time. "Here Marin," she said. "Keep them to fend off evil in the here and now. Remember that the future will one day be the here and now." It was only a few months later that I was to realize how prophetic her words were.

3.11

The bare bones of what had happened were clear enough and imagination could supply the necessary details. Mila was dead. And for a while Marta was inconsolable. She would not eat and neither would she pray. More than ten thousand Ottomans under Ahmed Pasha had moved from the East against Omiš. But just a short time before they were to strike, and while they were still encamped, Mila proposed a bold and fatal plan. She would feign infatuation with the Ottoman leader and let him take her. That a beautiful girl on the cusp of womanhood would volunteer to sacrifice herself in this way was incredible to me. That the elders would support it was a sign of their desperate commitment. With inestimable courage she strode into the camp and was brought before the Pasha. He could barely contain his good fortune. In having her he had her people, and this tribute was won before a single spear had been thrown.

After she was sure he was asleep within the tent, surfeited with lust and heavy wine, she took a torch from the carpeted wall and stealthily made her way to the gunpowder storage tent. If she heard a sound she would pause until the threat of it was gone. Oddly, a snoring guard sleeping by the entrance of the magazine enclosure sounded remarkably like her father. That was the last human sound she was ever to hear.

She gently removed a leather flap from a powder box and took a deep, final breath as she lit it. The torch glowed a fiery red as it burnt through the top covering of the powder keg. There was a light sizzling sound, and for a dread moment she thought the torch might simply fizzle out, but then the heavens unleashed colour and sound the likes of which only the gods could imagine at the beginning of time or at the end of it. It was done and finished and she was gone into the heavens.

3.12

A week passed. Marta and I were walking in the steep hills above the town.

"Why are you weeping?" I asked her.

"I am weeping for the many who have lived here and were driven away from this very coast, taken away forever. I am weeping for the families, for the misery, for the pain and trauma inflicted on them. I am weeping for their resilience, for their ability to be like the grass that is stepped on and springs back. I am weeping for the rape and pain and torture and senseless violence that took place here as we look upon this beautiful sunset. I am weeping for my beloved Mila whom I will never see again, never.

Ten thousand sunsets have passed and ten thousand more will pass. We are here now and will be gone soon but tonight I weep for all that is past and will come to pass on this night here on the mountain, on the barren karst beneath brilliant stars that have shone upon our ancestors as it does upon us now."

I drew my finger across her arm tracing the lines of the figure displayed there. "And here, what does this tattoo mean?"

"It is to remind me of who I am if all is taken from me. It is common in these parts. It is the mark of my people on my skin to give me comfort in times of pain and deep fathomless despair if I should be lost. With it I am never alone."

And then she brushed my cheek lightly, ever so lightly with her fingers. She pulled me gently towards her, and upon the hard karst stone that anchored our love.

I moved away from her for a moment and pulled off the heavy wool sweater I was wearing and spread it over the stone for her to lay upon. She smiled and closed her eyes, adjusting her body to mine. I heard her murmuring something that I couldn't make out, but then I heard her sigh and say my name in the most exquisite way. Marin. It was a sigh that sounded like a discovery and a surprise and a secret, all at the same time in that one word. No one had ever said my name like that before. I kissed her lightly on the lips and then felt myself falling as if from a great height.

Just then I felt a vicious blow across my back. I turned to see an old woman armed with a heavy stick and dressed all in black with a kerchief tied upon her head. She was crying out, cursing me, and raining blows down upon me. Her heavily wrinkled face was a splotchy purple colour, contorted with rage. Marta sprang up and ran away, as fleet of foot as a mountain goat. The old woman grabbed me by the ear and continued to shout obscenities, pulling me away with a strong arm until I broke free and ran down the mountain path.

Despite the mountain turmoil I felt a warmth and a heartfelt joy that stayed with me for days and nights after. When we saw each other at the dining table or outside in the front garden, I could see the joyfulness in her face, a bright joyfulness that mirrored my own. I left Omiš a few days later thinking I would soon return.

3.13

I was in Retro Zagreb, sitting on a park bench where, in the distance to my right was the equestrian statue of the first Croatian King, Tomislav. It was a cloudless day, cool but comfortable. My thoughts were random, images popping up without any train or sequence of thought. Mostly they were images of Marta in Omiš. Images of her smiling with the backdrop of haunting mountains high above the mouth of the Cetina River behind her. She was such a beauty, and I wished I was still there, but my mission was over. It struck me as odd that the very success of my work in Omiš could be the cause of my greatest unhappiness, for I had been told by Matija, to whom I had given the stones that Mila had given me, that I would not be returning to Omiš. He said I was to be homeward bound soon, having completed my mission and earned my fortune.

Marta was locked in the past, along with our unconsummated love, and I was a heartsick fool. I tried to think of something else but to no avail. The charms of the beautiful King Tomislav Park in front of me receded and I could see only Marta's wonderful blue eyes before me. Here I was, a millionaire several times over and yet, as unhappy as a pauper with a meal of grass in his stomach.

The next day I left for the Dalmatian coast. Within an hour, Josip and I were in a cafe on the Riva, Split's wonderful promenade fronting the ancient harbour. It was a cool, cloudless day with tourists chatting happily as they walked, marvelling over the sleek modern ships that were moored before us. Overhead, three gaily colored airships were moving northwards. Both of us were content with the day and our place in it. We were sharing a bottle of sparkling wine, and that made the day complete. The silence between us was agreeable, but a thought crossed my mind, and so I broke the silence.

"Josip, I've learned so much about Croatian history through the ages, the nation's nobility and the martial instincts that have saved it time after time, but there were times that were not noble, and indeed, were shameful."

Hearing those words, Josip sat bolt upright in his chair and glared menacingly at me.

"What do you mean? What time are you referring to?"

"Well, far back in the twentieth century, there was a time when Croatian fascists set about to systematically exterminate the Jews and the Roma, and many others at the behest of their Nazi handlers. Many hundreds of thousands were murdered."

Josip was furious and spat out his words. "The numbers were inflated."

"I've heard that before Josip, and I don't want to quibble over how many were struck down. Even one is too many. It was a sorry chapter and reflected badly on the Croatian character. Very badly."

Josip looked away for a moment, planning his rebuttal. "My dear Marin, you have no right to judge, especially considering your own Canadian history. No right at all." At saying that he drained his glass and poured himself another.

"What do you mean?" I asked.

Josip smiled wryly at me, regaining his composure before he spoke. He sat ramrod straight in his chair. "Every nation has its guilt, guilt that cannot be erased. The Jews of Croatia and also Canada's indigenous peoples. Have you forgotten them, Marin, or is your memory selective? Generations of native children were ripped from their parents' arms and incarcerated in educational institutions. There they were brutalized and sodomized and murdered with the tacit encouragement of the state. The political system protected perverts and murderers in their religious indoctrination centers. And the effects of that genocide remain today. A genocide committed against an innocent people and their children and grandchildren and great grandchildren for many, many decades. Let's not, as you say, quibble over numbers. Now, do you remember?"

The taste of the wine soured in my mouth. The blue skies were gone, replaced by gray scudding clouds that blocked the sun and promised a chill rain to come.

3.14

I used my free time to travel to Lika to do some hiking and revisit the place that I had first known as a boy with my grandfather. I was feeling nostalgic, eager to see some of the old sights we had shared together. I simply wandered about without any clear plan. The mountains beckoned, and I followed.

The entrance to the cave was quite wide, and there were rough stone steps that were uneven and made the descent difficult. The light disappeared behind me and the darkness before me was thick. I stopped in my tracks and waited while my eyes adjusted to the lack of light. It was cool and I could feel the moisture in the air. Unaccountably, I felt a feeling of dread. Slowly, I took a few steps deeper into the cavern, shuffling my feet rather than walking. I reached into my backpack and pulled out my antique flashlight. I held it up above my head and made a quick scan of the area in front of me. I was shocked at what the light revealed. My hand trembled as I moved the light across the floor of the cave.

There, before me, were dozens of alien bodies asleep on the cavern floor. Each of them was wearing a gray tracksuit. Remarkably, their arms were extended perpendicularly above their bodies. The index and middle fingers of their hands pointed upwards. They appeared to be reaching out to the top of the cavern with eyes closed. I looked up but could not see anything there. All was dark, and the illumination from my flashlight was minimal. I thought I saw something move above me but couldn't be certain. It was more a feeling than anything else because everything around me was pitch black, darkness upon darkness. Suddenly a drop of water struck the top of my head. It shocked me at first, but then I remembered I was in a cavern with stalactites on the ceiling, and they could be dripping water. I could not distinguish any shapes above me. There seemed to be a shimmer of paleness above me, but I couldn't be sure.

I used my flashlight to scan across the recumbent bodies once again. They looked like sleepers, unconscious, but with arms raised and pointing to the ceiling. They lay on what resembled yoga mats and between some of the bodies there were stalagmites pushing up into the darkness above them. It all felt unearthly, and I was anxious to leave the place. Carefully, I retraced my steps and returned to the entrance of the cave. I was confused. I didn't know what to make of what I had seen. My eyes smarted against the bright light of day. I heard shouting and above the crude steps that led into the cave I saw three Karstians crying out at what I assumed was the surprise of seeing me there. There would have been trouble for me if not for the intervention from an officer.

Several Karstian troops had suddenly appeared and surrounded me. Upon seeing the officer, they saluted. He returned the salute, his face tight and drawn. He gave a hand signal to them and they dispersed. They walked away as if the place belonged to them.

High above, a dark hawk circled in the heavens as the officer approached me.

"What are you doing here?" he asked sharply. "This place is off limits to anyone but Karstians."

"I lived nearby when I was a boy, and I used to play here."

"You could have been killed."

"But why? I was hiking, nothing more."

"Times have changed, at least here, near the caves. That is forbidden. Now, you must leave at once. You must go. Now."

I hurried away and struggled to make sense of it all.

3.15

Brujo and I were hiking along the coastal trail to Brela. It was a bright, cool morning with the sky the colour of a happy man's dreams. Along the way we rested by an old olive grove within a perimeter of stones. It afforded us some degree of shade and we made ourselves as comfortable as we could with our backs resting against some gnarled trunks. We looked out to the sea and shared a moment of quiet serenity. I noticed a golden-black butterfly flitting in the space between us. Brujo was smiling with his eyes half closed.

"That's good luck," I said, as Brujo's eyes fluttered twice and then opened.

"What?" he said.

"The butterfly, here between us."

"Better that we should be it and not confined within our own skin."

I hesitated for a moment trying to process what he meant, but I was puzzled by his remark and lost in the spaces between his words.

"How can we be it? There's an immense gulf between us and the butterfly, between our separate existence and its."

"An arbitrary distinction of your own making."

"How so? How can it be arbitrary?"

"You're making it so by refusing to permit a change. It's within your power, Marin, to let go of yourself and transform across the distinction between you and it. Look at how it's playing here, happy with us and the wide blue day around us."

Suddenly Brujo extended his arm and held out his hand, his index finger pointing to the sea in front of us. He was smiling and seemed to be waiting, sitting still and waiting. A moment passed, the butterfly flying about playfully. And then a most curious thing happened. The butterfly stopped and perched on Brujo's finger and folded its wings. Brujo brought his other arm forward and stroked the butterfly's enfolded wings. He did this for some time, clearly enjoying the experience. And then the butterfly flew away and disappeared into the shade of the olive grove. I heard a happy gurgle emanating from the back of Brujo's throat.

"Nice trick," I said. "How did you do that?"

Brujo simply laughed and dismissed my question with a shrug.

The Karstians

PART FOUR

09 June 10:00 2324

4.1

I WAS STANDING ON A HIGH point behind Makarska and just below one of the highest mountains in Croatia. I wasn't the first to wonder why the aliens wanted the country. The geology of the place was made up of ninety-five per cent limestone rock. Karst stone as dry as picked bones under the sun on the surface, and underground, hidden rivers that rise and fall with the movement of the seasons.

There were no caches of gold or precious minerals within the mountain ranges that nestled by the sea. What could they want with a tabletop of worthless stone and underground chambers that were dark and empty and insignificant?

But perhaps it was the spirit of the place that had always drawn predators to it. Imperial powers intent on taking what was not theirs. And now, aliens looking with covetous eyes on a spot of the Earth that entranced them and beguiled them with its beauty. Maybe that was it, the attraction of a place that had always beckoned the greedy and the rapacious. Hah! The crossroads of Europe had seen many a battleground and now the crossroads of the Universe would perhaps see another. I reached below to the ground on which I stood and picked up a small white stone and threw it down the steep slope of the mountainside. I didn't see where it landed.

As I made my way down the sloping mountain trail towards the harbour of Makarska I thought more about the aliens, the Karstians. What brought them here? What could they possibly want? I remembered seeing one of their diplomats exiting the government building in St. Mark's Square. He was alone. What struck me was his pallor. The man sorely needed sun on his skin. He was gaunt and looked grim with thin cheeks and hollow eyes. I watched him as he walked resolutely to the center of the Square and then saw him looking up at the famous tiled roof of St. Mark's Church for a full moment. There was a slight trace of a smile as he walked by me towards the Stone Gate. The name tag he wore on his chest read Sprague. He didn't even see me as I stood there watching him. As he passed by me, I felt a strange cold feeling move through my body that gradually dissipated as he walked further and further away.

A few days later I was back in Retro Zagreb. I arranged to meet Josip mid-morning in a corner cafe by the National Theatre. We sat outside and ordered coffee. The place was busy with tourists coming and going. He looked at me steadily for a moment and then began to speak.

"These Karst people are not to be trusted. Their offers of untold wealth are bogus, nothing more than sweet lies to keep us off their game. The Karstians are dividing us. It is an ancient tactic that has proven effective in the past. Just review your history. The Party of the Browns has already begun to draw plans for what they call the Clearances. Our people will be moved to the borderlands, the frontier areas, displacing our neighbours. While this is happening the Karstians will themselves be preparing for their own massive resettlement from their planet to here, and especially to the Karst regions. There seems to be a growing urgency amongst them. I don't know what has caused it, but we must prepare to meet it."

"How do we do that without sparking a bloodbath?"

A waiter returned to our table with a tray of two espresso coffees and a small wrapped chocolate to accompany each. Josip nodded and then took a sip of the bitter brew.

"We bide our time and then surprise them. Don't ask me how, not yet. We are still trying to negotiate some sort of common strategy with the Browns, and that isn't going well. We must have a common front. Your journeys into the past have proven successful, but more time is needed with those special objects that can provide us with an edge. Brujo is helping us in this regard."

I didn't have the faith that Josip obviously did in the magic things I had brought back with me from the past. How could a few objects, even exceptional ones, hope to counter alien weapons. I unwrapped the chocolate and held it in my mouth for a moment before taking a drink of my coffee.

"You have more faith than I do in the efficacy of old objects. Magical charms. Despite their provenance, how can they go against alien technology that has already shown what it can do. You seem to have forgotten what happened at Varaždin. Do you remember?"

"Yes, yes, certainly I remember. But I also remember old biblical tales of David and Goliath."

"A slingshot is no match for a smart bomb."

"Depends on who is on the working end of the slingshot. Technology, whether it be a slingshot or a bomb, or whatever, is subservient to the spirit of the person behind it. Human courage trumps technology."

I began to laugh in appreciation of this strange, good man who had the courage of a lion. I took a sip of what was left of my espresso and found that it was cold. I drank it to the dregs and looked across the roadway to the brilliant yellow colours of the theatre. As I did so a group of six Karstians passed by. They were laughing and looking about, pleased with the day and their place in it. They wore dark clothing that accentuated the pallor of their faces and hands. Josip looked away in disgust.

4.2

Indeed, things were getting very heated on the political front, with the threat of what the negotiating Karstians termed "erasures." This term meant that unless there was progress on the political front, a number of cities would be selected for erasure, and the certain death of a number of its inhabitants. Fortunately, a cooperative joint initiative was announced by the Sabor, the Croatian parliament. The gist of it was a mandatory pairing of a Karstian with a Croat. A kind of cultural exchange was then expected to take place to ameliorate any misunderstandings or prejudices between Karstian and Croat. Language was not an issue as the Karstians spoke an academic kind of Croatian with just the oddest of English accents. The acquisition of the Croatian language by the Karstians had been easy. A small circuit implanted in a chip in the brain and it was done. For officers only, of course. Also, it appeared that the Kartians greatly admired the history of the British Empire with its combination of ruthlessness and civility, and not a little mendacity. The Party of the Browns had sponsored the cooperative program and the Blues went along with the idea, and in fact were quite surprised that the so-called dinosaurs of the right had come up with such a progressive idea.

My pairing was with a young Karstian who introduced himself as Pipkin. The Karstians seemed to favour English names that were odd-sounding to my ear. He was tall and lean, with an athletic build, and a very pale complexion even for a Karstian. He looked as if he spent all of his time indoors. On our first meeting, under the clock at Jelačić Square, he suggested we simply walk about the city and see the sights. It was a brilliant sunny day and I saw him wincing from the light despite the fact it was early morning. It was then that I knew where I must take him first.

I escorted him towards Upper Town, having decided in my mind to get there through the Grič tunnel. The very moment we entered the passageway, built under Upper Town in the twentieth century, Pipkin actually sighed with delight and surprise,

"What! This is wonderful, Marin. I never expected to see such an ancient marvel. It is so intimate. We have nothing like it back home. Such a primitive imagination at work!"

"So you like it?"

"Like it? Wait until my comrades see this. It's remarkable!"

I was taken aback by his enthusiasm for the protective tunnel, constructed during wartime I'd been told. To me it felt eerie in its emptiness. There was nothing to it, nothing extra but an ancient lighting system. It felt cool inside and quite unremarkable.

"May I lie down here for a moment?"

"Certainly, go ahead," I said, somewhat puzzled. I watched him then as he lay down on the concrete floor. He held his arms out, perpendicular to his body with his index and middle fingers pointing to the curved ceiling. It was the same odd gesture I had seen demonstrated by the sleeping Karstians in the Lika caves.

"Oh Marin, thank you for this. What an experience! Second only to being in a cave. Thank you, my friend."

Soon we were out in the open again and Pipkin immediately put on his sunglasses. I took him to St. Mark's and he was quite impressed by the colourful roof tiles of the famous Church.

"Can we go inside?" he asked, removing his sunglasses.

"Yes, of course." There was no one else about, and we entered. He made his way to the Meštrović statue of Mary with Child. For the longest time he looked and looked at the sculpture, with his left hand on his chin and his head bent slightly towards his right side.

"It is wonderful. We Karstians feel that connection, that precious bond, and are one with it. There are so many churches, big and small, across Croatia. It will be easy to convert them."

I was stunned by his statement. "I don't understand Pipkin. What do you mean by conversion?"

"Oh dear. I'm afraid I am presuming too much. Once our leaders, yours and mine, have settled on the terms of the agreement and have paid the requisite tribute, we will begin our transformations. You see Marin, our priority is to adapt the caves, the Karst caves, to reinvigorate our population. First the men and then the women. Before we can do that, we will need transitional structures, and by that I mean your churches. We will empty them of art and adornments and benches until we have the space only. Then we will install sprinkling systems to coat the ceilings and walls with life enhancing moisture. Simple but effective transformations."

"No one has mentioned that," I said, with perhaps a trace of dismay.

"Not to worry. It will not affect your people too much. It may not even happen. Once the Agreement is ratified your people will leave Croatia for the border lands as we have stipulated. And your people will be rich beyond their dreams. But the price of great wealth, dear friend, is that you must vacate the premises, places like this very Church that will become ours. Of course, you will be free to take the artifacts and any and all items of importance to you to your new homes. All of these sacred buildings will be deconsecrated by your clergy and thereby become transitional structures for us. They will be re-fitted to a higher purpose. The conversions will become the beginnings of the new Karstian homeland replacing the old, decaying planet of our birth. You will secure our borders as you have for other empires in the past. We have studied your history closely. Just imagine. You and your people will become the majestic military fringes of the Karstian Empire. It will be a wonderful new world for all. However, we must have the actual Agreement in our hands before any of this can happen. Otherwise, we will be forced to resort to unpleasant erasures. What do you think my friend? Can we count on your support?"

I stood next to him, utterly astounded at what he had revealed in his enthusiastic monologue. Pipkin went on to tell me that a large group of ailing Karstians would be ferried by airship to Makarska to spend time recuperating in the great aerodrome there. The Browns had boasted of its cavernous size knowing the Karstian love of space beneath the ground. Understanding that I was affiliated with the Blues, he urged me to per-suade my friends to accept the offers of the Karstian negotiating team. We parted amicably though I was somewhat confused about where it would all end.

4.3

When I saw Pipkin next, at Zrinjevac park, his tall, lean body stretched out and at ease on a park bench, he had a dreamy look on his face. A magnificent plane tree offered shade. I approached him and stood quietly in front of him. I cleared my throat and that seemed to shake him loose from his reverie.

"Marin," he said with a note of delight in his voice. "I was just thinking about Karstia, about life there, and how different this place is. For certain, we will need a period of adjustment, but after that it's going to be wonderful. So much potential."

His voice trailed off and settled in a contented silence, and I could see how moved he was by the images and memories in his head. It was a splendid day. I sat down beside him.

"Tell me about Karstia Pipkin. I want to know what life is like there and why you want to leave such a familiar, beloved place, why you want to leave your home."

Pipkin smiled, clearly delighted at my interest. He nodded vigorously and then began his tale.

"Ah Marin, there were once splendid caves everywhere on Karstia, caves that our ancestors knew and loved. Incredible places where you could rejuvenate and gather strength. My memories are so rich and deep. But everything changes."

I could hear something infinitely melancholy and mournful in the tone of his voice. He went quiet for a moment and then began again.

"I remember as a small child following a stream or a river, following after it until suddenly it would disappear into the earth. The joy of it, the fun. The river would flow and then a hole in the ground swallowed it up just like that. And then I would continue my walk and to my surprise the river would reappear as if by magic."

The happy expression on his face fell away and was replaced by something grim and distraught.

"In my own lifetime I've seen the streams and rivers dry up. Great underground rivers and lakes were gone within the span of a few short years. No one was quite able to explain why. The great caves of Karstia became as dry as a white bone beneath an unforgiving sun. As children we would lie on the ground and raise our arms and point to distant planets and galaxies with our index and middle fingers. We knew we would find a second home, and now we have it.

The caves and chambers within the karst of Croatia are necessary to our well-being, our health. Unless we can have periodic access to the hollows within the stone, we die. And that is what happened. Our people began to die in droves. The choice was simple. Either we stay and die, or leave and live. A simple axiom and a proven one.

We searched everywhere within our galaxy. We found Croatia on planet Earth. The perfect conditions were here. Ninety-five per cent of Croatia is limestone rock. Our planet, Karstia, was only a third of that. But the water was disappearing at an alarming rate.

We looked to Earth, the water planet, and specifically its karst regions. It was perfect. But there was something more. Hundreds of thousands of years ago we Karstians emigrated from Earth. We had the technology while you humans were still foraging in the trees. A great environmental calamity forced us to leave. And so, we did. Another calamity, but this time on Karstia, forces us to return. We've come full circle now. We've come home and greet you as distant brothers and sisters.

We are four million strong, similar in numbers to your own. Together we can solve this impasse between us, and you will be our guardians at the borders, soldiers at the frontier. You are a stolid people, and we will support you. But the Karst will be ours once again. No matter whether it is ours by your agreement, or by our might. I hope it's the former. Otherwise, there will be blood. Help us, Marin. Help us by working with us."

I was astonished at his words and the thinking behind it. The man didn't recognize our sovereign right to our own ancestral lands. The Karstian elite wanted what was ours and had lied to ameliorate their takeover. I didn't believe there was gold for each and every citizen as promised. That should have been understood from the get-go. The very idea was laughably ridiculous. And without gold, we were to eke out a precarious living on the borderlands subject to handouts by the conquerors. If we refused there would be hell to pay. The clear irony of the situation was that we'd been in similar predicaments before, as a people. Ancient Croatian history could verify that. I was disgusted and angry at his bold ignorance, but I knew I had to dissuade him somehow.

"This is all so strange and odd, but I can tell you the vast majority of the Croats will not accept it without the promised gold, not ever."

"But they will have no choice. As I've said, it's a life or death matter for us."

"What do you mean?"

"The people either accept it or die, gold or no gold."

"You would kill a nation for limestone rock?"

"What choice do we have? We have not come this far to abandon our future."

"But you have lied about the gold. You know that's true. What else will you lie about? What will happen to us?"

"We may have lied a bit, certainly. Lies can be a diplomatic tool. We know history, earth history. The British Empire used mendacity to achieve worldwide dominance. Promises and plummy accents can go a long way. You're naive if you think otherwise, dear friend."

"How can you call me a friend after what you've told me?"

I could feel my heart pounding. I knew I had to remain as calm as possible, but everything within me railed against his arrogance and pride.

"You are still my friend. But that is personal. As a Karstian here in Croatia what I do is based on Karstian policy. And that is an altogether different thing from friendship."

"That policy is nonsense."

"How can you call it nonsense when things are moving ahead? Fifty thousand Karstian troops are garrisoned by the aerodrome and more are coming each day."

"Troops of occupation!"

"A new regime is all. I am being honest and open with you because you are my friend. Soon, our troops will secure government offices and all major transport hubs. Peace will be won with unconditional capitulation and acceptance. An ultimatum has been communicated to government parties and administrators. Just this morning as a matter of fact."

"And if there is no surrender?"

Pipkin shrugged and looked away as if by his words he had answered me fully. The expression on his face was grim, and beneath that there was a substratum of unbridled confidence and power.

4.4

From where we stood in the harbour, Pipkin and I could look up at the magnificent sight of the mountains that anchored Makarska to the mainland. In places, where the rock had fallen away from the mountainside, the wound left behind looked like streaks of exposed gold.

"It pains me to say this," Pipkin said frowning, "but we hold only limited amounts of gold. We had thought we could secure more, but unfortunately not. Oh, we have enough to make millionaires of the Browns and hope to do the same for the Blues, and the military leadership, but as for the general population, no. We are not able to do that. I reiterate that we are most sorry and apologetic.

We have promised the Croatian people that we would compensate them for their land, and rest assured we will not walk away from our responsibilities, from our sworn trust to a subject people. We know it will be difficult at first, and that's why we have ensured your leadership, political and military, will be compensated."

I couldn't believe what I was hearing. The beautiful day fell away from my eyes. The expression on Pipkin's face suddenly turned from one of commiseration to conquest. His chest appeared to swell with pride.

"Give yourself some time to think on it. We can only do what we can do. Our resources are limited. The alternative is not worth thinking about. Enough of this talk. Come, we can be back in Retro Zagreb within an hour."

4.5

I knew for certain that things had reached an impasse between the Karstians and the Croatian political elite, whether the Browns or the Blues. There was no dialogue at all. Nothing was happening. Not a single ounce of gold had been distributed by the Karstians. False promises only. There were all kinds of unsettling rumours floating about. I'd heard that people in rural Croatia were confronting Karstian troopers, demanding the promised gold. Reports of skirmishes were circulating in Retro Zagreb. The valuable tourist trade was dropping off dramatically. I could see for myself several huge blimps tethered to their mooring docks at the Retro Zagreb Aerodrome. Already, the only outgoing flights were tourists returning home to escape what appeared to be imminent violence. There was a feeling of dread in the air that was confirmed for me when I met with Pipkin at a pub near the Archaeological Museum. Ancient Roman columns and broken plinths were used as stone tables, tables with ancient inscriptions carved into the tabletops. I set my glass of beer upon one of them just as Pipkin entered the fashionable drinking spot. A handful of brave Asian tourists were the only other customers. I could see the waiter stiffen as he saw Pipkin enter. He was in full Karstian uniform, brilliant white with gold epaulettes and piping. He sat on a cushioned stone chair opposite me.

"Hello, dear friend," Pipkin said in his English accented Croatian. I rose from my stone seat and shook his hand. It was cold.

"Marin, I've been promoted. I'm serving as the Special Events Coordinator for senior officers. I'm now with the Marshall's personal retinue."

"That's excellent news for you. But Pipkin, I need to ask you what's happening."

"Well, you've probably heard. Talks here have stalled just as we were about to distribute limited amounts of gold to the political and military Croatian leadership. If they could only be patient, but that is not happening. Unfortunately, the Marshall has decided to embark on what he refers to as his Just Deserves Policy."

"And what is that?"

"Across Croatia certain historical buildings are to be razed and the building materials pulverized."

"But Pipkin, Croatia is a place where memory itself is set in stone."

"Be that as it may, the new policy has come into effect, and it mut be honoured. I was actually present when it commenced. Yesterday, at Nin."

"The policy is mad! The Church of the Holy Cross is one of the first in Croatia. It is sacred to the Croats."

I felt as if I could hardly breathe. A flash of red crossed my field of vision. I was furious.

"Not to worry, Marin. I did my research, and advised others as necessary. The old Church is safe for now. However, we may take another look at it if we don't receive full cooperation from your government. The church nearby is gone. It's been decided that your churches cannot be readily converted to our purposes."

Something in my heart dropped like an iron bird when he said that. He spoke of it as a matter of fact, objectively, as if it were nothing, the wanton destruction of a nation's history.

"I did think to bring you a small gift."

As he spoke, he pulled out a small bag from his pocket and pushed it across the table to me. For a moment it was stuck on a small protuberance atop the stone table. He pushed harder, and it was in front of me.

"I don't understand, Pipkin. What other church is gone? What church are you talking about?"

"St. Anselm's, yes that's the name. One of our demolition crews took it down completely. And the bag contains a fragment of its yellow dust. I thought you might want to have it."

I was appalled by what he had said. I placed my hand on the small bag he had given me, and I felt a wave of infinite sadness pass through me. The sacred place that had witnessed the coronations of Croatian kings was no more than a handful of yellow dust.

"No," I cried out. "What have you done? That church was the first cathedral in Croatia. Are you all mad? Croatian kings were crowned there. And you talk about policy. Madness! That's all it is. How could you be a part of all that Pipkin? How?"

I was stunned to see the perplexity on his face. His lower lip was trembling. It took a moment for him to speak.

"It's the policy of Marshal Leith. It is sacrosanct. Be careful. I can forgive your outburst and attribute it to emotion, but just this once because of our friendship. You cannot speak like that again."

A fierce look crossed his face like a sudden flash of lightning in the afternoon.

"Look around you. These stones are nothing but detritus from the past, nothing more. Your culture is not as old as Karstia, and you may be forgiven much because of that. These old churches are nothing but piles of stones given meaning by a superstitious, gullible people. Just like those old silly artifacts you collect from across the country. Put it aside, Marin. You are my friend. Help me to help you and your people. Do this and we can all live in peace."

The fact that he was sincere bothered me most. I sat there completely stunned. St. Anselm's was gone, gone forever except for a bag of dust on the stone table in front of me. Pipkin continued talking, but I didn't hear what he was saying. His lips were moving but I heard nothing. I was utterly lost in thought, confused thought, and then I felt his heavy hand on my forearm.

"You can help me, Marin. You've often told me about your work. I want you to know I've saved several objects from St. Anselm's for you, silver containers. They looked so ancient, with pieces of bone or something inside. Nothing important or valuable. But I need you to work with me, to help me in my new role as Special Events Coordinator. Marin, are you listening to me?"

He shook my forearm with his hand and waited for me to take notice of him.

"I know all of this is an unpleasant experience for you, but together we can save much of your heritage if you are flexible. There must be a strict application of the Marshal's policy. Marin, do you understand me?"

I shook myself awake, my mind still racing.

"You're saying that if I help you the destruction will stop?"

Pipkin shifted awkwardly in his seat and looked away from me for a tense moment.

"I can't guarantee that it will stop, but I know that together we can save much."

"What do you want me to do?"

"Well, you work closely with a number of government departments. You have access to geological records and the like. We don't want to redo the work already done. Many of our people are thrilled to visit the limestone caves that stretch across the country. As Special Events Coordinator, having these records would be a real feather in my cap. I could arrange for short term stays in these caves. We have scientific teams that could get the data for me, but that would take time, and I want to move quickly on this initiative. Can you help me, Marin?"

There was a pleading tone in his voice, and I was puzzled by that, but then I realized he wanted to expedite things so that the Karstian elite would be impressed by his work. From what I could gather so far, the Karstians loved dark, underground places. I didn't understand it, but I'd seen the excitement in Pipkin's face when he'd entered the Grič tunnel complex.

"I don't know if I would be permitted to obtain this information, but I will try."

Pipkin almost jumped out of his seat at this news, and squeezed my arm with affection.

"So you will help me with saving our cultural treasures if I do this for you?"

"Yes, so long as the political talks continue."

"Pipkin, you know I have no influence over that."

"Not to worry. Some of the gold is coming and that will push things along. Indeed, I believe I can even ensure you are rewarded in gold as well. Trust me, Marin. Are you with me?"

4.6

Less than two weeks after I had spoken with Pipkin, we were once again walking along the seafront promenade in Makarska. It was lined with palm trees and delightful modern open-air cafes that looked onto a protected bay and a small harbour filled with sleek yachts and strange futuristic-looking watercraft that I had never seen before. High above us, an airship sporting the red and white chessboard crest of the Croatian state moved majestically inland.

Pipkin was enthralled with the place and every now and then would stop to marvel at the towering, majestic Dinaric Alps range behind us and the dramatic limestone heights of Biokovo Mountain. Dozens of his fellow Karstians meandered through the old town of cobblestone streets as if it were their own. All of them were excited to be in the ancient town and several of them sported tourist guide tablets supplied by the tourist communications group. Unlike Pipkin who wore a gray tracksuit, they were dressed in attractive black uniforms, military in style and cut, with gold trim on the sleeves and collars. I learned later that the track suits were for the elite, for officers and high-ranking administrative staff. Both Pipkin and the other Karstians sported dark sunglasses against the moderate sun. The paleness of their faces contrasted against the dark peaked caps they wore. Their hands were a waxy white colour, almost translucent. It was their hands that disturbed me the most. There was a greenish cast to the whiteness of them that made you remember they were from another world.

But Pipkin seemed different. He was affable and well-spoken, though I watched what I said to him. I was careful and cautious. Beneath the polite veneer I knew he supported the ruthlessness that had ripped parts of Croatia apart. When we stood by the town's mile-long pebbled beach, backed by pine woods whose trunks showed the effects of years of strong winds, he laughed with sheer delight.

"You see Marin, we Karstians are like the wind, the invisible force behind these trees. We are silent and constant and yet always there, behind the scenes, even wonderful scenes like these."

At that he extended his arm in a generous sweep of the horizon, and then he bent down and scooped up a handful of pebbles with his hand and threw it out towards the sea. I could see he was caught in a vision of his own making.

"We will remake this place into something altogether different and even more wonderful. A place for us here and for always. And you, Marin, can help us achieve it. Talk to your people. I know you are well connected. Encourage them to act quickly and accept our terms. Your help will not go unrewarded. I guarantee you that, dear friend. We'll have the gold for your people soon, not for everyone but for a few. It'll just take a bit of time."

He threw his arm around my shoulders as if he were an old friend, and laughed heartily. His arm felt as light as a bat's wing. He was smitten by his own vision of the future, a vision that did not include me or people like me. I was to be somewhere on the periphery of things, on the fringes of empire along with my compatriots. All those serving on the frontier would receive additional compensation, at least that's what I was told. What struck me was that he had quietly alluded to there being some problem with the fortune promised in the ongoing negotiations. I remembered being told that every man, woman, and child in the Croatian state had been promised the equivalent of a million in gold. Croatian outliers too, from the diaspora, were to receive half that amount in gold as well. That included myself. The gold bullion was to be held in Swiss banks. As a surety, the leading political officials of the Browns had received their paper shares already. The Blues political officers had not yet received any compensation though they had been promised it was pending. I knew it was all a great and fantastic lie.

Pipkin turned his face upwards towards the broad massive face of Biokovo and smiled.

"Marin, can you imagine the wonderful caves within the Biokovo mountains? Enough room for thousands, perhaps tens of thousands of us. It feels so good to have arrived, and to see the potential all around. First, we will refit the aerodrome for our immediate needs and then move on from there. By the way I've noticed a few golden bare spots here and there on the slopes. What are they?"

"Oh, those are small slides off the mountains. It happens from time to time."

"I'll have some of our people look into that. It's on the outer wall of the aerodrome. It needs to be repaired. Not to worry, Marin. We'll fix that."

His remarks bothered me. The aerodrome he gazed at lay next to a slightly smaller and separate cavern, one that contained the model of Croatia, the one that I had flown over with Manda. Any activity in the aerodrome was sure, given time, to discover the adjacent cave and the secret model that was within it. The model held within it the mysteries of Blue Mist time travel and accessibility to different Croatian periods, its living history. It contained the very heart of the Croatian identity from its inception. I would contact Matija immediately with my fears.

A day later, at Pipkin's insistence, we were in the aerodrome. There were four large dirigibles tethered to the northern face of the cavern. Several much smaller airships were undergoing minor repairs on the eastern wing. Pipkin and I walked under the airships towards the eastern wall. Once there, Pipkin ran his outstretched arm against the wall of rock, admiring its beauty.

"This is absolutely wonderful, Marin. Look at the sheer face of it. With just a bit of work we can accommodate thousands here. Yes, thousands of us could have individual spaces up and down and across this face. And even if we need to expand, to enlarge the cave, there is more than enough room. The mountain range is massive and suited to our needs, ideally suited. Why you have air ducts everywhere! It's as if you knew we were coming."

Pipkin was pleased with what he was seeing.

"But what about our airships. What will become of them? You'll need transport for your people across the country, won't you?"

"Not to worry about us and transport. Don't forget we've come on a journey from the distant reaches of the Milky Way. We have our means Marin, more than you can ever know."

Pipkin was punching the air with delight. I had never seen him so enthusiastic, so energized. He clapped me on the back repeatedly, and then shook me by the shoulders. I feared for the future. I watched him as he ran towards a small band of Karstians in uniform and saw him share his excitement with them. I felt as if my world was collapsing.

4.7

Pipkin was beside himself with joy when I showed him a scale model of Croatia that revealed the location of caves and tunnels that had, in older days, provided transportation routes through the mountains. The model was about the size of a billiard table. We were in the courtyard of the Archaeological Museum that also served as a café.

"Marin, this is wonderful!" He ran his hand across one of the mountain caves that opened to his touch showing the interior in great detail. "We'll be able to accommodate thousands within that space. What a discovery!"

"Yes, I thought you'd find it useful. The one you're touching was called Sveti Rok, in Lika. In its day it was one of the main arteries through the Velebit Mountains. The tunnel contains two horizontal tubes, but of course there are many vertical chambers that will be ideal for your purposes."

Pipkin was ecstatic. "With this, your fortune and safety are assured my friend." He embraced me warmly and then shouted in triumph. "The Marshal's deputies will be most pleased when I show them the model."

"Is the Marshal in Retro Zagreb?"

"That is a state secret," Pipkin replied. "No one but the inner group and bodyguard command know of his whereabouts. He will want to see this in person I am certain."

"The model is portable."

"Excellent!"

"Oh, there is one more detail. In Lika, near the Bosnian border, there is an abandoned military air base from the ancient twentieth century era. There are spacious underground tunnels situated there, three and a half kilometers of them, that could support at least two thousand of your people. You must see it."

Pipkin looked at me with great affection and then embraced me.

4.8

I knew Marta would be shocked when I told her about Blue Mist travel, Canada, and the strange goings on in the future, but I was certain she would understand. Don't they say love conquers all? The afternoon I arrived in Omiš I could tell she was happy to see me, as I was happy to see her. She was a long-limbed, dimpled beauty that took my breath away. I suggested we walk to the beach, but she told me the old woman who had separated us the last time we were together would be following us. That vexed me but what could I do. Just to be beside Marta again was wonderful.

There was another fly in the ointment as well. Just as we set out a tall, blonde muscular youth started singing and following us, so that ten meters after Marta and me, there was the old woman dressed all in black with a headscarf, and ten meters after her, there was the youth. It has always been common among Croatians to express their heartfelt emotion through spontaneous singing. He was singing in a dialect I didn't understand, so I asked Marta what it was about. She turned crimson and smiled and said that he was professing his love for her. She said that he was very poor and that her family would never consent to their marriage. Still, he followed us and behind him two young boys were giggling and making a mockery of our strange parade.

As we stood at the far end of the beach and looked out to sea, I filled her in on who I was and where I was from, and I told her about Blue Mist travel. She was utterly dumbstruck and said for me not to joke, but to tell her the truth. She said that an elder had told everyone I was from Pula, from an important family there. She said that I was talking nonsense. She said to stop at once. I did momentarily, but started up again. I had to tell her the truth. Behind us the old woman stood motionless watching us, while the youth turned and walked back towards the Cetina River. He looked crestfallen and didn't even notice the two boys running around him and making fun of him.

I asked her what she wanted. She said a good life, with family and friends here in Omiš. She asked me point blank if I intended to marry her. She said she needed to know my intentions. I told her that I wanted to return to Canada with her. I did not want to live in ancient Omiš. That made her even more puzzled. She said I was talking foolish again, this nonsense about a strange place called Canada and Blue Mist travel. She looked at me in a way I had not seen before. She held up her hand and said she wanted to return to her home, that she had heard enough.

I felt as if I had been kicked in the stomach by one of the donkeys tethered near the harbour. The future I had dreamt of was gone. I just wanted to get back to Retro Zagreb and think things over. I wandered around the old pirate town completely broken, waiting for the Blue Mist airship to ferry me back to the city. In a few hours I was nursing my woes in a bar on Tkalčićeva Street, oblivious to the passing scene around me. Had I been so blind about Marta? Had I been fixated on a romantic, idealized love that was all in my head? Ah, the ambiguity of attraction, in love with a beautiful woman from the past, the pure past. I knew I could never live in ancient Omiš. Never. What had I been thinking?

I could just imagine what my friends in Retro Zagreb would think of my unconsummated Omiš dalliance. Beserka would laugh herself silly and make me the butt of jokes for my puppy love. And Manda would simply shake her head and feel sorry for me for not being myself, for not acknowledging who I was. Josip had once referred to me as the bečar or reveller of modern times. And perhaps most importantly I had not received permission from Matija to bring Marta back with me, to Retro Zagreb, and then on to Canada. Even if she had wanted to come, it was not a given, not at all. What a mess I had made of things, a complete and utter mess. The plum brandy burned momentarily as it went down my throat. What bothered me even more was that I longed to see Beserka or Manda walk down the storied street in front of me.

4.9

The first time I saw the Marshal I was not impressed. He was a short man with a paunch, very pale in complexion, and with an expression that looked as if he had just taken a bite of something extremely bitter and unpleasant. He and a small entourage were walking from Jelačić Square towards Tkalčićeva Street. The men around him, bodyguards I thought, were at least a full head taller and physically imposing. The Marshal looked anemic, hardly the avatar of a Milky Way empire. He waved and the crowd cheered, and a minute later he and his people were gone. The local people, on either side of the narrow roadway, melted away, chatting excitedly about the little man from the stars.

I thought to myself that if they knew that they would not be receiving their fortunes there would be trouble indeed. And on top of that, they would be banished to the borderlands and kept there as defenders of the Karstian homeland. The promised gold was a carrot that was dangled before their eyes, and a carrot that would prove costly to the Karstians when proved false.

Marshal Leith, as Pipkin described him, was a man to be feared and avoided, a man whose rise to power had left a bloody trail behind him. He was also an inveterate liar and during negotiations he would almost dare his opposition to confront him on any falsehood he brought forth. He would offer facts if he had them; he would lie outrageously if he didn't. The Karstian Empire he had helped to create was built on mendacity, on the use of lying as a diplomatic tool. The Marshal, it was said, was a devoted student of early twenty-first century Russian history, specifically the time of the dictator Putin.

Pipkin confided in me that it was rumoured the Marshal had poisoned a powerful contending rival. Shortly after the rival's death, several of his closest friends had unaccountably succumbed to a deadly virus. Charges were laid by the surviving families, but to no avail. The Council of Nine, the chief body of the Karstian State, appointed the Marshal as the Supreme Military Commander after an investigation found him innocent of all charges. The Chief Investigator had served under Marshal Leith in military campaigns a decade before. The Marshal was duly granted immunity against any future prosecution. Nevertheless, an atmosphere of suspicion and distrust lingered around his reputation.

Pipkin and I were sitting side by side in one of the storied blue trams that ran through the city. I could tell that he wanted to talk. We had become friends despite his conflicted nature. Since his promotion to Special Events Coordinator reporting directly to the Marshal's aide de camp, he was changing. I observed that his genial, open nature was being compromised by his new role.

"Yes, Marin, the Marshall has a checkered past. The Council of Nine has sent him here to achieve results and nothing less. Results at any cost. If you have any influence whatsoever, and if you can persuade your political leaders on a course of action that gives the Marshal what he wants, I suggest you do so."

Pipkin looked away from me for a moment, obviously in difficulty at what he was about to say. He shook his head, turned to me with a wounded expression on his face, and then began.

"The offer of gold bullion to every man, woman, and child recognized by the Croatian state was merely a ploy to gain mass support. Amongst the Karstian elite it was called fool's gold. Fortunes, however, will be given to Croatian politicos who back him. Marin, it was a lie, a grand lie, that the Marshall has used before in similar contexts. He has already issued an edict nullifying any agreement by the former governor, who is on his way home, disgraced and abandoned for not making progress fast enough. Of course, the Marshal knew the outcome beforehand. There was never going to be gold for all."

Pipkin was crestfallen. The tram bumped to a stop and passengers disembarked. There was a small queue waiting to board. In a moment the tram started moving again.

"But what does it all mean then? Why would gold be offered as compensation when there was never any intention to follow through?"

Pipkin laughed wryly. "The Marshall likes to be amused. It is as simple as that Marin. I'm sorry to tell you this, but it is the truth. And there's more to come, that I can assure you. Just wait and see."

Several weeks later I came closer to knowing what Pipkin meant. A great welcoming ceremony was held in Ban Jelačić Square. A number of dignitaries and notables, Karstian and Croatian both, perhaps thirty in all, arrived and ascended the portable escalator to the stage that had been erected. The Marshal was absent. Then, from behind the Ban's equestrian statue, there was a raucous cheer that arose when the Marshal's entourage suddenly appeared from a tall, yellow building that fronted the Square. Several imposing bodyguards cleared a path for the diminutive Marshal who strode onto the escalator and the platform. I was once again struck by how pale and small he was next to his guards and retinue. Disappointing was the word to describe him. After all the fanfare he looked so insignificant and trivial, though I was surprised to see him dressed in the colourful garb associated with Ban Jelačić. A splendid red cape covered his narrow shoulders.

Suddenly there was great applause and a heartfelt welcome as the Marshal's face dominated the great three-dimensional screen above the Square. The gray splotches on his emaciated cheeks caught my attention, but to be fair, the crowd was most generous in its applause.

He began to speak, but nothing could be heard. The retro sound system was not working. The Marshal spat out a few words to an assistant and within a moment the giant screen showed gold being distributed to a group of Croatians dressed in folk costumes. That was how it appeared. It may have been nothing more than a staged hoax. Each time one of the peasants was handed a gift of gold, a band of musicians strummed loudly on their stringed instruments in acknowledgement. No one needed to hear what the Marshal was saying. Just seeing the promised gold being given out was enough. Gold for patrimony was the order of the day. How could the Karstians be lying when the gold was right there on the screen for all to see? Surely it was a mistake and Pipkin was wrong.

4.10

"I remember the Marshal's speech verbatim," Pipkin said. "It was in an office at the Aerodrome. As soon as he entered the room, a sudden hush fell over the twenty-five senior Karstian officials seated around the conference table. Everyone stood and gave the traditional Karstian salute, arms raised straight out from the shoulders, with the index and middle fingers pointing horizontally. Marin, it was incredible. The feeling was one of fear and awe. I stood behind a General together with several other junior staff on hand to run errands and the like. The Marshal seemed to relish the uneasy effect he was having on the assembled officers, and he smiled knowingly. He was wearing a red cape over his shoulders that had reportedly belonged to Ban Jelačić. It was like a brilliant flame spread across his narrow back. Word has it that he simply took it from a museum in the old town. He certainly wasn't a prepossessing individual. His skin was gray and his face was wrinkled and wan. After some preliminary remarks focused on the logistics of getting arriving Karstians to the karst areas, he shook his head violently from side to side and then pounded his fist on the table. His voice was loud and sharp. I quote him."

"To date," he said, "the emphasis has been on transporting our people from the Retro Zagreb Aerodrome to the coastal regions. That will continue day and night. However, I have decided that all vestiges of Croat culture will be destroyed, utterly destroyed. Initially the plan was to convert the churches and historical architecture to our purposes, but with the discovery of numerous caves and tunnels, that was found to be not cost efficient. Indeed, many Croats would not have agreed to have their cultural heritage changed in this way, especially when the population was being moved to the border areas. You will continue to tell them that these buildings will be spared. I know you will find their gullibility astounding, particularly when it comes to the distribution of gold.

So, continue to promise gold and gain their trust with deception. You will find it easy. When people want to believe something, the truth doesn't matter. The desire to believe is enough. Once they discover that our gold reserves are minimal at best, there will be confrontation, but by then we will have our footholds and those feet will be pressing on their necks. The destruction of their past is essential. Every vestige of Croat culture is to be eradicated. Regardless of how many die, whether man, woman, or child, is irrelevant. You must see to it that they have no future here. They will inhabit only the borderlands. Nothing more. That is enough for these simple-minded fools. Incidentally, there is to be a parade of children in a few weeks centering around St. Mark's Square. Ostensibly to curry favour. Keep all of your troops away from the area. We shall see what we shall see.

In the meantime prepare your troops for general warfare, beginning with a contest of sorts. You must select a few of your finest warriors. I have in mind a gladiatorial contest between us and the Croats at Solin. It will be held in the amphitheater there. There will be dozens of warriors on each side armed with ancient weapons. See my first officer Artemis Sprague for details. I expect an easy victory, one that will convince the Croats of our military superiority. Please see to it that I am not disappointed. Thank you."

"That is exactly what he said Marin. I share this with you so that you realize what is happening. Together we can save lives, many lives, provided we support his plan. The Marshal will not quit until he has everything he wants. The numbers of the dead mean nothing to him. Can we work together on this? Will you help me move things forward?"

I nodded knowing I had to have him believe I would work with him. He was enthralled by the Marshal. Somehow, I managed a smile, and he gave me the traditional two-armed Karstian salute.

4.11

A week later Goran contacted me and said that there would not be any time travel activity for a few weeks, if at all. He advised me to keep fit and enjoy the free time that an absence of work offered me. Most mornings I would exercise in a small old-fashioned gym in the hotel. It had floor to ceiling windows overlooking the park with its boundary of plane trees. I loved the view I had of people coming and going in the retro time capsule that was Zagreb. I spent an hour on the antiquated Peloton stationary bicycle followed by some light weights and stretching that made for a good workout.

Just as I was leaving the lobby of the hotel, I saw Pipkin at the reception desk. I came up behind him and touched him lightly on the shoulder. Suddenly he swung around and almost struck me with his fist before he recognized me.

"Oh, Marin! Very sorry. I'm afraid my military training has made me preternaturally sensitive to threats, whether perceived or real."

"I'll remember not to do that again. My apologies."

"No, no. It's my fault. Ever since the Marshal arrived and has taken active command, the troops have become tense and hyper vigilant."

"Why?" I asked, surprised at the change in Pipkin's demeanour. He had always struck me as laid back and rather gentle. He had changed.

"That's what I wanted to talk to you about. Come, let's go for a walk."

He touched me affectionately on my arm, and we left the hotel. It was a cloudy, windswept day, but despite that there were quite a few people about, chatting and enjoying themselves. We began walking south. Soon we found a park bench near the equestrian statue of King Tomislav. A gray pigeon with iridescent neck feathers stepped towards us and then away, perhaps sensing we had no crumbs to give. Pipkin was not his usual exuberant self. He appeared agitated, a little distraught. He sat bolt upright on the wooden bench.

"I'm afraid there's going to be trouble, Marin."

I was always amazed that he spoke Croatian with heavily accented British English.

"What kind of trouble?"

"The movement of your people to the border areas. The clearances."

"Clearances?" I asked, confused by the term.

"The Marshall will lie and lie and lie until our forces can push the population of Croatia to the borders. But before that certain demoralizing activities will take place."

"Do you mean, as before, as in Varaždin, where people simply disappeared within a circle of death?"

"No."

"What then?"

"Your churches, your castles, your ancient sites, all of it, will be destroyed, utterly destroyed. Your history will be razed to the ground to undermine your spirit as a nation. Every last brick will be gone."

"How do you know this? You're only a junior officer, Pipkin. Even with your recent promotion as Special Events Coordinator, you're not privy to high level conversations where the fate of nations is discussed." I wanted so much to not believe what he was saying that I challenged him. It just couldn't be. I didn't want it to be.

"After he first arrived, I served on his bodyguard detail for a week. When the Marshall learned that I was the grandson of one of the serving members of the Council of Nine, I was promoted to Special Events Coordinator. I was introduced to him and that was that. After that he just didn't see me. I may as well have been a picture on the wall, a non-entity. The Marshal would hold discussions with senior Karstian officials and diplomats and be totally unaware of my presence. I heard first-hand what he said to his pock-faced deputy, a grotesque little man whose name is Artemis Sprague."

Pipkin stopped speaking for a moment and stared vacantly at the pebbled footpath in front of us. Then he turned to me and continued, his voice low and drained.

"You've been kind to me, Marin. I believe the times are going to get very ugly. Here is what you must know. The Marshal is absolutely ruthless and cunning. I personally heard him instructing Sprague to prepare a comprehensive list of all historical sites across the country. Everything. Churches, palaces, fortresses, towers, any and all structures that mean something to the Croatian soul. His avowed intention is to destroy your past, and leave nothing but charred remains behind. Nothing will be left but ashes and rubble. The architecture will be the first to go. And then, the things, the artifacts that contain the nation's spirit, your spirit, and the spirit of your compatriots.

He lies to gain time to get our troops in place. It was never his intention to use the people as border guards. He will use that lie to push you out and keep you in camps along the frontier. Sound familiar? History does repeat itself. Thousands of troops are arriving each day and are camping near the aerodrome. The Marshal has the power to destroy both the material and spiritual elements of your nation. He feeds on it and savours the destruction.

There's also a second edict he's put in place. He wants the personal details and whereabouts of historians, scientist, poets, and artists of every stripe. He intends to erase the cultural memory of the Croats, all of it, and leave nothing behind. Croatia will become a Karstian state that will establish a foothold in Europe. The takeover of all caves in Croatia will be a first step. Slowly but surely, my friend."

He grew silent, and then stood, touching me on the shoulder lightly as he departed, without another word.

Confrontation

PART FIVE

5.1

I'D TAKEN A SKY FERRY from the Aerodrome to Samobor and soon after landing I was sitting in the main square enjoying a double espresso and the signature dessert of the old town, the kremšnita. It was a block of vanilla custard topped by layers of flaky pastry. It was served warm and was a reminder to me that heaven exists in those pockets of human experience that are edible.

I had arrived early in the morning on a very cold day to get a feel for the ancient town before a clandestine meeting in the ruins of the old 13th century fortress. It took me a while to find my way there, as it was situated atop the surrounding, heavily forested hills that were quite steep. When I got there, I sensed the ancient power of the place despite its crumbling stone. I sat on one of the foundation stones and enjoyed the ambience of the place. Had it been evening or pre-dawn I am quite sure I could have spied a spirit or two among the stones. There were plans to rebuild it the way Zagreb had been reconstructed, but I liked it just the way it was. The broken architecture and the hands that had fashioned it spoke to its history far more than any reconstruction could have done. Some things are best left alone like this ancient fortress from medieval days. I felt the residual power in the spaces between the stones. It was a real treasure from the past, a treasure that lingered still, and was never lost.

No more than an hour later Matija and a group of people came up the trail, two of whom I didn't recognize. Four of the group were, from the look of them, bodyguards, judging by their huge size and hard, closed faces. They stationed themselves nearby, while Matija and the two I didn't know nodded politely as we made our way to a secluded spot to talk. It was to be a standing meeting.

It was Matija who began. He was one of the first people I had met after I had arrived in Retro Zagreb, and I had learned much from him. He looked drawn and exhausted, as if from several sleepless nights. After introductions all around, he began.

"There is no need for any preliminaries. There is now an imperative need to confront a new reality. The Karstians have effectively sidelined us. They are negotiating with the Browns both publicly and privately, and have suggested that the Blues support this initiative. We do not. We know that the Browns have no interest nor intention of working with us. None whatsoever. They want their hands on the spurious gold being offered, and to that end they will give the Karstians whatever they ask. Our sovereignty will be the first thing to go."

At that point Matija went very quiet as if a stunning reality had settled on him. The new people introduced to me included Ante, an older pinkish-looking man in his sixties with an abundance of thick white hair, and a young athletic-looking woman, Bianca, no older than eighteen. They looked away for a moment, obviously stifling their emotions.

"So," Matija continued, "we find ourselves on the cross hairs of a dilemma. To act or not to act. We must tactfully withdraw and plan for the worst. We must pretend to be outfoxed and avoid any confrontation for the moment. The Karstian ambassador, Henry Montague, second only in power to Marshall Leith, has ever so politely demanded that we form a working coalition with the Browns, and do it soon. The ambassador has threatened to let loose one of his more violent senior officers, a fearsome man by the name of Artemis Sprague, to move the agenda forward as he put it. He favors the Browns over the Blues because they are obsequious, gullible, and easily manipulated through bribery. They will do anything to curry favor including giving away the country. Divide and conquer is the imperial strategy that we know only too well after suffering from it for more than a millennium.

So, I am going to suggest that we back off and appear, like the Browns, to be subservient. That will give us time, valuable time, to sharpen our military skills because it is inevitable that there will be a reckoning."

He stopped speaking then and looked about, gauging the impact of what he was saying upon us. All of us were with him, and he knew it. He paused for a moment.

"Can you imagine! The Browns are rushing to the Karstian fold like drunken geese into fog, as the old saying goes, into the alien embrace of a people from a different world who love them not and will slaughter them if they do not do their bidding willingly. We have already seen their handiwork at Varaždin and undoubtedly there will be more object lessons like that before they are through with us. There will be many senseless deaths before they have achieved their ambitions. It is an old story, and one we know only too well." Matija looked up into the leaden gray skies as if he was seeking something that was hidden there. He shook his head slightly and then continued.

"And there are dangers lying before us. Grave dangers. Montague has requested access to view the caves where our airships and dirigibles are harboured. The Karstians are beginning to insist on preparing the caves as soon as possible for their own uses. But what they do not know and what the Browns themselves do not know is what lies in an adjacent cave to the Makarska Aerodrome, our model of Croatia with its built-in time travel technology. There too rest our Blue Mist ships that move from the present to the past, from here to there, to places and times that offer their secrets and artifacts. And objects that reach out to us across the centuries with the resonance of love and kinship and military prowess."

Suddenly Matija began coughing, a worrisome, deep rooted coughing fit, his shoulders heaving with the effort. He quickly covered his mouth with a handkerchief, flashed a warm smile at us, and looked directly at me as if peering into my soul.

"Marin, you have been the wonder boy in this drama. The Croatian outlier from Canada who has come to us at a critical juncture. That we found you is a great boon. Many thanks to you, dear friend. You were the only one of us who could travel to the past unhindered and become a part of it. Somehow, the rigors of travelling back in time left you unscathed, unlike us. The seer, Brujo, recognized your abilities long ago. Your consent, though it was conditional on financial remuneration, posed no problem. It is what it is."

In that moment I felt somewhat awkward like the Croatian mercenary that I was, but Matija spoke the truth, the money had brought me here, to the future, even though I was inordinately proud to be among these patriots. Back in the twenty-first century people believed that nationhood was dying out, but that was not the case, not the case at all, at least in this future.

"Yes Sir, I am happy to be of service, and I will do my best to further our efforts before I leave for home."

"And, of course," Matija said, "you will continue to enjoy our wonderful kremšnita." With a curt nod of his head Matija signalled that the meeting was over. Within the hour I was back in Retro Zagreb.

5.2

I was beginning to see things in a new light. It had taken me a long time, too long perhaps. I guess it was inevitable that my experience with Blue Mist time travel should bring me here, to this realization. How could it not? Things contained spiritual properties that were not accessible through rational thought, through linear thinking. Here I was, sitting on a park bench with the equestrian statue of King Tomislav to my right, thinking about Nin and Branimir's dagger. The early afternoon air was crisp and sharp. Few people were about. A lone jogger and an elderly woman walking with her brindled cat on a leash. Retro Zagreb was a reality, as much of one as the Byzantine dagger that I had seen unsheathed in medieval Klis. There was no way that I could have chosen not to see it. I remembered it clearly, its brilliant iridescent colours as it hung suspended in the bedroom I shared with a sleeping Marko. The dagger contained some sort of agency, some inner principle that was not animate.

Brujo was a key part in all of this. One of my earliest memories was when my grandfather had taken me to the cave in Lika, the place where I had first met Brujo. He had asked me to choose objects from among several that were arranged on a blue tarp on the floor of the cavern. Somehow, he knew back then which of those I would pick. He was the seer behind all of this, behind the gathering of objects in times past. The objects on the tarp were facsimiles only, not the real things. This I knew.

Brujo was special. He acted as a kind of non-technical adviser to the Blue Mist scientists and technicians. He knew things. I remembered the hike with him in the hills of Lika, and the wonderful conversation we had together. That same day, just before dinner, he had spoken to me of the strange power of things.

"You've come a long way from the boy in the cave. Those things in the cave that you chose were nothing but false copies, the Byzantine dagger, and the battle axe. You were intuitive and knew you had some special connection with these objects. Blood memory. Mila's two stones, their significance, would come later."

"But how will these things be used? What good are they?"

"The true objects and things of power contain spirits that can be accessed and released in times of crisis. Always remember, when we change the way we look at things, the things we look at change."

He stopped speaking then, almost as if he were giving me the necessary time to absorb his words. The first stars in the night sky were beginning to show themselves. Brujo smiled and gently placed his hand on my arm. His touch was incredibly light.

"You're a young man of great power and fortitude. However, you doubt yourself often, even after having witnessed strange events. You must put that doubt away now and move along with the times as they happen. You will make a difference that will echo long after you've gone. Remember, the past can help you find your way in the present, and in the future too. It is never finished. It is with us now."

I can't remember what we had for dinner. His words took my appetite away. He believed in me and that made all the difference in the world, retro world or otherwise.

A day later, Josip and I were walking towards Tkalčićeva Street when he stopped and looked at me hard.

"This side street," he began, "was once called Bloody Bridge. That was long ago when a stream ran under this street and people from the upper and lower towns fought over possession of a mill. Long ago. And here on Tkalčićeva Street there were brothels instead of fashionable pubs and restaurants. Ladies would saunter down the street parading their finery and the latest Vienna fashions. How things change." He gazed up and down the street in silent appreciation of the past and then continued his line of thought. "I have a question. I'm curious that you do not appear to feel fear. In several encounters I have watched you closely, and I do not see any sign of fear. Perhaps that is one of the reasons why you were recruited to help us. Am I right, Marin?"

"When I was a boy I felt fear. Craven fear. It started with two bullies at school. They would insult me and push me down on the ground as I made my way home to my grandparents' home. They would steal whatever money I had and throw my lunch in the gutter. After several occasions when I would return home bloodied and bruised, my grandfather quietly asked me what was going on. I told him. He nodded and was very curious about what I had felt when the bullying was going on. I told him about the hollow emptiness I felt in the pit of my stomach and the dryness in my mouth and the heaviness in my legs. He was very attentive to my feeling states. Slowly, he began to train me in ways to deal with fear. Over a few weeks I practiced what he taught me. He made sure I was very relaxed and gradually suggested that I change the fear I felt to one of excitement. He encouraged it, and so gradually I did it. I felt the excitement displace the fear. He said that fear was a gift you gave your enemy. He said enemies should not be given gifts. He said that I should give them a punch in the nose. And when I actually did it, the bigger bully cried with a bleeding nose, and the other one just ran away. When I told my grandfather what had happened he just laughed. Since then I've felt lots of excitement on different occasions, but no fear. There are always plenty of bullies around. And now we have the Karstians."

5.3

There was complete and utter darkness around the Solin amphitheater. It was relatively quiet, considering that about twenty thousand spectators were seated on the stone benches of the arena. People were rustling about in their seats eager to see the gladiatorial contest between the Karstians and the Croatian military elites. It was to be a fight to the death. The winning side, whether Karstian or Croatian, would receive major political concessions that would serve to break the stalemate in negotiations.

Suddenly a light source high above the center of the arena illuminated the darkness. It allowed me to see the faces of the people around me, but everything was still somewhat shadowy. People were whispering to each other though there was no need for that. I had the sense that something out of the ordinary was to happen here, even stranger than the imminent gladiatorial combat. It was just a feeling that travelled under my skin, pricking me to an awareness that I had not experienced before.

And then a kind of light show commenced. A round ball of light a hundred meters above the center of the arena suddenly shot down to near ground level and traced the circumference of the ancient ruins in such a manner that everything appeared sharp and distinct. This continued for several seconds until the light was extinguished somehow and a sovereign darkness ruled the night once again. After a moment, the darkness was pierced by cascading balls of yellow light that fell into the empty arena from a high central source and then on to the circumference of the amphitheatre with incredible speed. Everything was brilliantly illuminated.

From the northern and southern sections of the arena groups of warriors emerged. Perhaps two dozen from each section. Just then the light grew even brighter and brighter around the circumference of the arena and then upwards, in ever smaller circles, forming a brilliant cone of light. At the very tip of the cone the light was suddenly ablaze with colours of every hue.

Someone next to me on the stone bench sighed in wonder and leaned forward in anticipation of what would happen next. He smelled strongly of garlic and sour wine. I stood up for a moment and could see the lights of Split a few kilometers away. A spectator behind me put his hand on my shoulder and pressed down so I would not be blocking his view.

I looked towards the northern section and knew immediately they were the Karstian warriors. They were dressed in white with what looked like a hard plastic shell of some kind on their chests. They wore black helmets with dark visors covering their faces. Each of them held an ancient weapon of some sort, an axe, a spear, a short sword. I watched them closely as they fanned out in a wide semi-circle, and slowly, carefully, moved towards the southern section of the arena where stood the Croat contingent, dressed entirely in black from head to toe with the red and white checkerboard crest of the Croatian state emblazoned on their chests. They mirrored the movements of the Karstians and formed a matching semi-circle of their own.

I didn't know what to expect. Moments passed with nothing happening, no movement at all. The crowds in the seats began to grow restless and impatient for action. And then they met. Suddenly, one of the warriors in white raised a spiked steel club above his head and then brought it down heavily on the shoulder of the stunned Croat warrior who fell heavily to the ground and then ineffectively raised a short sword to counter a second fatal blow.

The first encounter seemed to ignite both teams, and then all hell broke loose. The opposing warriors drew their medieval weapons and clashed in the ensuing chaos. Iron rods and spike-studded clubs glittered in the perimeter of light surrounding them. It was difficult to follow all of the action in the blood-letting and violence that took place in the very center of the ancient Roman amphitheater. Oddly, the floor of the arena seemed to be made of thick glass or plastic of some kind that was transparent. A bright light could be seen beneath the plastic covering. It showed a gladiatorial scene from the Roman past. It was like a supercharged diorama with what appeared to be real figures fighting to the death. The light went out and I was once again seeing the real combat taking place before me.

I focused on one Croat warrior who cried out in triumph as he dispatched one of the opposing warriors with a swift dagger thrust to the heart, piercing the plastic chest plate. Then he grabbed the battle axe of the dying combatant to fell another Karstian beside him with a savage, swiping blow to his knees. Very quickly it appeared that most of the bodies on the floor of the arena were dead or dying Karstians.

Just at that moment a half dozen fresh white warriors ran into the arena to help their fellows who were getting the worst of the melee. As they did so a matching number of Croat warriors entered the arena from the rear side and joined their team in striking hard at the new group of Karstians.

The battle went on with great intensity for some time until several of the Karstian soldiers threw their weapons down and surprisingly begged for mercy. The crowds in the stone bench seats, most of them Croats, shouted in victory. I stood up and cheered with them and then one of the upper galleries erupted with intense light blinding us for a moment.

I observed there was a group of Karstian dignitaries in the enclosed upper gallery just above from where I was sitting. They were all of them dressed in white. One of them, a short thin man with his face averted, seemed very angry from the way he was rocking back and forth from his heels to his toes. I'm sure it was Marshal Leith though I did not see his face clearly. He was motioning erratically with a large stick, seemingly beside himself with rage. His gallery was enclosed so there was no sound coming from it. I was breathless with excitement. The brutal medieval-style combat had lasted, I think, no more than twenty minutes. People were cheering and running down the stone steps to the arena to celebrate with the victors. There were no white warriors to be seen there. The Karstian survivors had left, and their dead had ben summarily carted away along with the five Croatian fatalities. The Marshal and what appeared to be several of his bodyguards and attendants quickly left the gallery area, pushing ecstatic Croatian bystanders out of the way.

5.4

I looked around at my familiar hotel suite. Soon the room would be a memory only. Opening a closet door I saw my old clothes, the clothes I was wearing on my arrival. They were freshly laundered and ready for me, for my departure.

Things of great moment can happen suddenly. On the very eve of my departure to Canada, I was informed by Goran that Matija wanted me to attend a brief ceremony in St. Mark's Square. He simply gave me the message and left without further ado. Matija was in Makarska meeting with his war cabinet. He wanted me to witness and report on the Karstian reaction to the event. There was to be a parade, one dubbed the children's crusade, as part of a Croatian peace initiative. Children, four to ten years of age were to congregate in the Square, and then parade around the ancient church in a bid to save it from anticipated destruction by the Karstians. Other churches, in other parts of Croatia, had already been destroyed. Pipkin had advised me not to attend. He said that Sprague, the Marshall's Deputy, wanted to make an example that would mark Karstian resolve throughout Croatia. Pipkin didn't know what Sprague intended, but he said he was told by a well-informed friend that it would be an event that would never be forgotten.

I wanted to make a brief appearance and then head towards the Aerodrome where my chartered Blue Mist airship was waiting. With any luck, I would be back in Hamilton that same evening, enjoying a pint at West Town tavern with Peter, and talking about the future and my millions accruing interest in the Bank of Montreal at Bay Street and Main. I had accomplished my mission and there was nothing more for me here in Croatia. Marta was unattainable, safely ensconced in the past, a place where I did not want to live.

Matija had been impervious to my repeated requests to travel to Omiš and return with Marta. Indeed, many of my friends and colleagues were privately dismissive of my putting my personal needs ahead of those of the Croatian state. That was my dream, my hopeless dream. Matija said that the consensus among the scientists was that Blue Mist technology was not advanced enough to bring Marta to the future, and he knew that I did not want to live in the impoverished past, in Omiš. A fortune was waiting for me in Hamilton, and I had earned it. I felt free. I had completed my work, and except for my attendance at the children's crusade, I was on my way home.

The moment I left the hotel I was totally surprised at the size of the crowds that had gathered in Zrinjevac Park. On the roof of the gazebo, there were two youths cheering and waving Croatian flags. There were homemade signs made by children from all over Croatia, from Osijek, from Vukovar, from Karlovac, from Pula, from Zadar, from Šibenik, from Split, from Makarska, from Dubrovnik, from every corner of the nation.

I saw one doting parent lifting his blonde child into the air to afford him a better view of the festivities. The cherubic child was dressed as a sailor with a straw hat upon his head. Another child, perhaps seven years old, plucked yellow petals from the bouquet he held and threw them at passersby. Everything appeared well organized. Parents stood to one side of the light ropes that separated them from their children, ropes that kept the growing rows of children in order. Slowly but steadily the great crowds moved towards the upper part of the city. Many of them wore garlands of flowers that I imagined would be given to the Karstians waiting at St. Mark's Church. I joined one group of parents and moved along with them, carried in the flow of the happy throngs. There was great excitement in the air and joyful voices everywhere, young and old. I was happy now to be part of it, on this, my last day in Retro Zagreb. I felt choked up as a wave of unbridled love surged through my chest. What a time I had had! If only Marta could be with me.

A party atmosphere filled the air as we walked towards Jelačić Square. I couldn't understand why Pipkin had advised me not to attend. After all, the children of Croatia were bringing tribute in the way of flowers to give to the Karstians. What did this Sprague person have in mind? The children were there to protest the destruction of churches and to request the gold that had been promised. Flower petals covered the ground that we walked over. The crowds stopped momentarily by the Stone Gate where the Croatian monitors took charge of the swelling groups of children as they arrived.

Once we reached St. Mark's Square, Karstian troops dressed in white uniforms began to herd the children around the Church. Guardians and parents were quietly re-directed to the side streets bordering the Square. On one of the corner buildings the stone face of Matija Gubec, a Croatian peasant hero, had been adorned with a garland of red roses. The petals that had fallen to the ground beneath the corner wall sculpture looked like spattered drops of blood. The crowds pressed forward until the sheer numbers of the advancing groups came to a halt. Tens of thousands of children stood stock still while the troops separated the adults from them. There weren't any Karstian dignitaries in sight. A dozen Croatian officials stood on a raised platform waiting for their Karstian counterparts to arrive. I felt a sudden chill run through my body as I was pushed by the crowds into a small palatial portico just off the Square.

I recognized three of the Croatian officials standing on the platform, the very ones that had recruited me in my apartment in Hamilton. I had not seen them since then. The woman's name was Inez, and the big man Darko. The portly man who had sat in my rocking chair was Boris. They wore tight political smiles on their faces as the crowds of children pressed forward below the structure they stood upon. Pipkin was nowhere to be seen. That surprised me because his role was Special Events Coordinator and this was certainly a special event. The government buildings around the Square appeared to be deserted.

Groups of children dropped their bouquets of flowers in front of the massive door of St. Mark's, and then made a circumnavigation of the Church, moving in a clockwise direction. They were singing and laughing as they walked, with the older children guiding the younger ones along. The organization behind the event was quite impressive and the behaviour of the children exemplary. Pipkin and his Croatian counterparts deserved high praise. Never had there been an event like this before. I took a moment to take it all in. It was magnificent.

And then I noticed Karstian troopers abruptly leaving the Square and pushing aside the children brusquely as they made their way. When I saw that, a feeling of dread passed through me. Something was not right. In a moment or two not a single Karstian could be seen in the Square. I watched in wonderment as a dozen burly bodyguards escorted the Croatian officials, including the elegant white-haired Inez, the physically imposing Darko, and the stout gentleman, Boris, from the platform and away from the parading children. They seemed as surprised as I was at the sudden turn of events.

Suddenly I heard a strange, high-pitched humming in the air. When I looked towards the Square, I saw an orange rope of light coming from the open door of the Church. It moved slowly and wove its way around the Church and around the children. It appeared to be about a meter off the ground and no thicker in diameter than a garden hose. In rapid, snake-like motions it quickly encompassed all of the children that I could see from my vantage point in the portico where I stood. The urgent press of the crowds kept me where I was and I could not move forward. I was trapped. Parents and guardians were shouting, madly confused at what was happening. The humming in the air was replaced by a terrible roaring sound from above the Square adding to the general chaos. An elderly woman wearing a black head scarf dropped to her knees in front of me and cried out in prayer, raising her frail arms to an indifferent heaven. Incredibly, I saw St. Mark's appear to cave in upon itself and disintegrate before my eyes. Children disappeared in the turbulence of air and fire. Red and white tiles from the famous roof of the Church fell into the maelstrom of flesh and stone. Within moments there was nothing in the Square but mounds of steaming yellow ashes and pulverized masonry materials. I cried out in horror at the terrible scenes of utter carnage and destruction. Oddly, the roaring sound suddenly stopped, replaced by an eerie silence that hung suspended over the Square.

Everywhere people were screaming for the lost children. Many fell to their knees hoping for some impossible reversal of what they had seen. I pushed my way through the crowds, through stunned parents and guardians, confusion and terror written on their faces. I could not believe what had taken place. After some struggle I crossed Jelačić Square and made my way to my hotel. I knew in my heart I could not leave. An event of such magnitude changes lives and my old life was forfeit now. I would not be going home to Hamilton as I had hoped. At least not yet.

In the hotel lobby a shaken concierge handed me a sound note from Matija. Before I could access it, the concierge bolted out of the lobby and onto the street and Zrinjevac Park beyond it. A large monitor behind the lobby reception desk showed throngs of people crying out in horror at what had happened. St. Mark's was gone, obliterated from the face of the earth.

Then I realized why Pipkin had advised me not to attend. He knew full well that something terrible was coming down. I went to my room and heard the sound note from Matija. In a calm voice edged with fatigue and grief he requested that I postpone my return home as I was needed in Croatia. He asked me to meet with him as soon as possible. He coughed loudly, and then I heard no more.

5.5

I met with Matija late that afternoon in a second-floor apartment on the west side of Flower Square. The city was in chaos as news spread of the massacred children. Crowds walked aimlessly not knowing where to go or what to do. Matija's face was ashen gray as he stood next to a window overlooking the Square and the statue of a warrior poet. A gray pigeon sat atop his head.

"You saw what they did, Marin. Who could predict such evil cruelty? Thousands of our children incinerated in a single moment. There can be no more futile negotiation. That time is gone."

Matija looked away for a moment composing himself and then coughing violently into his handkerchief. He looked very ill and appeared unsteady on his feet. He motioned for me to sit, and then he sat opposite me.

"We need you, Marin. We need you more than ever. Can you extend your stay here? We will compensate you, of course."

"There is no need for additional compensation. I will stay and do whatever I can to help. Of that you can be sure." I felt awful that even on the eve of what would have been my departure I was still regarded as a mercenary of sorts, an outlier who came for the money.

"Excellent. It is now a question of our sovereignty or our death. There is nothing in between."

He smiled at me warmly and then continued. His voice was tired as he spoke and edged with anguish.

"Within the last three days the Karstians have destroyed much of our spiritual heritage. The Church of the Holy Trinity in Karlovac, the Church of St. Michael in Osijek, to name a few. But today's carnage was something we did not anticipate. We are at war. There is no turning back and I am sick at heart."

His complexion was very pale, and I could plainly see that he was very ill.

"What can I do?" I asked.

"Our retaliation must be swift and sustained throughout the country. A small elite force is on its way to the Lika caves as I speak. Brujo has told me that you have been there before and are familiar with the terrain. Several hundred Karstians are within the cave complex revitalizing, as it were. Yes, that is the word they used: revitalization. They must be destroyed. Commander Beserka Matić has requested your assistance. Your skill in retrieving memory objects is well known amongst a small group of us. We need that skill set. With your consent, we can have you there within an hour. An airship is waiting on the roof."

I swallowed hard and stood before him, humbled. "I'm ready, Sir."

Matija smiled broadly. "I am simply Matija, Matija Radelja. I am not to be addressed as Sir."

He stood then and embraced me. As I held him I could feel his thin body trembling and the physical effort it took for him to stand and hug me.

There was a sharp knock on the door and Goran entered the room, not waiting for someone to answer and open the door. It was as if he knew beforehand of my decision to stay and fight. On our way up the staircase to the hotel roof Goran briefed me on the situation in Lika. A small contingent of Karstians, about twenty in all, guarded the entrance to the caves that were filled to capacity with hundreds of sleeping Karstians. He said we were in need of a strategy and smiled ruefully.

Less than an hour later I was in Lika. I met Beserka at a tourist hotel in Gospić. It seemed to me once again that I was merely an acquaintance to her, nothing more. That bothered me, especially when I realized it shouldn't have troubled me at all. Our sexual encounters were just that. We certainly weren't friends.

After a perfunctory nod acknowledging my presence, Beserka summoned a waiter and ordered coffee for us. She began speaking abruptly in a harsh tone.

"My understanding is that you are adept in the handling of memory objects, or rather memory weapons, that can be used against the Karstians. Correct?"

"Yes. I am familiar with such objects."

"Good. Do you have them with you?"

"No. I do not Beserka."

"You will address me as Commander Matić. You will report directly to me, and to no one else. Is that understood?"

"Yes," I said, in as formal a tone as I could muster.

"Well, where are the objects? I want to see them now."

"I believe they are in Makarska."

"Well, that certainly does not help us, given the present situation, does it?"

There was an edge to Beserka's voice as she spoke to me. It covered a barely controlled anger that she did little to hide.

"Goran has given me the context we're faced with."

At that moment the waiter served us coffee, and then Beserka waved him aside.

"We need something now, right now. We need to show them that a line has been crossed. Our brave children are gone. We will pursue the aliens to the very mouth of hell. Tonight we strike the guards, but I'm afraid we will rouse the sleeping Karstians when we do so. Any thoughts, Marin?"

"I've been to the caves before, Commander. The karst is like a great petrified sponge. We need to contain them within the caves. We cannot allow any of them to escape. We have to prevent that by any means."

"Tell me something I don't know."

Suddenly she swept the coffee cups aside in a fit of anger. A waiter suddenly appeared hearing the sound of broken cutlery, but she dismissed him with a cursory wave of her arm.

"We must get rid of the guards. I know what we can do." As I explained to her what I had in mind, I thought I saw the trace of a smile cross her lips.

A short time later she summoned one of her officers to organize a small elite force to dispatch the Karstian guards. That night we struck them, and struck them hard.

At midnight a hundred of our men fanned out in front of the cavern entrance. They were positioned behind three low hills. All of them, I had been told beforehand, were wearing night vision contact lenses. I couldn't make out the type of weapons they were carrying. They looked to be laser pistols of some sort. They were dressed in hooded black uniforms.

Several of the Karstian guards were speaking in low voices. Others were asleep on what appeared to be camp beds of some sort. A few of them were snoring heavily.

Suddenly there was a coughing sound from one of our men. The Karstians snapped to attention and three of them advanced towards our position. The moment they did so our attack began. Several shots rang out and the three aliens fell lifelessly to the ground. In a pincer movement the Karstian guards were surrounded and cut off and killed in a barrage of firepower, but not before two of them ran into the cave shouting alarms. All of the sleeping Karstians were roused into full and sharp consciousness. Suddenly there was a moment of silence as the Karstians realized they were imprisoned. We could hear muffled shots from within the cave as some of the aliens blasted away at the inside of the sealed stone door, but to no avail. The Karstian engineers had done their work too well. It served our purposes exactly.

I nodded to an officer to light the dozens of torches we had ready for the next phase of the operation. Then our soldiers grabbed the torches and sprinted to every small opening atop the exterior of the cave, and dropped their smoking torches onto the desperate, screaming, coughing Karstians below. Within an hour there was nothing but silence. Hundreds of dead aliens lay entombed below.

It had been my idea to use the torches to destroy the Karstians with smoke. It was a tactic the Vikings had used to kill the hapless Irish when they retreated to their caves after a Viking raid. As a boy I had played atop and below the cave complex and knew every hole and fissure. I shared that knowledge with our soldiers. Now the job was done, and none too soon.

That morning I reported to Beserka in her hotel suite. She beamed at the good news. I had never seen her look so ecstatic. She paced back and forth, excited, and charged with energy.

"So, they are not invincible. And the bodies are there, within the cavern?"

"Yes," I replied. "Apart from the guards, that is. We killed eighteen of them outside the cave entrance, and their bodies are in a makeshift morgue."

"Good. Make sure we have several of their uniforms. They may come in handy."

I was just about to leave when she approached me and placed her hand upon my shoulder in a gentle fashion. I recognized an expression on her face that I had seen before.

"Follow me," she said, leading me to the suite's bedroom.

"Yes, Commander."

"Marin, within the confines of my bed chamber, you can call me Beserka. Now, we will celebrate the victory in the best way possible."

I'm sure she could see the puzzled look on my face and she laughed heartily. Once in the bedroom she turned off the lighting and then pushed me roughly onto the bed. In an instant I was totally aroused. I ripped off my clothing until I was completely naked. It was a kind of madness that possessed me when I was with her. She was on me in a moment and ran her hands frantically over my body. I was breathless. I'd forgotten how desirable a woman she was, despite her mind games. The world around me receded until there was nothing left but a pungent darkness.

I could not resist her, and she played with that fact, luxuriating in it. I would have followed her to the end of the world if she wanted. Her skin felt cool to my touch as I caressed her. Nothing else mattered to me but the way she felt above me in the charged space between our bodies. She pressed down upon me, and I felt an abundance of pleasure that was beyond measure. She placed her arms around me and held me captive in an embrace that made it hard for me to breathe. I heard a gurgling sound emanate from her, followed by several sighs and then silence. Suddenly she pulled away from me and waited. I could see nothing in the darkness, but then I felt the long curves of her body as she encircled me with her legs and arms and then together we fell off the bed laughing. After a moment I cradled her in my arms and placed her on the bed, her silky hair brushing against my face as I did so. In a frenzy of movement her lips covered my face with kisses and seconds later we moved into each other oblivious to anything but our union. A small eternity later I felt my body shudder, and I drew away from her, exhausted and spent. She was like a lithe cat stretching in the fecund darkness around me. I pulled away from her but she was not finished. Over the next hour we rekindled our passionate encounter, and then finally, we were done. It was over. I could hear her dressing and then she departed, a flash of light bursting through the darkness as the door opened momentarily and then closed behind her. As I lay sated on the queen bed, the commander between my thighs flagged and then fell. Beserka was gone.

5.6

Things were beginning to happen at breakneck speed. The little bit of gold that was distributed to the Brown politicians and a few others was too little, too late, and everyone knew it. The Karstians had taken over the Makarska Aerodrome and were using it as a transport hub in linking the Retro Zagreb Aerodrome. All tourist activity was suspended. Indeed, on the promenade and ancient streets of Makarska confused tourists wandered about, desperate to find a way to return to their homes.

Airships were confiscated and used by the Karstians to carry hundreds of their people to caves across the country. The aliens were refitting the caves to take on new functions as medical facilities. Incredibly, as the Karstians laboured to accommodate their compatriots, they had not yet discovered the huge adjoining cavern that contained the miniature model of Croatia and the time travel secrets it held. That discovery would only be a matter of time.

5.7

I met Pipkin at a café in a mostly deserted Flower Square near the centre of Retro Zagreb. He looked tired and paler than usual. I sipped on my cappuccino while he ordered a double espresso. Disappointment was etched on his face. There were no preliminaries in our conversation. He looked hard at me and got right to the point.

"I know that you knew about the Lika caves Marin. Did you participate in the massacre?"

"No, I did not," I said flatly.

"Did you advise someone in this matter, someone who perpetrated the crime?" His voice was strained and empty of emotion.

"Of course not," I said, looking away from him. I dared not tell him the truth. Pipkin was my friend, but he was a Karstian first, and he could have me imprisoned at his will. I continued to look away, focusing on a gray pigeon looking for crumbs under the next table.

"Ah Marin, you're beginning to lie like a diplomat, but you're not yet adept at it." Pipkin shook his head slowly. There was a trace of a wry smile on his thin lips. "Everything has changed. Things have taken a violent turn, and that will continue. And now you have become my enemy. It is all so confusing. You know I must report you, unless you can give me some names."

"You could have told me what was planned for the children," I shouted out. "I remember your suggestion for me not to attend. Tens of thousands of children were slaughtered. Why did you not tell me? Why Pipkin? Why did they have to die? What manner of man or beast are you? How could you have been silent?" It was difficult for me to get the words out fast enough. A flash of red crossed my line of vision, as I listened to Pipkin speak in low measured tones.

"The Marshall is under great pressure to begin the clearances, to push your people to the border lands. The only exceptions will be people like yourself who can help expedite our work. Hundreds of Karstians, sick Karstians, are already being transferred to the Makarska cavern. Many more will follow. If you can help me Marin, I promise you'll be spared."

"Spared? What do you mean?"

"The first priority is to identify as many caves and makeshift underground facilities as possible. The Marshall has already given the go-ahead to raze the churches and significant historical buildings. Nothing will stand in the way. Your culture and heritage will be destroyed. You can mitigate the number of deaths by helping us. I know what's happened is horrendous, but you can still save many, and save yourself as well. I can vouch for that."

"Yes, but I will be a traitor."

Pipkin made it all sound so reasonable. I was stunned by his revelations. Just a day earlier I was thinking about Hamilton and home, and now it was gone, perhaps gone forever. Marta too was gone, for I would not be joining her in Omiš. The losses were everywhere around me and mounting. My world was crumbling before me. I heard my voice telling him that I would think about what he had said, and then made some excuse to leave. I needed to see Matija.

The entire country was in shock. No one could believe what had happened. The children were gone forever and no amount of tears or vain cries to heaven would bring them back. People wandered about the downtown parks and squares, listless and stunned.

Long lines of tourists were queuing up at the main railway and airbus terminals, frantic to leave. Fights broke out as people jostled for spots near the front of the lines. I wanted to meet with Matija but could not secure an appointment. His office told me to stay close, advising me to keep a low profile. I needed to do something, anything. I knew Pipkin was expecting to hear from me within a day or two regarding the identification of additional underground areas for the growing number of Karstians arriving daily. It sickened me to think that he thought he could buy my loyalty with a bit of gold and my personal safety, as if that mattered in a world gone mad. Matija would know what to do, and how I could be useful. That very day I received a call from Josip to meet at a favourite outdoor bar on Tkalčićeva Street, lying in the shadows of the twin spires of the Cathedral. So far, it had been spared from demolition. I wondered how much longer that would last.

Only a handful of people in various stages of inebriation were there when I arrived. Josip was already seated. I took a chair opposite him and sat down. For the longest time he didn't say a word. He just looked at me shaking his head.

"Ah Marin, welcome to our brave new world where children are blown to bits as they bring flowers and smiles to their murderers. Welcome to Retro Zagreb. Welcome to the new Karstian world that is about to erupt and change us forever." He stopped speaking then and poured himself a stiff shot from the bottle of plum brandy on the table. He pushed the half empty bottle towards me and signalled a waiter to bring a glass.

"What do you think is going to happen?" I asked.

"People have lost their children. What matters to them now? They will do whatever they can, with whatever they have, to avenge the massacre. The Karstians will systematically destroy the churches and our culture and anything they think will make us come to heel. But they will soon learn who we are. Of that you can be sure. First, however, we must destroy the head of the snake, the Marshall. Already, Matija has empowered commando units to seek and destroy the Karstian leadership. Your memory objects will be useful at last. He has ordered that these weapons be sent to us from Makarska. Special handlers, under your guidance, will be tasked to manipulate the objects at the right moment, once the Karstian elite is located.

Your friendship with the Karstian coordinator, this Pipkin fellow, will need to be exploited. We need to know the whereabouts of the Marshall and his direct subordinates. Do you know him well enough to secure this information, Marin?"

I explained to Josip what Pipkin had asked of me in exchange for compensation and my safety. He rubbed his hands gleefully, and then laughed sardonically.

"Oh, you can be sure you will find caves huge enough to accommodate them all. Wonderful!"

Now I would be betraying Pipkin as he had wanted me to betray my people. In a time of war friendship is a fickle thing.

5.8

Matija sat behind a polished oak table in the ballroom of the Esplanade Hotel in Retro Zagreb. Before him, resting on the tabletop, there was a dagger in its sheath, a battle axe with its blade in a dark brown leather covering, and two small oval-shaped stones. These were the memory objects I had recovered from the distant past, from Nin, Senj, and Omiš. I felt a tremor of keen anticipation run through my body. It was good to be so near the precious objects.

Standing around the table were Josip, Beserka, Goran, Manda, and two others that I had met in Samobor, Ante, a white-haired senior in his late sixties and Bianca, the young athletic looking woman with the build of a gymnast. I also recognized the three senior Croatian officials who had recruited me in Hamilton, Inez, Darko, and Boris. There was also a military presence outside the ballroom that I took to be Matija's bodyguard contingent. Matija coughed violently into his handkerchief and then nodded to Manda to begin the meeting.

"Please take your seats," she said. "I will be brief. My purpose is to give you a demonstration of what these remarkable objects can do. You will not share this privileged information with anyone. You will remain in your seats until the demonstration is over. Lights out."

The very moment that pitch-darkness covered the room the hilt of the dagger began to glow with a brilliant emerald colour illuminating a circular space above the weapon. Manda then proceeded to remove the dagger from its sheath and hold the blade above her head for an instant. The moment after she did so, the dagger hung suspended in the air on its own. Manda placed the sheath on the tabletop. And then a shadow that resembled smoke, dark curling smoke, issued from above the dagger. There was just enough light settling around the dagger to see the lengthening smoke-like shape grow into what appeared to be a hooded, masked person dressed in a loose black outfit with billowing trousers drawn tight around the ankles. The evolving shape moved gracefully in a wide circle above the table and near the ceiling of the ballroom until the creature, or whatever it was, swooped down suddenly and grasped the suspended dagger by its hilt. It whirled about at great speed throughout the ballroom. The hand that held the dagger seemed to be a part of it, an extension of it, as the masked figure sped about. The bodily shape was eerie and menacing. It appeared to leap about and stop suddenly, and then leap again at great velocity. In the bit of light available I saw Manda strike her fist three times against the tabletop in rapid succession. The figure and dagger soared up to the high ceiling and then down again to where the empty sheath lay. The dagger entered the sheath blade-first followed by the creature that grew smaller and smaller and flowed into the opening until it was lost from sight. Before Manda could present demos on the other memory objects several of our officers burst into the ballroom shouting that a large Karstian force was on its way to the Esplanade. Matija was spirited away, and everyone made a quick exit. I saw Manda collect the memory objects and race towards an exit. Somehow they were on to us.

5.9

It was a bitterly cold February day. The skies were metallic gray and unforgiving. I followed the crowds moving towards St. Mark's Square. There were whispers around me that a traitor was to be punished, someone who had challenged Karstian rule. A large crowd remained bottlenecked at the Stone Gate entrance where a dozen Karstian troops were checking for weapons of any kind, as carrying weapons was forbidden. The faces in the crowd were sullen and curious as to what would happen. St. Mark's Church was gone of course and cleansed of the mounds of ashes and debris of the Children's Crusade. The Square actually seemed spacious and open, except for a white tent-like structure on its northern side. Around the Square itself a cordon of Karstian military police were stationed at intervals to prevent anyone from entering the space contained within. An old-style banner was positioned atop the tent. It read "King Matija Gubec the Second."

Suddenly, the tent covering was pulled away and there, sitting in an ox cart, was a pale, emaciated man in chains. With a shock of recognition, I saw that it was Matija, my Matija, my leader, and my friend. I looked around with horror. No one around me appeared to know who he was. I moved closer, straining against old-fashioned hemp ropes. One of the alien guards struck me with a truncheon, and I moved back quickly.

From where I stood, I watched as a Karstian official placed an iron crown on Matija's head. I recognized him as a man named Sprague, one of Marshall Leith's retinue. Then, with a snap of his fingers, he signalled to two of his henchmen to carry out the next act. Together they dipped a huge bucket into a smouldering cauldron and hoisted it directly over Matija's head. His eyes were wild with fear, darting from side to side, and clearly terrified at what was about to happen. As molten gold was poured over the rough iron crown that Matija wore, his horrific cries soared above the empty space of the Square. I realized with a start that the Karstians were putting on a parody, a tragic replay of the fate of the original Matija, one Matija Gubec, sarcastically called the peasant king. My instructors had told me that he had fought against the greed of the feudal nobility in 1573, and had been publicly humiliated and executed in the same spot exactly, in St. Mark's Square. It was an object lesson of what would happen to any opponent. The next moments were a blur as huge draft horses were brought forward and chains were fastened to each of Matija's limbs and one of the horses. He was pushed off the cart and lay for a moment on the cold stones of the Square, looking up at a gray, indifferent heaven. The past was present again, a future past. A signal was given and the chains tightened as the great horses moved slowly in different directions. Matija screamed in a cacophony of pain, breaking the taut silence that hung over the Square. It was merciless torture for all to see. One of the horses bolted, causing the others to quicken their pace. One of them ran headlong into a group of Karstian troops, pulling what was left of Matija into their circle. I turned and left the place, my tears blurring my vision as I sought the sullen peace of my hotel. As I came near the Stone Gate, I looked up and saw the spiked rooftop ornament that Brujo had once told me was to fend off evil witches. The irony wasn't lost on me. I vomited twice as I made my way through the cursed streets.

5.10

Goran told me what had happened amid a flurry of curses and wild cries. After Matija's death the Blues appointed Darko Yamich as Prime Minister with Inez Jakovac as his deputy. That had not gone down well with Boris Hodnik who promptly defected to the Browns and did the unthinkable. For gold and Karstian protection he sold out his people. Not only did he reveal the location of the Croatian miniature model in the Makarska cavern, but he'd also tried to bribe several of the scientists without any luck. He knew nothing about the operation and maintenance of Blue Mist airships. Manda had said that Boris had absconded with the three memory objects that I had brought from the past. It was incredible the harm he had done. The names and families of the Blue Mist team were identified and were now being hunted. Goran went silent then and looked away from me utterly despondent and sorrowful.

Apart from Goran and Josip, I didn't know who else knew that I had been recruited by Matija to act as a double agent, but Matija was dead and that worried me. Would others know that I was not a traitor like Boris? That remained to be seen.

Just as we were being hunted, we hunted them. All over the country there were skirmishes between Croats and Karstians. The rallying cry of *Remember the Children* could be heard on the lips of patriots everywhere. Weapons were in short supply, but that was why Matija had asked me to join the Karstians. The intelligence I could gather would be invaluable. Matija had also given me a tiny capsule "in case of imminent torture," he had said. That made me very serious in a second.

I already knew where thousands of Karstians were situated, in the cave and tunnel locations I had given Pipkin. If suddenly these areas were to be attacked, Pipkin would know that I had been the informer, and that would be the end of me. In that regard the tactical solution would be to synchronize the attacks simultaneously. We would have to attack all of the caves and tunnels with great force and power in a single moment. Nothing could be left to chance.

I knew what I had to do. I was determined to retrieve the memory objects Boris had stolen and to discover the location of Karstian armaments.

Those were my two greatest objectives, and with Boris perceived as mentally deranged, at least momentarily what with talk of magical objects and time travel, we needed to act quickly before they discovered the truth. That same day, after my meeting with Pipkin, I contacted Josip and asked him to create a medical file prepared on Boris's mental health. It had to be convincing and extend over several months. The record must also be complemented by Boris's brilliance as a political organizer and strategist, the brains behind the Blues political party. He must be presented as a loose cannon, certainly, but one pointed in the right direction. Goran later told me that Josip was beside himself with mirth when he learned of my ploy. He is reported to have said "God bless Canada!" A day later I had a very impressive video and digital file on Boris's life in my hands. In addition to that, there needed to be factual evidence on my own past. That I was born and raised in Lika, Croatia in these modern times.

The next morning I met Pipkin as usual at his seventh floor office in the Retro Zagreb Aerodrome, but he had a worried look on his face and that wasn't usual for him. The majority of the time he was smiling as if he'd heard some good news or a funny joke. Far below his office I could see a Karstian airship landing on the runway. Several of them arrived each day with hundreds of Karstians arriving on each of the flights. They never seemed to stop coming.

"Hello Pipkin."

"First Officer Sprague wants to see you."

"What about?"

"No idea."

I followed Pipkin as we made our way to the top level of the Aerodrome and passed through security. Pipkin didn't say a word, and for him that was unusual. Two bodyguards frisked us once more. We were waved through to a large, open space overlooking the runways. Floor to ceiling windows revealed several Karstian airships parked on the perimeter of the Aerodrome. In the distance we could see a dark green range of mountains. A tall, lean man was standing with his back to us as we entered. He turned to face us and I recognized him immediately. It was Sprague. Though I had only seen him on two or three other occasions, he had left an impression on me. There was something severe and menacing in the look of the man. Pipkin saluted.

"First Officer Sprague, I want to present Marin Dukovac."

"Ah yes, the latest traitor."

Pipkin and I were both taken aback by the man's rudeness. An awkward silence ensued until it was broken by Sprague's cruel laughter.

"Please forgive me, Marin. The information you have provided to us on the caverns and tunnels has proven invaluable, but I have not had much experience with traitors, so you will pardon the momentary reservation before embracing you."

"Yes, Sir," I said.

He pointed to two chairs in a corner of the room by way of an invitation to sit. He remained standing.

"First things first, gentlemen. Boris. Our first traitor has regaled us with amazing tales of time travel and magical objects and no end of strange and wondrous happenings. I'm told he expected you to corroborate his stories, even to the extent of his having recruited you in a faraway place called Canada. I'm also told that you declined his request. This is all very unseemly and we need to get at the truth if there is such a thing. Ah, but we have someone you know, someone who is said to have recruited you along with Boris. Allow me." He touched what looked like a watch face dial on his wrist and in a moment a tall woman, obviously beaten and tortured, was dragged into the room and made to kneel before Pipkin and myself. I recognized Inez Jakovac at once. The two guards who had brought her to us departed. She was in no shape to offer any resistance.

I kept my composure and looked past her, trying not to reveal any emotion whatsoever.

"This woman is very stoical and it will be a challenge to unlock her secrets, but unlock them we will. You can count on that. So far, she has confirmed nothing and Boris has said she is a liar like you. Any words of wisdom for us, Marin? Anything at all?"

I used the moment as Sprague walked about to secure the poison capsule from my breast pocket and secret it into the palm of my hand. I stood up abruptly then and slapped her with all my force depositing the pill into her mouth with a flick of my thumb as I did so. A trickle of blood fell from her lips. Pipkin pulled me back forcibly into my chair, and as he did, I kicked her violently across the side of her head. I thought I saw a gesture of recognition in her eyes at what I had done, but couldn't be sure. At least there was no sign of a capsule on the floor between us. I knew the speed of my physical actions was a tribute to the training I had received from my physical skills instructor, Frane. I only hoped it would offer a softer escape route to the doomed woman. Sprague nodded gleefully when Inez cried out in pain.

I turned to face Sprague. "All I can say is that Boris Hodnik is in dire need of a great deal of psychotherapy. What he has told you is nonsense. Travel to the past to find magical objects? This is sheer fantasy. Oh, and he has also talked of recruiting my services in search of these special things. He has said that I am from Canada, from the past. How can that possibly be? And as for the military potential of a dagger, an axe, and a couple of stones, I wonder at the gullibility of anyone who believes this rubbish."

Sprague touched his watch once again and the same two guards dragged her away. "Ah yes gentlemen, rest assured we will investigate Mr. Hodnik's credibility on these matters. That work is being done as I speak. However, his work on planning and preparing the way for the clearances, for moving the population to the border areas has proven most useful, so we will see what we shall see. And you, Pipkin, what are your thoughts on all of this?"

For a moment Pipkin was frozen, and appeared quite frazzled, his mouth slightly ajar. Finally he spoke. There was a slight tremor in his voice. "I do not think it is credible, Sir. I believe it is hogwash as they say and no reflection on Marin and his excellent work with us."

"Perhaps, Pipkin. Perhaps. Before I take any of this forward to Marshal Leith I want you to make certain of the facts whatever they are. We will continue our discussions with Inez Jakovac, the Deputy Prime Minister of what we can now call the Resistance, the former Blues Party. I am sure we will have closure soon on these and related matters. That is all, gentlemen."

5.11

Several days later I had still not received the promised gold nor any special security though I knew many of my former colleagues must have imagined the worst, that I was collaborating with the enemy, the Karstians. Pipkin simply shrugged his shoulders, and said it was forthcoming. We were busy day and night with remodelling activities associated with the caves and tunnels that would reinvigorate the Karstian people. My personal concerns were a small matter he said, and he asked me to be patient.

One night as I was leaving the Sabor government office late in the evening where Pipkin and I sometimes worked, two masked men accosted me and pushed me to the ground. It was just at the entrance to the Stone Gate and I wheeled around from the cobblestone floor and kicked at one of them, breaking his knee. The other man struck me with a small iron rod cutting me deeply on my chin. Somehow, I grabbed it from his grasp and struck him on the top of his head. Two passersby suddenly appeared and shouted loudly. The two made their escape, one of them hobbling on one leg and the other clutching the top of his head. I ran through the gate eager to be at the lighted roadway nearby. I knew it was not a random attack or robbery.

5.12

I knew I had to get near the memory objects to activate them. Just as I had with Manda before she could give her demo at the Esplanade, I needed to be the living connection, the host. I simply had to handle them briefly and then transfer their powers from one hand to another hand, literally. Boris hadn't counted on the memory objects possessing an awareness of friend and foe and the distinction between them. When he ran off with them he thought he had their powers simply by holding them. But of course he didn't. That remained with me or Manda. Pipkin and Sprague had dismissed the memory objects as bunk and Boris as some kind of lunatic despite his usefulness on moving the population to the border areas. Pipkin had asked me to review the documentation regarding Boris's sanity which I did. Josip had done excellent work in falsifying the records. Pipkin had also reviewed my own records which proved that I was born just outside Gospić in a village called Ribnik and nowhere near the country called Canada. Amid great peals of laughter he confided that if Boris's version of my recruitment had been true, it would make me hundreds of years his senior. Pipkin thought this utterly hilarious. I just hoped that Sprague and his gang of thugs couldn't get at the truth or parts of it through torturing Inez Jakovac. She had the poison capsule and I prayed she would use it.

5.13

I learned that Josip was in hiding at a safehouse overlooking the great market a stone's throw from Jelačić Square. I was surprised that he was in the center of the city, but sometimes the best place to hide is in plain sight. He looked anxious and worn from lack of sleep. I could tell he was worried about his mother. He had told me he had tried contacting her earlier several times but to no avail. Then he abruptly changed tack and began speaking.

"Do you remember when Manda was giving a demo on the memory objects at the Esplanade? She had started with the Byzantine dagger and was about to continue with the axe and stones when the Karstians were at the door. Our bodyguards held them off while we escaped. Boris was entrusted with the objects and he fled to a safe house, but as it turned out, he never made it there. We found out later that same day that he defected to the Karstians. He gave them everything, all of it. The miniature model, the Blue Mist technology, and the objects. We found out later that Manda had destroyed parts of the model, parts that enabled Blue Mist travel. The Karstians didn't know what they had. Boris tried to explain it to them but to no avail. They scoffed at the very idea of time travel and magic objects. They attributed it to our feeble minds and gullible nature. They discounted it all. Boris attempted to show them the military capabilities of the objects but he is a traitor and the objects didn't respond to his touch. The objects aren't conscious beings of course, but they feel character and his touch wasn't right. It was off. He thought Manda had given him copies or facsimiles of the objects. Of course she hadn't. At the time she didn't know he was a traitor. Nor did anyone. But when the Karstians broke into our Makarska cavern, everyone soon knew. The Karstians were more impressed with the size of the cavern and its potential as a revitalization center than the intricacies of the model. Had they had the imagination to realize the immensity of the model they would have been stunned. They thought it was just a clever toy of sorts. Some toy!"

"And I understand that Boris gave them your name, and those of others involved."

"He did. He gave them your name too. You would be on their kill list if it were not for the intervention of your friend Pipkin. Matija was brilliant in having you appear to be a traitor like Boris."

"Yes."

"We need you to find and bring us the memory objects. We know Boris has them, and you can get close to him through Pipkin. We need those priceless objects more than anything now. It will put you in grave danger. Can you do it?"

"I will. Not to worry."

A sharp knock at the door froze us all for a tense moment. Josip unlocked it to find Goran standing there, his face a mask of sorrow.

"What is it?" Josip asked.

"I am sorry, so sorry."

"What? Speak man!"

"Your mother is gone. I am sorry to tell you. We found her this morning, inside her kitchen."

"What do you mean?"

"She is dead, tortured, my friend."

Josip's legs buckled under him, and I caught him by the elbow before he fell. Goran and I helped him to the leather sofa where he sat mute and in shock. His eyes were downcast. After several seconds, he spoke. "How tortured?"

"Perhaps later we can talk."

"Now! How tortured?"

"Beaten and raped and cut up with sharp kitchen objects. There is evidence from the lacerations across her body that she struggled. I am so sorry Josip."

Josip stared at the floor and nodded. Moments passed in silence, and then Josip rose from the sofa and walked to the window overlooking the

Dolac market. The place was bustling and alive with color and motion. The gaily decorated familiar umbrellas, red and yellow, over the market stalls were brilliant under the early afternoon sun. The sounds of hundreds of cheerful people buying market goods was like a balm to the soul. It was such a contrast to what we were all feeling. It didn't seem right that life should go on normally and happily a few stories below us while our insides were being torn apart by Goran's revelations. Suddenly, Josip turned away from the window and began speaking in a calm, neutral voice as if nothing terrible and utterly horrific had just happened in his life.

"And now to our work at hand. We must go after the snake's head. That's where we must strike. Planning begins here and now."

Within minutes Josip was identifying roles for each of us and calling for others to join us. His attention to detail, all within tight parameters of action, was a marvel to me. He tasked Goran with receiving clearance on the overall plan from Darko. I was to secure the memory objects from Boris and try to determine the whereabouts of the Karstian elite. A small elite team would join me. Josip seemed to be totally energized by the planning work. I had never seen him more alive and vital. Through the long afternoon and evening he didn't touch a drop of alcohol. He said that he had sent a team to retrieve the Meštrović statue from his mother's courtyard. It was a special piece of sculpture as I knew, and one that he said warranted further examination. I had a full agenda and left the safehouse early the next morning to begin my work.

5.14

I went to the Aerodrome in Retro Zagreb mid-morning where I was to meet up with Pipkin. I had digital data on the locations and size attributes of several caverns across the country that were ripe for conversion into Karstian health centers. Pipkin was pleased when I shared the information with him. He said that I would be receiving payment in gold within the week, and that I was to be supplied with two Karstian bodyguards once the agreement was fully ratified. That information troubled me as Karstian security guards compromised my ability to do the work Josip had assigned to me. Not that it mattered, but I also wondered if I would actually receive the promised gold. Just as we were finishing up, I saw Boris smiling and approaching us. He looked the same as always, portly and pink, with a full head of thick white hair.

Pipkin was positively delighted with the chance meeting. "Ah, Boris," Pipkin said, "you will be happy to see your compatriot once again. Like you, he has joined our ranks, and we welcome his expertise."

"But of course. I was one of the three who recruited him from Canada. For gold and glory. Now we are both rich."

It took all of my inborn strength to smile at the traitor and pretend he was like a friend. How I loathed the man.

"Marin, you are just the man I wanted to see. The memory objects that I took from Manda are not working. I tried to give Officer Sprague a demonstration but nothing happened. In fact, it's made me a laughing stock. And the Blue Mist travel that you have experienced, can you confirm that those flights actually happened. I think Manda and her scientific team have tampered with the model and the time travel airships. None of it is working. Please confirm."

There was a frantic note in his voice that I had not heard before, and I could see that Pipkin was alarmed. Both he and Boris waited for me to speak. I knew that now was the moment of truth or deception, depending upon how you looked at it.

"Boris, you're confusing me. What's this talk of Canada and memory objects and time travel? I have seen the model of Croatia in the Makarska cavern, but nothing more. Have you been indulging in some plum brandy by any chance?" I glanced at Pipkin and saw the trace of a smile cross his face.

Boris turned ashen gray for a moment and I saw his lower lip tremble "Why you, you're lying. You're an outlier from Canada. You have remarkable abilities that allowed you to travel back in time and retrieve objects, things of great value militarily. Why are you lying Marin? Why?"

"I'm sorry Boris, but I have no idea of what you're talking about. Surely this is some bad joke you're playing on me. Like you, I've defected from the Blues and there is great stress in coming over to the Karstians, but we must be calm and cool. We are hunted men. We can't let the tension and stress defeat us."

At the very moment I stopped speaking, he lunged at me and missed, falling to the floor in a paroxysm of rage. There was a light white foam coming from his mouth as he convulsed in a sudden fit on the floor. Two attendants came by and helped him to his feet. He was very unsteady and dropped to the floor again. He kept shaking his head and glaring at me, speechless and still stunned at what I had said. A wheelchair appeared and took him away.

Pipkin shook his head in disbelief. "Yes, Marin, I had heard some scuttlebutt about what he was saying about you and magical objects, and travel to the past, but I didn't know what to make of it. It all sounded so far-fetched that it was discounted as nothing more than nonsense. Maybe Boris was trying to impress us somehow, but obviously he's under incredible stress and that certainly proved to be the case here. What is this place called Canada? Do you know of it?"

"Just a bit, but I understand it's very cold there."

5.15

Darko had asked Goran to arrange a meeting with me at my hotel. I was feeling down because, through Pipkin, I was aiding and abetting the Karstian takeover of Croatia, and I hated it. I wanted to do what I could to defeat the Karstian child-killers, and then go home to Hamilton.

"Ah, Marin," Darko said, after embracing me warmly, and kissing me on both cheeks. "You are helping the cause, and we thank you for it. Matija always spoke of you highly."

When he embraced me, I felt small within his powerful arms. He was one of the biggest men I had ever met. He reminded me of Marko, the gentle giant whom I had met in Nin in ancient Croatia.

"My actions are those of a traitor. I supply Pipkin with the location of caves and safe places for the Karstian elite. And still, the churches and cultural artifacts are being destroyed, erasing our identity. I am simply accelerating the destruction of our nation."

"The Karstians believe you are a traitor. But we know you are a great patriot. We want you to continue in your role until we can destroy the alien leadership."

He was very busy and couldn't spend much time with me. He cautioned me to be careful in my dealings with Pipkin, saying he was not to be trusted. He believed that Karstian assassins were actively pursuing our people, including the names of all Blue Mist personnel that Boris had given them.

5.16

From what Pipkin had told me, the Marshal and his retinue would travel from place to place, never staying more than two nights for fear of assassination attempts. Darko would be keenly interested in this information. Much to Pipkin's satisfaction, I had identified several ancient road tunnels similar to Sveti Rok in Lika. Among them they included Brinje, Mala Kapela, and Učka. These tunnels had once served Croatia when it needed swift passage through the mountains. Now, several of these tunnels were already being renovated to serve as revitalization centers for the hundreds and thousands of Karstians recently arrived in Croatia. Pipkin was thoroughly elated, most especially when I spoke to him of the underground warren of rooms and vaulted ceilings of Diocletian's Palace in Split. The huge cellar had once served as a sewage reservoir in ancient times. He saw immediately that it could be used as an extensive safehouse for the Marshal and his senior officers. I also dropped the suggestion several times that it might serve well as a military depot for the Marshal's elite bodyguard. He nodded his head vigorously upon hearing this and left immediately to begin preparations on adapting the venue for military purposes. Ironically, I too could readily envision how the ancient Roman palace might be ideal as a killing ground for memory objects given the scale and scope that the palace offered.

Two weeks later we were there. All of the exits from the underground palace were blocked. Slowly, we made our way through the maze of small rooms. Fortunately, it was well illuminated, thanks to the aliens. Beserka was in the lead, clutching her weapon with both hands. I could see she was excited by the hunt and thoughts of revenge. All of Croatia was an armed camp with half the population intent on destroying the Karstians regardless of the cost in lives.

"Commander," I whispered. "Allow someone else to act as point person. You're too valuable to lose. Let me. Please." She glanced back at me with derision, and kept advancing into the small rooms of stone. Josip was beside me and nodded each time he moved forward from one room to the next. The excitement in the air was taut and tense. Suddenly I saw Beserka drop to the floor and fire off a round from her laser weapon. Three aliens fell to the ground, their bodies instantly shredded by the blasts of her fire. Pools of blood spread beneath them. Everything was silent for a moment. Josip and I were crouched low on either side of the doorway, waiting to hear from Beserka. Seconds passed, and then oddly there was the smell of sour cabbage. It baffled thought until I remembered cabbage had become a Karstian delicacy. Pipkin had raved about it. Just ahead, Beserka scuttled backwards on all fours to the room Josip and I were in, shouting for us to take cover. There was a sudden explosion and the rooms ahead of us were blocked by the debris and dead aliens. Josip swore. We knew that the Marshal and his bodyguards had escaped death. There would be another day.

5.17

A few days later in Retro Zagreb I met with Josip again. He pulled me aside and spoke to me as we looked out over the busy Dolac Market. His voice was calm and reassuring. I realized how much I had missed him. It's heartwarming to me that when you see a friend after an absence, how precious it is to hear their voice, its familiar tone and cadence. You realize then that the friendship is part of the fabric of your very soul.

"The Meštrović sculpture, Marin, do you remember it, that day we had lunch in the courtyard at my mother's home? The strong, seated woman with the book on her lap and the secrets she revealed to us."

"Yes, of course. The history of Croatia. I recall the three-dimensional video clip that was so real to me."

"The Karstian thugs tried to destroy it but could not. Come with me for a moment."

Josip took my sleeve and ushered me into an adjoining room where the sculpture rested on a stone plinth. It was the sole object in the room and dominated it. He ran the palm of his hand across the bronze book and waited for a moment. Suddenly, images appeared, violent images of Josip's mother being assaulted and worse. I tried to look away, but Josip's harsh glance insisted that I fix on the scene and witness the full scale of its depravity. It was there just above the open book, an image of Karstians laughing and shouting obscenities. There were five of them attired in the white military dress of the Karstians. With a shock of horror, I recognized one of them, the leader, Sprague, the Marshall's right- hand man.

Josip nodded and looked at me. "Those images are seared into me now. I cannot forget, and I will not forgive. Enough, let's talk more elsewhere." Josip ran his hand across the book once again, and the images disappeared.

Somehow, the sculpture was the repository of incredible events, and not only historical records. I couldn't believe what I had just seen. And Sprague, the very devil of a man, had led these beasts. Revenge would come soon enough.

5.18

First Minister Darko Yamich had authorized a six-person squad to find where Boris and the memory objects were located at the Aerodrome. The key objective of the mission, led by Goran, was the retrieval of the objects at any cost. Darko realized that I needed to accompany the squad to ensure the memory objects were authentic ones and not merely facsimiles. I would join the squad on the pretext of needing to meet with Pipkin. I had already been given the necessary clearance to visit the Aerodrome and the squad was able to access Karstian uniforms and kits from Beserka's military operations center. Boris was to be brought back alive if possible. They held out little hope for Inez as I had told them of her condition when I saw her at the Aerodrome and that I had supplied her with my poison capsule. A secondary objective was to find the location of the Karstian armaments and destroy them if we could. I hoped that we would return with our mission accomplished.

The next day we entered the Aerodrome without incident. I showed the Karstian gatekeepers the requisite digital documents and it was done. I asked for the team to be escorted to Boris Hodnik's office. What I didn't count on was Pipkin being there, meeting with Boris. Several Karstian guards were also present.

"Marin, why are you here? I hadn't scheduled any meeting with you."

"I wanted to see the memory objects for myself to determine their veracity. I should have contacted you but I was eager to check things out." Boris's face turned crimson. He was breathless.

"Marin you are an imposter and the greatest liar! You are here to disrupt things. Nothing more." He recognized Goran immediately despite the Karstian uniform and was about to shout out when Goran pulled out a laser pistol and fired. A tiny circular red dot appeared on Boris's forehead for a second or two. He looked surprised, his mouth slightly ajar, and then fell to the floor. Pipkin cried out in horror and knelt beside Boris as the squad pulled out their weapons and ordered the Karstian troops in the room to cast their weapons down. Pipkin stood up, confused, not understanding what was going on.

"Marin!" he cried out. "What is going on? What have you done?"

Goran grasped Pipkin by the back of his neck and held his pistol beneath his chin. "Where are the memory objects?" he shouted. He ordered our squad to search the office for the objects.

"Pipkin," I said. "Tell him. He will kill you otherwise."

"There, in the cabinet opposite the door. The second shelf."

In a moment I held the dagger in my hand. I raised it high and then balanced the hilt of it in the palm of my hand. I withdrew my hand and it hung suspended until I replaced it in its sheath. Mila's stones were in a leather bag with a light blue cloth separating them. I removed them and touched them together. They made a light, familiar scratching sound and then stopped. The battle-axe felt warm to my touch, and the incised tattoos a welcome sight. These marvellous things were ours once again. I nodded to Goran. Pipkin just stared at me in disbelief.

"Where is Inez Jakovac? Where is she? Quickly! Tell us now," I said, almost not wanting to hear what I feared.

"She died suddenly during interrogation, the very day you were here last. I can't believe you're doing this, Marin. Boris was right. You are a traitor, and maybe the other things he said were true as well, as fantastic as they are. You were my friend, and you've betrayed me."

One of the Karstian troops on the floor attempted to touch a dial on his wrist, probably to alert security. Goran and his squad fired their lasers at the Karstians, killing them all. Goran ordered Pipkin to lead us out of the room and begin our escape. With Pipkin's card, we locked the chamber behind us. Goran and I followed Pipkin as quickly as we could, desperate to leave the Aerodrome with the objects in hand. Safe passage out of the Aerodrome was ours. Fortunately, Pipkin and I were known to the security staff and permitted to go wherever we pleased. Goran's squad was seen as just another level of Karstian security. I watched Pipkin closely. He was trembling with fear. He flinched when I placed my hand on his shoulder.

"It will be all right. Not to fear. You'll be all right."

"You betrayed me, Marin. You could have been one of us."

Very soon we were on the ground floor and ready to depart the Aerodrome in one of the shuttle vans serving the Karstian military. But then Goran stopped suddenly and looked menacingly at Pipkin.

"Where are the armaments kept?"

"What do you mean?" Pipkin said, his voice terrified.

"Your heavy-duty weapons, the ones used at Varaždin and to destroy the ancient churches around the country. Where are they kept?"

"I'm not sure," Pipkin squeaked.

"You have three seconds," Goran said, in a dry, level tone.

"They're stored in the outbuilding at the far northern end of the runway. The yellow building with the security perimeter around it."

"Good. Take us as near as we can get." Goran then issued commands for the squad to assemble a small portable missile launcher that was no bigger than a carry-on piece of tourist luggage. A large group of Karstians was approaching us at a run from the Aerodrome. Within a few moments it was done. The launcher was assembled and then the single missile contained in the weapon was fired immediately by one of our team. Goran and the rest of the squad continued to fire their lasers at the advancing Karstians. Suddenly a great explosion erupted from the outbuilding and the sky turned dark gray. Pipkin fell to the ground and I dove near him, protecting the memory objects that I carried in a leather bag over my chest.

"Get into the shuttle now!" Goran cried out. And then Goran, Pipkin and I, and two of the squad members leapt into the shuttle and fled at top speed. The rest of the squad, four of them, had taken cover behind a military vehicle and fired in a desperate last stand against the Karstians who were blasting away at them. I heard one of them cry out, "Remember the children!" Multiple explosions could be heard, all of them coming from the outbuilding. The afternoon sky appeared almost dark as we sped away.

The mission to the Aerodrome had been a success except for the death of the squad members. Perhaps it was inevitable that some of us should die. Most everything had gone well. We had the objects. Boris had died without revealing our Blue Mist secrets, and technologically advanced weaponry was destroyed. Now we were on an equal war footing, at least for the present. We had Pipkin, and we could learn much from him. I did not want him killed. Despite his flaws, I liked the man. He was Pipkin. He was my friend.

5.19

There were perhaps no more than three hundred Croatian warriors remaining at the Klis fortress, while there were upwards of forty-five thousand Karstian troops surrounding the base of the mountain on which the fortress was built. A few more days at most and the fortress would be in Karstian hands, or so they thought. A simple equation, nothing more. It wasn't the first time Croats had faced seemingly insurmountable odds. Within three days, according to Pipkin, Marshal Leith planned to visit the famous site, and he demanded of his officers that the fortress be taken, hopefully surrendered before he arrived. My task was to deliver the three memory objects to the besieged fort and hopefully enable the defenders to break through the Karstian ranks and demoralize the invaders. As I was told, history had not always favoured the Croats, but more often than not they held their ground and routed the would-be usurpers. Marshal Leith wanted a clear-cut victory and nothing less. The Karstians could have pulverized the place, perched as it was on the very top of a mountain, but they wanted it as a war prize, like the Ottomans from ancient times past. They wanted to parade any survivors along the Riva Promenade and through the streets of Split in order to make a mockery of the military history of the war weary Croats. But, there was a plan afoot and I was the means to an end. An ancient tunnel beneath the hill offered access to the top level of the fortress, and I had sworn to Prime Minister Darko Yamich that I could do it. I felt the excitement of imminent action growing within me.

The narrow tunnel was crumbling in places and a foul, musty odor bothered me somewhat, but two hours of steady crawling with a pack on my back brought me to a pile of stones that blocked an ancient door. It felt good to have the objects near me once again. I cleared the stones away and used a rock to pound away on the door. I did not know if anyone could hear me. I continued to pound away at the door and then place my ear against it hoping to hear voices or a sound of anything at all. Perhaps they were quiet, thinking I was a Karstian trying to get in. For the longest time I hammered wildly at the door and then sat exhausted resting my back against the stone wall of the narrow tunnel. Everything was eerily quiet for the longest moment and then the sound of men shouting and striking at the door from their side. I cried out my name and said that I was one of them, one of their very own. Suddenly, a streak of light showed itself on the top edge of the door and moments later the door fell in one big heap beside me. A couple of men pulled me out at last and began laughing at me, stone dust having covered my features completely.

They slapped at my clothes until I was reasonably recognizable once again. And then they sat me in a regal looking chair and asked if weapons would be following me. They were desperate for weapons of any kind. Despite the urgency they faced, they brought me some stale bread and tart wine and a cheese that squeaked as you ate it. it was the best they had. I devoured it like a hungry jackal.

When I showed them the objects and explained their provenance, I could see the skepticism and disbelief in their faces. I removed Branimir's dagger from its sheath and held it high for all of them to see. I remembered a much earlier time when I had held it. I was in a room in this very fortress with my friend Marko, but that was in medieval times. I returned it to its scabbard and then showed them the covered battle axe Nikola had gifted me in Senj. I removed the axe blade from its leather sheath and held it triumphantly above me. They were not impressed. They had seen many like it. It was nothing special to them, a common axe, nothing more. Against Karstian guided laser weapons what could it do? Nothing much. I heard some whispers and then silence as I replaced the axe cover and set the weapon down on the oak table. When I showed them the two rocks, Mila's rocks from Omiš, I heard titters of nervous laughter from several men nearest me. For some of them that was the final straw. Were they to throw a couple of rocks at the Karstians? Someone guffawed and let out a hoot of derision.

A Captain, a short, stocky man with only one eye, stepped forward, pushing others aside, and in a challenging voice cried out, "What is this nonsense? We expected weapons, modern weapons that we could use in a last stand against the Karstian devils, and you show us these museum pieces! Curse you for this!"

"Give me some little time," I replied. "In a few hours it will be nightfall and I will show you what they can do. Let me have a dozen of your best, battle tested warriors. I need to work with them. Can you do this for me?"

The Captain shouted out a few commands and a dozen men gathered around me, waiting for instruction. The rest of the larger group departed to the lower levels of the fortress. Everyone knew that time was running out, and that the Karstians were planning an all-out assault to be launched some time over the next day or two. Laser ammunition was more precious than gold and officers began preparing for a final defense. There was a palpable tension in the air.

I asked my group of men to believe in me for a few hours. I didn't talk about Blue Mist time travel or how I had come by the memory objects. That would have burdened their credulity too much when time was limited and precious. I spoke to them of the powers inherent in things that contained the memory residue of leaders and warriors of high character. I spoke to them of the transferred touch within the things I had brought of persons long dead. This residue or power could be passed on to others of similar character and virtue and manifest itself in battle action. I said I would show them what these objects could do, and to suspend their disbelief for a little while, not long. They glanced at each other not knowing what to believe, but they stood there wanting to believe, and that was the most important thing. I planned to give them a demo similar to the one Manda had given at the Esplanade in Retro Zagreb.

My demo began when night fell. We were in the largest room of the fortress. A few torches were lit and the men sat on the ancient stone floor curious to see what would happen next. I asked them to stand and form a circle. There was the scent of cooking smells from the Karstian camp at the base of the fortress hill. The pungent smell of sauerkraut was in the air, and I saw a few men swallow involuntarily wishing they had such food before them. But they looked to be hard men and recently at least accustomed to privation.

I began with the battle-axe. I removed the leather blade cover and then passed the long-handled axe around the chamber. I could see the familiar tattoo-like designs on the handle and I thought of my friend Nikola from Senj who had given it to me. I asked everyone to hold it momentarily and then pass it on to the next man. When everyone had touched it, I took it again and stood with it in the middle of our circle. A few men moved forward closing the circle even further. I raised the blade high and waited. Nothing happened for several moments and then something like a curl of smoke issued from the top of the axe. One of the men gasped when he saw it. I withdrew my hand from it, and the axe remained where it was, suspended somehow above us all. Several of the men cried out in wonder and awe at what they were seeing. The smoke curled around the long handle and then beneath it, and in a moment the shape of a man, cloaked and hooded, could be discerned holding the axe. Only his eyes could be seen, and then only a glint. He wheeled around in billowy dark pants and then floated effortlessly into the air above us. His movements seemed choreographed and graceful, but with a speed and power that was incredible to behold. The axe was like an extension of his body and scissored the air, criss-crossing it every which way. The dance-like movements continued for several moments and then finally, the axe hung suspended in the air once again. I moved into the center of the circle, extended my arm, and retrieved it, replacing the axe blade in its sheath. Now the assembled men knew its power and what it could do in the right hands.

I removed the second object, the Byzantine dagger, from its sheath, and here again, I passed the memory object around, making sure everyone held it. It followed a similar pattern and movement to that of the battle-axe, beginning with traces of curling smoke arising from the hilt and then culminating in a human shape that wheeled and circled around the chamber like a madman, sometimes appearing to be looking at us from the ceiling of the great room. When the dance-like actions were completed, I took it again and replaced it in its sheath. I could feel its power course through my body, and I trembled.

Nothing remained to show them other than Mila's two stones. I doubted myself for the first time because I had never witnessed their power, the power of the two stones. Mila had tossed them to me on a mountainside in Omiš as tokens of friendship, and I knew their provenance then, but I had not seen what they could do in battle. The men gathered around me in a tight circle and waited. They looked at each other in apprehension. I held each stone, one in my left hand and one in my right hand, and unthinking, I brought them together, touching one against the other lightly. Nothing happened. I knocked them against each other again, a little harder this time, and I heard a sharp squeaking sound as they made contact. Again, I struck them against each other, and a louder rock-solid sound emanated from the rough contact between them. And then I pounded them against each other with force. I did this repeatedly not thinking why. I just did it. And then, I heard a distant, rumbling sound coming from the far end of the chamber where I had emerged from the cave tunnel. I turned to look behind me and saw the pile of stones that had blocked the tunnel entrance suddenly rising, clacking against each other as they did so. The men were dumbstruck as they saw it. I continued to knock the stones in my hands one against the other and watched in amazement as hundreds of stones rose upwards, and then stopped. They hung suspended in the air. After a pause, I struck my stones sharply three times against each other, and when I did so, the mass of stones hanging in the air beneath the ceiling fell to the stone floor in a great clatter of thundering noise. There had been no human shapes of warriors arising from Mila's two stones. Nothing like that at all. Just the sheer power of rock speech as it issued from stone contact.

Intuitively, I realized that outside the chamber, in the stone courtyards of the fortress, the effect of thousands of pummeling stones would be colossal. Some of our men would die. Certainly. That could not be avoided. But many more would escape amid the chaos and confusion of battle. We would break the siege and bring the war to them in ways that they could not fathom. Any doubts I had were gone. I felt a growing excitement move through my body as we planned the outbreak from the fortress.

We opened our gates in the middle of the night and withdrew from the fortress. A vanguard of the dozen men the Captain had given me led the way. We moved stealthily with two of the men wielding the Byzantine dagger and the battle-axe respectively in the front rank. They were to hold on to their weapons as long as they could, the phantom warriors released after the first Karstian blood was shed. If either of our men were to fall, they were to pass their weapon on to the next Croat warrior following them. Behind them, just behind the front rank of twelve warriors, I would have the stones ready to be released. I carried them in a canvas sack across my shoulders. The rest of our warriors would follow behind me in a tight formation, five in each rank. Only a few of them possessed laser pistols and ammunition was scarce. The rest of them held spears and long-handled knives they had taken from the fortress museum behind us. Our main objective was to get beyond the Karstians and move towards Solin and then Split. The secondary objective was to destroy as many of the enemy as possible.

The Karstians were so sure of themselves that they had only a few guards posted outside their tent encampment. We ran straight at them, our lead warriors slashing at them with the dagger and battle-axe. Suddenly shouts rang out alerting the sleeping Karstians of our attack. They came out of the tents in their underwear with laser pistols blazing away, killing three of our men in an instant and several of their own in their mad rush to counter us. The men wielding the Byzantine dagger and battle-axe were able to slay about a dozen of the Karstian troops before they fell. Their weapons were taken up by men behind them who held the memory objects high as the phantom warriors emerged from the hilt of the dagger and the top of the battle-axe. The two phantoms remained unseen in the darkness and bloody chaos of battle. Our men continued to strike down any opposition and move quickly down the hill towards the ancient road leading to Solin.

Several men fell to the ground in front of me, so I removed Mila's stones from my bag and struck them forcibly against each other. The sharp knocking sounds could be heard clearly despite the desperate cries and shouts of the Karstians, totally unprepared for the bizarre attack they were facing. As I continued to run, I banged the rocks together as hard as I could. It was near pitch darkness so I couldn't see much at all, but suddenly I heard a strange, whooshing sound on either side of me. I could just make out a faint pallor against the dark above me and to either side of the rows of men around me. One of the Croat warriors cried out that hundreds and thousands of stones from the hillside were rising and forming a canopy above us. I strained my eyes to see what he was talking about, and there it was. Stones of every size, big and small, some of them shards and pieces of limestone, were suspended above us, hanging in the near darkness of night. We continued moving down the hill as fast as we could, and as we did so, more and more stones formed high above us. I didn't stop striking the stones against each other for a second. And then, instinctively, I struck them three times as sharply and abruptly as I could. Immediately, the stones above us began to move away from us and shower down all around us, creating havoc in the Karstian camp. There was no place to hide for them, none of the hard plastic tents strong enough to protect them from the avalanche of stones falling from the heavens. Some of the Karstians shot at the stones with their laser pistols. They were not even deflected. The stones pelted down on them regardless. There were screams of terror as the Karstians began to run looking for shelter but there was none to be found.

They were running for their lives and dropping by the hundreds around us. Those who weren't killed by the Niagara of falling rock were bludgeoned insensibly and rendered unable to fight. I looked towards Split. A faint light was beginning to show on the horizon. The scent of blood was in the early morning air. No one could have anticipated the carnage that the mass of stones had left in its wake.

The entire hillside was with us, denuded of shale. There were bodies everywhere. I'm not a religious man though I was born and raised a Roman Catholic. It just didn't stick, but I said a prayer of thanks under my breath. We were escaped and free. The Karstians were routed and destroyed. Marshal Leith would not have his celebrations this day or the next. The victory was ours.

5.20

Pipkin and I were walking near the base of Biokovo. We were hiking up the mountain. The tourists had left Croatia and so the majesty of the place was ours. The sun was bright and high overhead, spilling over the karst landscape like a giant's generous gift. I picked up a small stone and felt its warmth in my hand. Despite all that had happened between us, we were still friends. Somehow, our spirits were in synch, and we were comfortable with each other. Opposite sides, yes, but on a basic human level we were just friends. He had his mission. I had mine.

Fortunes had changed. Now, he was my captive. I didn't tell him that a day earlier I had initiated a multi-pronged attack on the caves and ancient road tunnels used by the Karstians as recuperative centers, centers that I had identified for Pipkin. As we had in Lika, we poured incendiary devices down openings in the karst stone after ensuring any exits were blocked. Thousands upon thousands of Karstians were killed. There were no survivors. The strategy had been simple. The caves and tunnels were lightly guarded. Croat shock troops had taken them out easily and then our engineers had blocked the entrances used by the Karstians and any other openings that might have offered them means of escape. It was then that smart fire bombs were released into the cave and tunnel systems. It was over soon enough. The children who had died in the ill-fated children's crusade were avenged and the spirit of Matija reigned supreme.

And not a single memory object had been used. News of their existence had galvanized the fighting spirit of the people. It was as if the ancestors had suddenly sprung to life again. A simple dagger, a tattooed battle-axe, and a couple of stones had made the difference. The majority of the Karstians must have been terrified when they heard of their resounding defeat at Klis. How could it be, they might have thought, that inanimate things, mere objects from the past, a kind of black magic, could wreak havoc of this kind? Initially it must have struck them as nonsense. It was not to be believed. After all, Karstian science, technology, and culture, was far superior to the blighted Croat sensibility. But yet the Croats had triumphed. And this even after the lesson the Karstians had given the Croats at Varaždin. Perhaps, some Karstian intellectuals might have thought, the murder of Croat children had crossed a line, but children become adults, and adults could kill. So better to kill them all if need be. The old Croatian world was Karstian now and would remain so. Now there must be a final confrontation, one that would force the upstart deranged Croats to come to heel, memory objects or not. That was the kind of thinking they may have indulged in.

Pipkin picked up a small stone and tossed it behind him.

"Marin," he said. "Will you release me soon? I need to supervise the ongoing transition of the caves and tunnels. I am sure a trade can be arranged."

It puzzled me that he was so naive in the ways of the world. He hadn't anticipated what had happened. Croatia would not be a Karstian convalescent colony. Never. But I played along with his thinking. "Perhaps in a few days. These things take time and diplomacy." Even now, the massacre of the children didn't seem to phase him. He saw it as nothing more than an unfortunate fact of war, retaliation for Croatian intransigence.

I noticed his skin colour was becoming very pink. The Adriatic sun was giving him the base of a suntan. "Soon, but I need to know where other munitions are kept. The outbuilding at the Aerodrome was a good start. Now, where are the others?"

"Marin, I can't tell you that. I've given you what I know. That's all."

"My dear friend, you must. Otherwise, I'm afraid, my compatriots will use other measures similar to those you used against Inez Jakovac."

Pipkin grew very silent then. His imagination of what would happen to him kindled his fear. The expression on his face turned to one of dread. He stood up, looked at me with bitter disappointment, and said "I really don't know." Suddenly, a small dark red dot appeared just above his left eye, and then he dropped to his knees and fell backwards, dead. Pipkin was gone.

Within a moment Sprague appeared with a laser pistol in his hand, smiling. He was flanked by three Karstian troopers with their weapons at the ready. "That man deserved to die. A traitor like yourself, giving intelligence to the enemy without even being touched. He gave up the memory objects, which still another traitor had given us. He advised you of the weapons warehouse at the Aerodrome. We couldn't allow him to live even though he was one of us. And now for you my friend, we have a different agenda. We will not rush it. I can promise you a quicker death if you give me details of the Croat strategy. If you do not, that will still be OK. Your pain will be my pleasure."

One of Sprague's men handed him a wooden stick. Sprague tied a knife to one end of the stick and ran his finger along its blade. A few tiny drops of blood appeared on Sprague's finger which he licked away. Two of Sprague's men tied my hands behind me and pushed me hard on the ground. They tied my ankles together and then stepped back, deferring to Sprague. Sprague wiped his blade across Pipkin's beige uniform and then studied me for a moment before he spoke. There was the hint of a smile on his gray face.

"If you are forthcoming, things will go reasonably well. If not, I am afraid you will not like the experience. I came across a common expression from ancient times I suppose. *Death by a thousand cuts.* Have you heard of it? I am sure you have. A cliché that has come unmoored from its original meaning, but we will do our level best to restore it to its original meaning, won't we. So, let's begin."

Sprague began with a barrage of questions most of them dealing with the location of weapons across Croatia. I told him I didn't know, which was true, but nevertheless he poked me with his sharpened stick. He didn't cut deep. He just stood over my body and stabbed me, again and again. It seemed to me he didn't care if I gave him the correct answers to his questions or not. He would strike at my mid-section and then my foot or my arm. I cried out to the blue heavens above me but my screams were lost in the depths of the sky. Sometimes he would instruct his men to turn me over so that he could cut my back or my tied hands. He was methodical and manic. He was entirely focused on my torment and completely indifferent to my cries for him to stop. At some point I lost consciousness, and when I awoke Sprague and his men were gone, as was Pipkin's body. My hands and ankles were no longer tied. In the distance I could hear the noises of war coming from the nearby cavern where the model of Croatia was kept. One of my wounds was deep. I was in great pain and could hear myself moaning. My clothes were smeared with my blood.

I began to crawl up the mountain. The major bleeding from my wound had stopped. I remembered seeing faces above me. Someone had tended to me and staunched the wound. They did what they could and then left quickly. They needed to escape a battle nearby. I don't recall seeing a face I knew.

I continued to press forward as I crawled up the mountain. It was far steeper than the heights, the escarpment, behind my apartment in Hamilton, a world away from here, away from this place, and from this future time. I felt I would never see Hamilton again. Each movement I made as I dragged myself up was painful. My legs and arms pushed against the shale and scattered stones. Sometimes, just when I seemed to be making progress, my awareness deserted me and I fell into a void that was neither sleep nor rest nor any other state that I knew. Someone must have taken pity on me and given me a sheepskin jacket. It afforded me some degree of warmth as night fell and the wind abated. The stony terrain scraped against it and sometimes a piece of stone pierced the wool like a random dagger. Once I thought I spied a red-tailed hawk flying high above me, but I wasn't sure. Maybe it was a vulture. I wanted it to be there, vigorous and vital in the heavens, soaring above me, but perhaps it was just a dream and nothing more.

Suddenly I remembered Josip telling me about a Roman Emperor, Trajan, who had a huge column erected of his martial victories. From preparations for war to combat, the column depicted events that spiralled upward in stone, commemorating his greatest feats of warfare. Memories become stone. What a monument we could build I thought, of our war with the Karstians. I remembered the early days when we actually believed negotiations with them could lead to peace and wealth for all. But that was not to be. If your enemy believes he is superior to you, he will lie and play loose with the truth in order to confound you and make you doubt yourself. The Browns were the first to go down that stony path, but to be fair, many of the Blues followed readily enough. Lies and deceit and greed led to war and death.

Once you know this, and once you've experienced it, you win a grim freedom that allows your most terrible actions to become honourable after a time. You glorify in the hatred your enemy has given you, and reason falls into a deep abyss and leaves you with a shredded kind of truth.

I was so tired, but I knew I must keep on moving. This body of mine had taken so much. I needed it to do a little more, just a little. Below me I saw traces of red, smears of red across the rock. It was my blood. I dragged myself up. I would stop now and then. My breathing was heavy. I felt myself drifting off as my eyes closed. In the daytime, the sun blazed through the brilliant blue skies, and the wind was steady and like a blessing. The night winds were like a madman's curse and chilled me to the bone.

The images came in the darkness. I didn't know if I was dreaming them or if I was awake. They came unbidden. Strange images that spiralled into the darkness. Images of men and women and children moving over mountain passes, reminding me of the ancient scenes at Josip's mother's garden, the scenes with the Meštrović statue. Images of warriors in battle. Images, and then sounds of people laughing and singing and dancing. Strange images and yet familiar. I was a still point in the darkness and in my mind's eye there was color and substance and form. I followed the images until they stopped suddenly, and I was once again a broken body on the side of a mountain overlooking Makarska.

I was conscious again of the heaviness of my body and the pain in my torso and arms and legs. Surely death is better than this I thought. I lifted my arms and pulled myself a few inches ahead. It didn't seem as if I was making much progress, but I was. Pulling and pushing and scraping ahead, I moved against the mountain and then I would stop for a moment, or what I thought was a moment. Time was lopsided here and variable like the Blue Mist that had carried me into the future and into the past, but I didn't have the luxury of that fine technology nor the companionship that came with it. My choices had brought me here to this painful solitude, and I was one with it.

Even so, the stones gave way before me but not before they pierced and cut me like tiny daggers. The feel of the sun and the wind and the stone was my connection with heaven and earth. I drifted into a different primal consciousness that was dark and formless and without sound or colour. I would see a flush of rose, the merest flush of rose that clothed itself into an image that guided me to a new place and time.

Times when I thought I was awake, moving images crossed my field of vision. The images appeared to be spiralling just ahead of me, as I crawled and followed in their wake. I was able to crawl at times and was thankful for that. I would feel a small surge of energy and then I would twist and turn my body to make headway.

At first the images were of people I knew and loved, my parents and grandparents and friends from my Hamilton time. Seeing their smiling faces and movements took me away from the mountain of stones beneath me for precious seconds until the pain circled back and held me in its claw like the talons of an eagle.

Some of the images surprised me. They were from distant times, people engaged in all kinds of activities. I could hear nothing but I could see faces and forms that somehow were familiar. Men and women, girls and boys, dressed oddly to my eyes but familiar nevertheless.

Often images of battle would be there, in front of me, strange and terrible vignettes that were brutal and sharp. Flashing swords and spears thrown with great skill at enemies close and menacing. The images, all of them, were like the memories I had experienced in my Hamilton time, close and sharp and real. It was as if even the most distant images in time were my own, memories from a far and long ago past. Scenes from a millennium ago or a second ago were mine, remembered times that I had known and shared with others. I was connected to all of these and more, living truths, as real as the pricks of pain that pierced through the tattered sheepskin jacket I wore.

The images, the memories, were not sequential or chronological events. That baffled me at first. I was trying to make sense of something that had to be approached differently. They just appeared and then disappeared, without rhyme or reason. It was as if from the depths of my consciousness image memories were being released and bobbed erratically to the surface of my awareness. A dark sea was offering brilliant colours and forms that transformed everything.

All of a sudden I felt so tired, so very tired. I tried to raise my arm to cover my eyes from the brilliant sun overhead, but I couldn't. I turned my head and rested my left cheek against the stone. Cool winds blew around me, and feeling them made me forget the pain in my body. Sensations only. Soon, even these would be gone, lost in the crossover.

I closed my eyes and a host of memories and images fluttered under my eyelids. Everything was red-gold for a moment and then slowly I could make out forms and faces and scenes that I knew, walking with Marta in the hills above the harbour at Omiš. The wealth and warmth of Marta's smile. And then Beserka straddled above me on my hotel bed in Retro Zagreb, satisfied and exhausted after a night of debauchery. Whenever I blinked, a new image sparked into my awareness. A flash of red-gold and then a memory as sharp as the living reality and imbued with colour and movement and feeling.

Suddenly I saw my grandmother's loving face as she served me scrambled eggs and coffee in her sun-bright kitchen. I saw the streets of Hamilton, below the escarpment, where I walked in my old life. And then I saw the miniature model of Croatia within the mountain behind Makarska, with Manda lying atop me, her mouth on the nape of my neck, the weight of her against my back. Images piled on other images. The iridescence of the Byzantine dagger suspended before me in the room at Klis. Nikola's battle axe with its tattoos incised on the shaft. Mila's stones. The wrinkled face of Brujo stroking the wings of a monarch butterfly. The slumbering Karstians within the Lika cavern as they dreamt their dreams of renewal and empire.

All of these people and places and things that were as much to me as the fingers on my hands. Somehow, I was processing these images for a final reckoning. All was connected. All was related, and I was alive only through my connections with them. I was nothing beyond my relationships. Invisible bonds tied me to these people and places and things. I was as much a part of them as they were a part of me. Not one part of me was separate, nor isolated from the relations, the connections.

I didn't think it would be like this. Dying. So strange. It took me what little strength I had left to make it here, to be here, right here, on the top of the mountain, just after dawn. In front of me, the sea and the islands shone in the distance. My body was resting on my left elbow. It was cold and windy, but I hardly felt it. The pain came and went, like my consciousness, in and out, back and forth. I had made it here, and after all of this time, I was almost ready to go. But this living moment was mine, and mine alone. It had taken me three days of crawling, maybe longer, to get here. Dragging and pulling myself, inch by inch, up the mountainside from the bottom. I was cut and torn in so many places. My sheepskin jacket was a bloodied mess. Yesterday I didn't know if I would make it, but I did. The shale and stones beneath me were as sharp as ten thousand knives. But even here, I saw beauty in the far distance and beauty beside me in the brave purple wildflowers.

And then another series of strange images crossed my field of vision, images that were unfamiliar to me, and yet I felt I was connected to them, strange, smiling faces beckoning me forward to join them. I extended my arm, but then the strength in me faltered and my arm dropped like a stone. I felt someone of great power reach down and cradle me in his arms as if I was a small child. It had taken me a small eternity to get here, but now I felt a freedom and a kinship with the powerful presence above me. I turned my head to gain a better look and saw a man's countenance smiling down upon me. He had long copper brown hair and golden skin. But what struck me was the expression of compassion on his face and the deep positive emotion that I felt he was extending towards me. I'd forgotten the pain in my lacerated body. It was enough for me to be with this powerful man whose kinship I felt singing in my blood, the blood of humanity, and of all

the gods within us. I raised my arm to touch his golden cheek and then fell
back, fell away from the time and place I inhabited on the mountainside to
a darkness that was as rich as a womb, and I gave myself to it.

Epilogue

PART SIX

6.1

ALL OF A SUDDEN, A flash of golden light covered everything in sight. Oddly, I felt energized. I felt comforted by the presence of this golden man. He was wearing sandals and a white linen robe. He smiled at me, a warm, familiar smile, as if I were a brother or a close friend. He gently touched my wounds and with his touch the pain lessened. The pupils of his dark brown eyes were dilated. I took a deep breath.

"Who are you?" I asked, in a tone of wonder and awe.

"A man from the future, the far future, beyond Retro Zagreb. I'm here to take you there if you wish. But we must leave soon to attend to your wounds. Otherwise, you will die here on the mountain within minutes. Brujo has sent me." The golden man took hold of my hand and gently pulled me to my knees. A strange disk-shaped aircraft hovered a few meters away. The choice was mine.

I hardly knew what to expect, but I went with him, this Golden Man who had come to save me. I guessed I must have been unconscious for some time for when I awoke, I felt much better and my wounds had been treated. A thick transparent gel covered my entire body. Overhead, a soft white light illuminated the large room. It felt peaceful to lie on the bed and simply wait for someone to come.

It was a shock to me when the Golden Man entered the room with Brujo at his side.

"What, Brujo! How good to see you! I never dreamt I would see you again." I was ecstatic to see my old friend once again.

He placed his hand on the bedsheet that covered my foot and smiled warmly. "You are with us now in this future time and your strife is over. Never more the killing and hate and greed."

"Yes," the Golden Man said, "you have come just in time from the killing fields of the past. All that is gone now and a new world beckons."

"Where am I?"

"A future Croatia, 2824, in the same place as before but different, far different than the time of the Karstian invaders that you knew in 2324. You have come home to a new life." Brujo's voice was warm and reassuring as he spoke, and then he gestured to the Golden Man to speak.

The Golden Man ran his hand across the wall, and there before us, down a steep mountainside were stands of tall trees covering the slopes. In the far distance were islands and a turquoise sea that I immediately recognized as the Dalmatian Coast near Makarska. I raised myself from the bed to see better but fell back in pain.

"Be careful," the Golden Man said. "You are healing, and need to rest before any exertion. It will take a few days, no more. We brought you back just in time. Another hour on the mountainside and you would be dead. Brujo knew where you were and informed us. Welcome, my friend."

"What of the Karstians?" I asked.

"They are gone, those who could. Those who couldn't, have died." Brujo shook his head. "Such waste, but we believe those times are gone now, gone for good if we can help it."

"And my friends, Josip and Goran and Beserka, and Manda, and all the others, are they with us? Are they here?"

"They are in the future past, as you were, in Retro Zagreb. They survived the battles and now they are starting to rebuild a nation, a nation of restored churches and schools and playing fields. They believe you died on the mountain, and they grieved for you, Marin. They loved you."

I turned away from Brujo for a moment and thought about what he had said. I felt a sense of immense loss, but also of joy that they had survived. A tear rolled down my cheek, and I smiled.

I had so many questions that I needed answered. My head was swimming despite the security and safety I felt in the presence of these two good men. "Are we safe here finally? You said the Karstians had left. So then, we are free at last. Brujo, what kind of place is this?"

"It is a new period in mankind's history, and we, in Croatia, are in the vanguard of it. The old times of invading armies and raw force and power are not to be found here. Love and tenderness rule the day. We have vanquished hate and violence and it is not to be found within our borders. Ruthless militarism has been transmuted into sport, competitive sport. A new day has dawned and murder and greed are banished within our borders."

From the amused, kind look on his handsome face I could see the Golden Man was reading my mind. "Marin, give this place some little time. It is not a utopian fantasy. It is the result of centuries of trial and error. Things got out of whack when brute force crushed delicate sensitivity, when the bully powers ruled the day. Can you imagine the lost time and stunted human development that arose when raw power simply wiped away subtle, new growth and sensitive, delicate, responses to life and the environment. And that's been the case for most of human history. The Romans, the British, the Russians, so many lost empires, swallowed up in the abyss of time. Just think about it. Look how it all starts. Conquerors don't come out of the womb ready to brandish a sword and strike down some hapless bystander. Not one human baby, not a single one, would last several days without delicate sustenance and nurturing by a mother or caregiver. It baffles thought. And not one empire would last without the common grass that, seen as grain, feeds all manner of life, whether human or otherwise. Just think about the vast riches of lost cultures and civilizations that were tossed aside in the rape and murder for gold and slaves. Entire indigenous tribes were wiped off the face of the earth. The Karstians, led by Marshal Leith, would have destroyed the Croatian people if they could. But they couldn't. The Croatian spirit won out. They have never been conquerors, but they will fight defensively to the last for what is theirs. Meštrović knew this as did Radić and countless other Croatian heroes."

Brujo sat on the edge of my bed and gazed out the floor-to-ceiling window at the islands and the azure Adriatic Sea. The wink of a bronze-coloured sail moved slowly towards the Makarska harbour. The town below seemed larger than I remembered with strange new architecture having replaced the high rises along the coast.

"Look where we are Marin," Brujo said. "Look at the sea and sky and lands below. This is our home now, a place of peace and joy. In ancient times brute force was everything, but we have evolved, we have come away from that legacy of hatred and ruthlessness. For millennia, the paradox of human nature cursed mankind with war, but we fought against that, fought against our innate predisposition towards violence, and look where we have come. Laughter and harmony have supplanted hatred and greed. We are leading the world."

I didn't know quite what to say. The next few days were a revelation. No one had need of money because everyone had more than enough to live on. Accommodation and food were givens. People were free to pursue their innermost goals, provided it didn't impinge on the freedom of others. Regardless of the field of endeavour, whether the arts or sciences or sport, each man or woman could live his or her own destiny. For the first time in human history mankind was free.

It was remarkable how well my wounds had healed. The gel rejuvenated my skin and I felt vigorous and robust. After three days in hospital, I was discharged and given a small apartment near the ancient market in Makarska. Brujo would visit often and smile at my countless barrage of questions.

"But surely Brujo this is a utopia for the privileged few. This sunny, happy place surely cannot banish greed or crime. Some people will always want more than others. It is a fault of human nature to never be satisfied with what you have. Wouldn't you agree? Why should this place be any different?"

Brujo walked out on to the large balcony that overlooked the sea. It was mid-morning and the sun was beginning to strengthen. He glowed with reddish-gold health, and though I knew him to be an old man, he seemed to me to be ageless in many ways. I loved the man for he was the last living connection with my grandfather. Just to be in his presence felt like a benediction.

"Ah Marin, you challenge so much. Nothing is perfect. But still, we must try to make human life better. The potential is there. Because there are migrants on the borders of our country doesn't mean we shouldn't try. Other countries are looking to us for solutions. And slowly, we are finding them. It is taking time, but we are moving steadily ahead and bringing those we can into the fold. The alternative is misery and war. And we have seen what that can do, haven't we?"

"The Karstians certainly brought that home to us. Yes, indeed Brujo."

I mused over his fine sentiments for some time as I gazed out at the sea watching several seagulls flying towards shore. I knew Brujo was right according to his instincts, but deep within me I feared that not being ready to face adversity, to face an enemy with resolve and hard weapons, could lead to destitution and death, human instincts be damned. I kept my thoughts to myself, but I could see that Brujo had misgivings about what I truly believed. That's why he was such a remarkable man. He could read people, and respected different systems of belief.

I'd been there about a month before I realized what I must do. I wanted to return home, to Hamilton, Canada. Brujo and the Golden Man were in a different future world, one that I could never live in happily. It was out of my reach though I prayed for its success. Both Brujo and the Golden Man understood completely. They would arrange Blue Mist travel to Retro Zagreb for me and then on to Hamilton. I would breathe a great sigh of relief when I was finally on my way home. I was an outlier, but a grateful one, for I knew where I was from and the people of my past and future. Croatia was singing in my blood. All that remained was to visit some old friends from the Retro Zagreb future.

15 July 10:30 2324

6.2

I'd arrived in Retro Zagreb at mid-morning and was greeted with astonishment and joy by Goran and Manda. There was good news. Almost all of the Karstians had left and a great rebuild was underway. Much was destroyed. Churches, historic buildings, museums, and cultural artifacts, all of these and more were gone. Fortunately, human memory and three-dimensional records enabled artists and engineers to begin recreating the lost legacy. Goran apprised me of the military costs and related matters. For instance, the Blue Mist technology had been preserved and was functioning reasonably well though at reduced capacity. Goran assured me that an airship was available for my return home in a few days. The Karstians scoffed at claims of time travel but they had witnessed what the memory objects could do at Klis and elsewhere. Josip, he said, would inform me of what was to happen with the memory objects. He said his goodbyes then and said he would let me know when I would return home. He said he was sorry to see me go, but that I had accomplished much and would be remembered. However, there was some unfinished business.

6.3

The safe house, located on the slopes just off Tkalčićeva Street, overlooked the restaurants and pubs below. I was ushered into a grand room where

I saw Josip. He looked up from his work and howled with surprise and delight. We embraced and kissed each other on both cheeks in the traditional Croatian way.

"Marin, my dear friend, we thought you were dead. No one knew what happened to you in the last days of the war. Everything was so chaotic. Dozens of skirmishes and battles were going on everywhere. We learned from a Karstian prisoner, a former bodyguard of Sprague's, that you had been tortured and left to die on the mountain behind Makarska. But here you are, looking well and recovered from your ordeal. I've been told you are on your way home. We will miss you dearly. But I have a surprise for you." He gestured for me to follow him down a corridor and he stopped before an oak door. He opened the door slowly. I was shocked to see Sprague sitting tied to a metal chair. He looked up and cursed me when he saw me.

"I demand to be released," he said. "I am a Karstian diplomat, a senior adviser to Marshal Leith. You have no right to hold me here."

I was surprised at his defiance. He spat out his words. Josip gave him a withering look and just smiled at him, intrigued by his behaviour.

"You've got him Josip. You've captured the beast."

"Yes, I have. His own men gave him up, though after some duress."

"Stop this nonsense. Let me go. Now!"

"What are you going to do with him, Josip?"

Josip smiled at me. "Do you want some time with him, after what he did to you?"

I shook my head. I did not want to go that way.

Josip nodded his head. "I understand. He knows what he's done, and he must pay. But I remember a saying that seems to me just right and I wanted to share it with you. *We prove ourselves better than our enemies by not being like them.* Now Marin, you must leave. I wish you well, dear friend, and I hope we can meet before you leave us."

As I left, I heard a whimper from Sprague. I turned and saw his head drop to his chest. He knew his fate was sealed. I closed the door behind me. Walking down the corridor a shot rang out. It was a pop-like sound followed by silence. It was done. Just then I felt a light touch on my shoulder, and I turned to recognize Ante and Bianca. I had first met them in Samobor. It seemed a world away. We chatted and I learned they had captured Marshal Leith. They had found him hiding out alone in a filthy outhouse in Karlobag. We embraced warmly, happy to see each other one last time.

6.4

I was walking downhill from the Old Town. Beserka knew I was following her, as she herself was following Marshal Leith, but she didn't care. She was beyond all that, beyond everything that linked her to what you could construe as morality, to what was right and to what was wrong. I believe that Marshal Leith really thought he was going to return home to Karstsia scot-free as the saying goes. The First Minister, Darko Yamich, had promised him safe passage home if he and every last Karstian left the planet within a fortnight. Not one vestige of their temporary and deadly incursion into Croatia was to be left behind. Leith was a man who believed that deception and lies were diplomatic tools, yet ironically he held Darko to his word that he and his senior officials would be allowed to leave. Of course, all Karstian weaponry and technology was to be relinquished. So, while his entourage followed respectfully behind him, Leith played the tourist and asked to wander through the Grič tunnel on his own.

Beserka waited a moment outside the tunnel entrance and then went inside, several paces behind Leith. Three of the Marshal's bodyguards had tried to stop her but she waved them off brusquely, and they knew better than to cross her path. I guess what happened was to be expected, but no one really anticipates these things. At least I don't. I imagined it though, and I couldn't be far off from the actuality. Beserka was one of the finest warriors that a warrior nation had ever produced. Centuries of warfare had shaped her thinking and created a formidable warrior. In my mind's eye I saw her. Dressed in her Commander's dark blue uniform she followed him with the certainty of what she must do. The walls of the tunnel were completely covered in swaying, curtain-like material that an artist had fashioned. I had seen the opening exhibit a few days before. It was remarkable. If you touched it, the material drew back as if in human contact. And then, it enveloped you in its folds and the effect was exhilarating. A feeling of euphoria swept over you and the joy you felt was palpable. I could see Leith running his hand across the material and relishing the experience, with Beserka several paces behind. The outcome was inevitable despite the Croatian assurances.

I'm sure Leith did not expect to see anyone within the tunnels, but there she was, grim and focused. There may have been a terse dialogue.

"Who are you?"

"I'm here for you."

"But I'm under the protection of the Croatian state."

"Yes, you are. But I'm an individual and stateless, as are the dead children. Do you remember?"

Leith would have reached for his hidden laser pistol as Beserka ran towards him. He may have discharged his weapon but he couldn't have aimed properly, the curtain around him billowing out as Beserka plunged her stiletto blade into his heart. Suddenly, a tiny red dot appeared on the cream coloured curtain covering Leith, and then it grew larger and larger becoming a great jagged circle. There might have been a gasp of surprise and then silence, as Leith knew he would never see Karstian skies again. A crumpled heap of a man fell to the ground and it was done. Beserka would have taken one of the branching tunnels to escape just as his bodyguards stormed into the tunnel complex. But they could do nothing without weapons. That's how I imagined it, and it couldn't have been far from the truth.

As for the memory objects, Josip had found the perfect resting place for them. They were safe and well hidden in Meštrović's History of the Croats sculpture. The Byzantine dagger was there within the pages of the bronze book. The battle-axe was aligned vertically with the head and spine of the woman. Mila's two stones were encased within her joined hands. The objects were at the ready should they ever be needed again. Since the day of his mother's murder Josip had not taken a single drink. He told me it didn't agree with him anymore. Perhaps it never would. He was a great friend and I would miss him dearly. He had hoped I would stay in Croatia but my home was in Canada and I longed to return. Croatia was singing within my heart and so much a part of me that I knew there would be no separation between here and there, between Croatia and Canada. My identity was dual and could be nothing less. I was, after all, a Croatian Canadian.

6.5

After he left, Manda approached me in a serious manner and began speaking in a very formal tone. She was dressed in a dark blue uniform that accentuated her stout, yet curvaceous figure. I remembered our last meeting in Omiš that was far less formal.

"Marin. Welcome. I am glad that I am among the first to see you. I need you to provide me with a thorough debriefing on your mission with the Karstians. It will take two days. We will meet in Omiš beginning this afternoon. I've arranged military transport for us. I assume you are free, without any other obligations?"

"Yes, certainly. I don't know how much of what I can tell you will be useful to you but I will try my best."

"Good. Your best is all we can ask. I will meet you at my apartment at 3:00 pm. I'm sure you remember it. The driver will take you to the Omiš Aerodrome, and you can walk the short distance from there."

My return to Omiš was bittersweet. The small Aerodrome, together with the imposing restaurant tower, formed the nucleus of the modern town. I decided to walk around the old pirate haunt for a bit before I met with Manda. The old town with its twisting serpentine streets had always beguiled me. I thought about Marta, centuries dead, and wondered if she had lived a good life, had married, and had children. Perhaps her descendants walked these same streets as I did now. Memories of lost love dogged my steps. I turned and walked along the Cetina River looking up at the mountains that had witnessed so much history, a great deal of it violent, but now peaceful and quiet. I realized now that I could never have lived in Marta's past, just as she could never have lived in my future, whether Retro Zagreb or Hamilton. They were different worlds. The memory of her beauty pierced my heart. I shook the thoughts from my mind and walked resolutely to Manda's apartment near the tower. There was some final work to be done.

Manda and I chatted idly for a moment or two, talking of friends we knew in Retro Zagreb. She was very informal and dressed casually in a form-fitting outfit that complimented her abundant figure.

"So Marin, are you ready to leave us?"

"I've done what I could, and I miss home. It's time. Where do you want me to start with the debriefing?"

"Start right where you are. Just there, stand by the sofa, at least for now." We were in her living room. The curtains were closed though it was only mid-afternoon.

"I'm sorry. I don't understand where to begin."

"Begin with the briefs. After all, it is a debriefing that I requested of you."

"Sorry, but I still don't get it."

"Silly man, do you have briefs in Canada?"

"Briefs?"

"Underwear."

"Is this some sort of joke?"

"It was meant to be, but I guess Canadians, even Croatian-Canadians, lack a sense of humour."

Rather belatedly, I got the joke. I broke out into a great guffaw of laughter and fell backwards upon the sofa. Her ruse had taken me completely by surprise. My debriefing began then and there, and went on for some time with a minor venue change to her bedroom at one point. Manda was not only a leading scientist. She was also a punster of the highest order.

The two days I spent with her were wonderful. I discovered that she was incredibly powerful. Preternaturally strong. In our lovemaking she would wheel me about with a physicality that astounded me. My body weight hardly mattered to her. When we danced in her spacious living room, she was like a whirling dervish holding me in her arms completely, sweeping me off my feet, until panting, we fell on the floor in each other's arms.

At the same time she was ever so tender. Several times she reminded me that I was a dead ringer for her deceased husband, only younger. She would tell me things about him with a wistfulness that was heartbreaking to hear. The tears would run down her rosy cheeks and she would turn away from me, embarrassed at the display of emotion. We weren't in love with each other, but it was a close friendship, and honest. What more could you ask of anyone? She said I was what the Croatians called a bećar, a word without a precise translation. A kind of reveller, a lover I suppose. Close enough. Once, she held my face in both her hands, and said that I should be who I was, nothing more. She said she would miss me especially in the afternoons.

6.6

My last night in Retro Zagreb was with Beserka. She had insisted that we spend the evening at my hotel, the Palace. I hardly knew what to think. It was a strange relationship, and I would miss her. She knew me and I knew her. We weren't perfect and it was lust, not love, that fueled our friendship if you could call it that. For killing Marshal Leith she had been stripped of her military rank and honours. At the inquest she had merely shrugged her shoulders at the verdict and said she would have done the same thing regardless. The parents of the massacred children were angry at the First Minister for his disciplinary action against her, but revenge was not policy in the new Croatian state. A page had been turned and would stay turned. The Karstians had left but things would never be the same again.

The last night of our lovemaking was, if anything, wistful. Anyway, that's how I remembered it. A kind of melancholy nostalgia for a lost time. We were gentle with each other as if we realized we would never see each other again. Our lovemaking that night was like a little death. It was vigorous, as always, but tinged with sadness. Though we had survived and were alive after the Karstian battles, this tryst would be the last. I would always remember the cool touch of her body, its curves and coiled power. After we had made love she lay quiet for a time and then turned to me.

"Marin, you are a romantic fool. I heard about your love for the woman in Omiš. What was her name? Marta, I believe. Fool that you are, you wanted to bring her from the far past to the future. But it was not allowed by Matija, and at any rate she would not have survived. Besides, I understand she didn't want to leave. She wanted to remain where she was, and have you with her. Correct? You don't have to say a thing. You idealize love. You were in love with an idea of her. That's all it was. Besides, in Omiš you would be poor. You would not have your ten million. You would be wiping your butt with dried cabbage leaves. Such a fool you are."

And then she laughed as if to emphasize her cutting remarks.

I didn't say a word. I could hear the dripping sarcasm in her voice. It surprised me that she had known about Marta, just as Manda had. There were no secrets among these Croats. All of a sudden I wanted to get away. I wanted to leave and not have my emotions analyzed by a woman who knew me only too well. I wanted to go home, as quickly as possible. But I lay there petrified, staring up at the vaulted ceiling, a little numb and lost. Somehow, I fell asleep and awoke in the early morning while it was still dark. I reached out for her. She was gone. My hand ran over her pillow and I felt a spot of dampness there. I realized in a shock of belated understanding that the spot was the result of Beserka's tears. Beserka had wept. I buried my face in her pillow and took in the scent of her hair for the last time, and then my own tears fell.

15 July 18:30 2024

6.7

I realized that I had taken my last Blue Mist journey. Those days were gone. The airship hovered above the old sports field for a moment and then descended lightly to the grass on the north side. The door sprung open and I leapt out. A stand of cedar trees separated the field from the adjacent tennis courts. It was dusk and the great field lights were not yet on. No one was about to witness my arrival. I patted the fuselage and walked away from the airship. I didn't look back.

I couldn't believe how excited I was to be home. There were no lights on at Peter's place. I scribbled a note for Peter to join me at West Town Bar & Grill and slipped it under his door. Then, after getting into some new clothes, I hurried to the pub, a short five-minute walk away. Locke Street was humming on a sultry July night. I was parched. There was a booth available with a large window overlooking the street. Sports memorabilia covered the soft pine wall boards. Peter and I had often sat there. I took a seat and ordered a pint, a light lager. Just as the slender fresh-faced waitress returned with my drink, I saw Peter's smile as he caught sight of me from the street side of the window. He came into the pub and we hugged each other. There was a warm silence for a moment and then an avalanche of words fell between us.

"It's great to see you again, Marin, after all this time. I haven't spent any of the money you gave me, not a nickel. We'll do it together. You've got a ton of mail waiting for you, most of it from the Bank of Montreal."

"That money was for you, and there's more coming, much more. Don't worry about a thing. I've been waiting for this time."

"Where were you? Where did you go?"

"Peter my boy, you wouldn't believe me if I told you."

"I'm just glad to see you back. By the way, a few of the ladies have asked about you. They missed you. I told them you'd be back."

"That is music to my ears. Now it's time to raise our glasses, the first of many. Cheers!

Živio!"

Acknowlegements

Special thanks are owed to Laurie and David Buchar who provided comprehensive editing and valued suggestions on the text. Any errors that escaped them are mine and mine alone.

Love and gratitude to my son Marco for his contribution in making the novel better than it could have been otherwise.

Heartfelt thanks to Mike Caterini for organizing literary readings at the Judge.

Author photograph by Ward Shipman.

About the Author

Frank Buchar is a writer of both fiction and non-fiction in North America, Europe, and Asia. He's written for a variety of publications such as the Globe and Mail, the Hamilton Spectator, and Canadian-Croatian literary magazines. He uses fiction as an incisive tool to probe and explore past times, places, and people.